LOVE in Prime Time

LOVE in Prime Time

Avery A. Voss

DEDICATION

To all the dreamers and lovers who dare to chase their hearts' desires. This book is for you.

Contents

Chapter 1

December 11, 2011
Bucharest, Romania

THE LOUD POP of a champagne bottle echoed off the lobby of the imposing building, drawing cheers from the small crowd Alexandria turned just in time to see Nando pouring the sparkling wine into plastic glasses.

"Guess we're starting the party early!" Alexandria said, taking a glass from Nando and handing it to Marilyn, who kept her other hand in hers.

"Sorry, I couldn't wait any longer! I thought we could use a little toast before the wedding ceremony." Nando, one of their closest friends, gave an embarrassed grin and held up a bottle of champagne with a flourish. Marilyn laughed as she watched some tiny bubbles dance in the air. Her nerves were starting to relax.

"You're unbelievable, always finding a way to break the tension." Their friends gathered closer, forming a tight-knit circle.

Nando handed them each a glass and said, "To Alexandria and Marilyn, may your love story be filled with laughter, joy, and more champagne than you can ever drink. To love in all its beautiful forms!"

"To love! Cheers!" Everybody raised their glasses.

"To us, and to the best friends anyone could ask for," Alexandria finished the toast, hugging Marilyn around the waist.

"Shhhh!" An elderly woman stepped out from behind the door. "Save some of that enthusiasm for the vows." Her stern gaze was softened by her indulgent smile. She put her finger to her lips and closed the door again. Nodding respectfully, they stifled their giggles.

They were kept waiting in front of a massive wooden door. Its dark surface was decorated with intricate designs and patterns that spoke of centuries of craftsmanship and tradition. It was a symbol of the importance and significance of what lay beyond.

Alexandria whispered to Marilyn, "I can't believe we're here. And we still don't really know what's going to happen, what the ceremony will be like."

Marilyn smiled, squeezing Alexandira's hand a little tighter. "That's what makes it special, love. It's our ceremony, our way of doing things. Unconventional, just like us. We'll figure it out together." She gave Alexandira a soft kiss on her cheek and Alexandria hugged her to warm her up. It was cool outside.

"Excuse me, it's a little cold in here; would it be warmer inside?" Alexandria asked a woman who walked by with a schedule. She had just told them they were next.

"Love will keep you warm," she replied hurriedly to the general laughter of the group, and then disappeared down the corridor.

It was a chilly December day. The sun's dim light tried to break through the thick clouds. It had snowed lightly that morning and the streets were covered with small, white patches. Alexandria did not like winter.

Summer was her time. It always seemed to bring a sense of joy and vitality when the weather started to warm up. Rituals like clearing snow off the car early in the morning, shoveling the driveway, and not slipping on icy stretches of streets and sidewalks, made her daydream about moving somewhere where it was summer all year round.

But today was different. The weather, the season, the snow—none of it mattered. It was the sunniest day in her soul. The day she'd been waiting for all her life, the day she felt she was exactly where she was meant to be. There was no fear, no disbelief, just a sense of wholeness and completion. Every failure, every trial, every heartache made sense because they had brought her to this perfect moment. And she had to live it fully, consciously, savoring every minute—every second—because she wanted to remember this day forever. Today was the day when their happiness would be sealed by their vows. And once they said yes, their fairy tale would unfold.

Suddenly the doors creaked open loudly, revealing the impressive interior. As they were welcomed inside, solemn music began to play while a soft female voice recited in the background.

"Beauty is a form of genius. It is even more than genius because it needs no proof. Beauty tortures us; beauty tortures us; torture us; torture us. Higher, deeper, more, most."

Alexandria felt like she was attending a play, watching what was happening around her and to her. She didn't feel as though she were in her own body.

She and Marilyn were led slowly forward by a young girl. They approached a small altar. The young man standing behind it smiled and began.

"The life of a human is an endless passage through time and space. And undoubtedly the most beautiful, the most magical moments are precisely these passages…the passages through which we give the most and receive the most. Passages called love."

A young girl approached the couple and held out a tray of four small bowls.

"I invite you both to provide the other with a taste of life's essential flavors."

The girl quietly gave them directions. Alexandria dipped her finger into the first bowl, which contained honey, and placed her fingertip gently into Marilyn's mouth.

"Sweet," she commented. Marilyn did the same for Alexandria. The second bowl was salty. Again, they accepted the bowl, dipped their finger in it, and offered it to the other to taste the salt. Sour and spicy came next.

"I now invite you to cleanse your bodies," the young man intoned. The girl handed a piece of carrot to Marilyn and Alexandria and motioned for them to eat it.

When he said, "Let us activate our spirit," the girl placed little pieces of cooked noodles in the women's hair.

"To love is to vow; to love is to deny. To love is to renounce. Repeat after me," the young man instructed. They repeated what he'd said, and he continued.

"I love you, and I vow to you all that you are. I love you, and I renounce everything that is not you. I love you, and I vow to you, the one I love."

Alexandria and Marilyn again repeated his words. The girl handed them each a glass of champagne and whispered, "Bottoms up." Doing as they were told, they each downed all of the champagne in the glass.

"Please, the rings." The man handed each woman a ring and asked them to exchange them, each putting her ring on the other's finger.

"Marilyn, do you take Alexandria to be your wife?"

Marilyn looked Alexandria in the eye and said, "Yes."

"Alexandria, do you take Marilyn to be your wife?"

Alexandria smiled and also said, "Yes."

"Newlyweds, you may now kiss each other. Congratulations!"

Everyone started clapping as Alexandria and Marilyn exchanged their first kiss as a married couple.

"You're mine now—enough with your bachelor life," Marilyn murmured as she held Alexandria in her arms.

"You too," Alexandria laughed.

"Alright, you two! Time for some pictures. We need to capture these moments forever," broke in Alexandria's best friend, Mel, her voice brimming with excitement.

Nando stepped forward. "I've got my camera ready to go. Let's do it here; the light is perfect."

Alexandria turned to her friends and announced, "Hey, everyone, make sure you're in some of the shots."

Mel smiled in agreement. "Listen to the bride! Let's make these pictures as memorable as the day itself."

"Okay, everyone, get in close! Brides, you look at each other and pretend we're not even here," Nando instructed from behind the camera.

Mel nudged him. "Hey, Nando, can you pop another bottle of champagne? We need some action shots!"

"I'll get right on it! Get ready for some epic

photos," Nando said enthusiastically as he grabbed another bottle.

He popped the cork, champagne bubbled over, and Alexandria experienced a whirlwind of sensations—love, fireworks, applause, and happiness all at once. She still couldn't believe she had married her soulmate, the love of her life. Holding Marilyn's hand, she was ready to begin this new chapter as her wife.

The group walked together downtown, where they planned to take more pictures. They crossed the street, laughing and exclaiming as if the world were theirs. On the way, they passed a Christmas market that was lavishly decorated with twinkly holiday lights. The market was crowded with people enjoying the bazaar, drinking Christmas wine, and eating sausages. The crowds were delighted to see the brides pass by, and called out their congratulations.

"Where are your grooms, girls?" someone shouted.

"No grooms. The girls love each other, and they tied the knot today," replied Nando with a smile. Same-sex marriage was not legal. People were more open these days, and accepting of gay couples, but it was still a bit of a surprise to actually see two brides on their wedding day.

A street musician on the other side of the street interrupted the Christmas carol he was playing and started playing the wedding march. This festive gesture delighted the couple and their guests, who started dancing around him.

"Congratulations, girls! I wish you all the happiness in the world. The next song is for you too," the man said as he played the last chords of the wedding march. Across the street, a reporter was interviewing random passersby, capturing viewpoints for his morning show.

Mel, who was opening her wallet to leave a donation in the musician's hat, nodded over her shoulder in the cameraman's direction to point him out to the brides.

"Check it out, across the street. You don't want to get caught in the shot, do you? I imagine your parents probably watch that show."

"No, you're right. Let's get out of here." Marilyn's eyes widened as she tightened her grip on Alexandria's hand.

"We're not worried or anything. They're not homophobes," Alexandria said, pulling Marilyn along, her pace quickening. "But we don't want our families finding out about the wedding from some random TV show."

"The world is changing," Mel assured them as they walked away. "People will see you two today and think, *Wow, that's beautiful*. It's only a small number of people who are still stuck in the past—but let's not waste our time worrying about them because love always triumphs in the end, and today is a celebration of just that!"

After their downtown photoshoot, they got in a luxury car, which was specially decorated for the occasion with white and blue ribbons and balloons, and a string of empty beer cans attached to the bumper. Heading to their apartment for the reception, Alexandria kept looking at the wedding ring on her finger, still unable to believe it was true.

"Thank you for making me the happiest woman in the world," Marilyn said, her voice breaking into Alexandria's thoughts.

"A year and a half ago, when I first saw you in the studio, I never could have imagined we'd be here today. I remember that first moment," Alexandria mused, her voice soft with admiration. "You had this incredible charisma. Your blue eyes, they were so striking. You had the most delicate features, almost like an angel. And that gorgeous wavy blonde hair? You just radiated femininity. You were magnetic."

"You're making me blush," Marilyn told her.

"Every curve of your body was perfectly divine, and your skin...it looked as soft as velvet. You were just...perfect. I couldn't take my eyes off you."

"This is the happiest day of my life. I love you." Marilyn kissed Alexandria tenderly.

The newlyweds stepped over the threshold of their home together, embarking on their new chapter as wife and wife. Their friends followed them. Their place was decorated in soft white with light blue accents. Twinkling lights and flowers adorned every corner. The air was filled with the scent of fresh flowers and vanilla.

"Hey, I need to go check on the appetizers in the kitchen," Marilyn said, glancing at the tray of snacks on the table. "Can you take care of our guests for a bit?"

"Absolutely! Go, I've got this." Alexandria squeezed Marilyn's hand before turning to their friends and announcing, "Enjoy the party, everyone!"

As Marilyn disappeared into the kitchen, Mel poured a glass of wine and, her eyes shining with happiness, said to Alexandria, "The ceremony was absolutely beautiful. The vows, the setting—everything was just perfect."

Alexandria hugged her and said, "Thank you. We wanted it to be special, something that truly represented us."

"I'm very happy for you two. I've never seen a couple so in love." Mel nodded, taking a sip from her glass. She moved closer and whispered in Alexandria's ear, "Be careful this time. Don't repeat the mistakes from your past."

"I know," Alexandria said, looking over Mel's shoulder as her wife emerged from the kitchen with a tray of new appetizers.

"And don't forget that she is your wife…but also, she isn't." Mel took another big sip from her glass and ensured that Marilyn had moved in a different direction before continuing, "Everyone here is excited about your wedding, and you give hope to everyone that love exists, but it was a symbolic wedding. It's not real; it's not legal."

"Legal or not, it's real in the ways that matter." Alexandria smiled, but a little insecurity pinched her inside. She continued firmly, "Our love, our commitment—that's what counts. One day, I hope the law will catch up to our love."

Chapter 2

2006
Bucharest, Romania

"HEY, YOU MUST be Alexandria, right?" A large man carrying a yellow folder smiled as he walked towards her in the small café. Another man of similar build followed behind him.

"Yes," Alexandria replied, shaking hands. "Nice to meet you." She'd seen an advertisement posted on her college campus for a job, an assistant videographer. There weren't many details about the internship, but she decided to give it a shot and called the number listed. She'd gotten an interview, which was at a café near the studio. Alexandria was surprised by the location, but excited to get the interview.

"I'm Nando, I'm the chief cameraman, and this is the lighting technician. I'm happy you came," said the man with the folder, as they both took seats across from Alexandria. "I hope you don't mind meeting here, but we prefer it to be informal," he continued while flipping through a few papers. "We don't shoot news or serious journalism; we entertain people." Nando smiled and paused for a moment. "I'll explain to you more about the job, but why don't you tell us something about yourself."

He took another look in the folder. "I see that you're studying videography?"

"Yes, cinematography, and film and video production. I'm set to graduate soon," Alexandria answered proudly. "I don't have a lot of experience yet, but I saw in the ad that you were looking for an assistant videographer, so I gave you a call." Alexandria sat upright in her seat, her posture exuding confidence despite the butterflies in her stomach. "I want to start gaining practical experience in television or production."

"That's okay, we're looking for people with or without experience," the second man, who had been quiet until this moment, responded.

Alexandria cleared her throat and continued. She wanted to be direct with them, but not too forward. "To be honest, I've been to two other interviews already, one for a news show and one for a political show. I'm interested in any genre at this point, so that I can get real, practical experience. Theory is interesting to me too, but without the camera and the spotlight, it just wouldn't be possible to make the magic happen, would it?"

"True," said Nando. glancing at his colleague with a tiny smile. "I can see you're motivated." He looked back at her again and closed the folder. "Our television station produces a new, innovative, one-of-a-kind entertainment program. We broadcast twenty-four hours a day, seven days a week over global satellite. It's essentially a twenty-four-hour show that is broken into four smaller shows, which make up our shifts. All the crew rotates out each shift."

Alexandria hadn't expected the job would involve working at night, so she made sure to clarify that part. "So some of the shifts are during the night?”

"Correct. But new employees usually start with day shifts. The night shifts are a little bit more dynamic and complex, so we work with a more experienced team. Is that a problem for you?”

Alexandria was getting more curious about what exactly they broadcast that required filming all night. "I don't think that would be a problem for me. What exactly are you filming?”

"Every show includes five to eight girls who dance, smile, wave to the camera—you know, have fun on-camera. The girls speak on headphones to viewers who watch the show from all over the world through a satellite.” His voice was serious and professional. "The conversations between the girls and the viewers are private, not audible to other viewers. A sound engineer selects the music for each show and that's what viewers hear.”

The lighting technician added, "From time to time, the girls might say a few words on air. Say hello to a viewer, or introduce themselves, something like that. This is all coordinated with the director.”

"Yeah,” Nando waved his hand and continued, "We have pay-per-call lines that viewers use to call into the show. People from different countries around the world can call in and chat, have someone to talk to, share how their day was…sometimes they might even get a little naughty with the girls they see on screen. We have regular viewers who call every day and always talk to the same girl. They become like close friends and feel a strong connection because they talk with each other every day.”

"Or some people talk to a different girl every call. We even have female viewers,” the lighting technician again interrupted Nando.

"Sounds interesting," Alexandria said. "You said the night shift is more complex. What is the difference between the shifts?"

"At night, the show gets a little hotter," Nando said. "It's more erotic. The girls can dance more provocatively and even take off some of their clothes. They can also touch each other—but we have very strict rules. The line between erotica and porn is pretty thin, and if things cross that line, we could be shut down and face legal consequences. As you know, porn is illegal in Romania." Alexandria was listening with her mouth just a bit open. "If you're cool with all this, I suggest we head over to the studio to check it out," Nando said with a smile. "The studios are across the street."

Although Alexandria hadn't known the nature of the job earlier, she'd become intrigued while they spoke. Something drew her to the opportunity and she wanted to know more.

"Sure, let's go."

~

"What cameras do you shoot with?" Alexandria asked as they walked together to the building where the studios were located. "And do you change the lighting every day?"

"All the equipment is new," Nando responded, showing her the way. "The cameras are high-definition, Sony. For lighting, we use a mix of tungsten and fluorescent lights. ARRI and Kino Flo are our go-tos. Sometimes we change the set if the director has a specific idea for the show, or a theme they want to work with."

He opened the back door of the building, one that Alexandria had passed by a few times before but had never really paid attention to. The inside of the building impressed her. It was actually a large warehouse with several different studios.

"It's quite different from the other television studios I've been to before," Alexandria said, walking slowly and admiringly, like a kid in a candy shop.

A young man walked by, nodded, and smiled, saying to her, "Hey, how's it going?"

"At the other studios I've been to, people seemed serious, busy…even grumpy," Alexandria whispered to Nando. "I like the energy and vibe here."

He gave her a friendly smile and pointed the way to the main studio, where the show was being broadcast. She stared in astonishment.

"This décor is new. As you see, it's very stylish—black and white."

He pointed to the On Air sign, which was lit in red. The floor was mirrored glass, and imitation jewels hung from the ceiling. Two women sat on a white leather couch in the middle of the room. While one woman danced, others were seated on high-backed chairs, and a third spoke into a microphone. All the women used headphones placed behind their ears to talk to viewers. Some of the women smiled when they saw Alexandra in the corner of the studio.

"Are you going to jump in?" a woman asked her. She was heading toward the studio, seemingly returning from a break.

"She's not a model!" Nando laughed. "She's

applying for the cameraman position."

"Really?" The woman smiled at Alexandria. "Good luck, I hope you get the job. The camera crew is mostly men; it would be great to have you here." She signaled to a young man behind one of the cameras that she was about to enter the frame.

Alexandria liked everything she'd seen, and the idea of filming erotica at night seemed interesting, even though she saw this as a professional challenge. She knew that at the entry level, she couldn't be too choosy about how she got her first work experience in the profession. She was hoping they'd give her the thumbs up.

"About the salary," Nando said, leading Alexandria to a small breakroom. "We make our money based on the calls and text messages we get during the shift. The viewers pay a lot for this experience. We charge them per minute and it's pricy. If we do a good show, if people are interested in the girls and the lines are full, then the profit for the company is good. A formula calculates how much each of the employees will make, based on percentage. It's a good strategy because if we do our job well, we're making more money, right?"

"Sure, that makes sense," she answered.

"Take a moment to think about whether this is something you'd be interested in," Nando said, looking at his watch. "We've got a few more interviews lined up before the end of the week, and if you make it through, we'll give you a call. I'm glad you came." He shook her hand and led her to the exit.

Right afterward, Alexandria called her mom to tell her about the interview, and how much she hoped she'd get a job offer.

"I think it's a terrible idea. Most likely they film porn! Places like this end up raided by the police, and the people who work there end up in jail. You're so young—you're going to ruin your future and it's going to be on your record forever! And what are you going to tell people if they ask you where you work? What will I tell your father?" Her voice became more anxious as she added more details. "You have other options. What's wrong with filming the news or politics? It's much more prestigious."

"Oh Mom, don't exaggerate. It's nothing like that, and this is just for entertainment. It's much more innocent than you think. Your opinion matters to me, but I have to be honest: if I got the call that they wanted to hire me, I would start right away. You just have to trust me—everything will be fine." Alexandria didn't have any doubts about this opportunity. "And you don't need to give Dad details about what I'm doing. Just filming advertisements."

~

A few days later Alexandria received the call she was waiting for. The news was good, and everything was going according to plan. Her first real job was exactly what she'd dreamed of, and despite her mother's worries, she felt like the content of the show was a sort of bonus. Deep inside, she felt intrigued, even if she wasn't able to truly identify why.

"Take Camera Three," Chill said while preparing Camera Two.

"Got it." Alexandria stood behind her camera, which was mounted on a heavy-duty tripod. She touched the headphones that were hanging on the side.

"That's our connection with the control room." Chill said as he nodded at the headset under her hand. "In the control room, we have a video switcher. That's the main tool the technical director on the video mixer uses to switch between different camera feeds." Chill was also a new cameraman. He had been hired a month earlier, but he already felt experienced. He was average height, thin, and always wore wide cargo pants and black T-shirts featuring metal bands.

"Yeah, they showed me the control room."

"The director calls the shots," Chill continued. "They're watching all the camera feeds on multiple monitors. When the director wants to switch to a different camera, they'll call out the number of that camera. For example, 'Ready Camera Three,' and then 'Take Camera Three,' he presses the button, and you're live."

"I can't wait," Alexandria smiled as she checked the settings on the camera.

"Always try to find something interesting going on in the studio. Be ready with the next frame and keep it steady. Make sure you always have focus."

Alexandria loved the media production industry. Her passion for photography and videography began as a hobby when she was a girl. Now she was living her dream.

"What about Camera One?" Alexandria nodded toward the camera in the corner.

"That's the wide shot. It shows the whole studio. On the daytime shows that don't have a special theme, we use it just like that—without a cameraman. But when there's more going on, there's supposed to be one more guy here," Chill responded, checking the lights. "Are you going to take night shifts?"

"I don't think so. They told me only experienced cameramen work them."

"Yeah, most likely you'll cover the daytime shows." Chill waved and went to the control room to check the cameras.

Alexandria liked the feeling of being in a studio, of holding the camera in her hand, of seeing the lights and spotlights…she loved being part of filming a project.

~

At the end of the shift, Nando arrived and stood in the back of the studio. Alexandria noticed him and thought that maybe he was there to see how she'd done on her first day.

"How was the show? "Alexandria heard his voice behind her. She shifted her headset microphone away from her mouth and said, "So far, so good."

"Great!" He came closer and checked her tripod. "Is this tripod moving smoothly? I think we might have to do some maintenance on it." He didn't wait for Alexandria's response before shifting to, "Hey, I need to ask you for a favor."

"Sure!" Alexandria couldn't imagine what favor she could do for him.

"If you're not in a rush, can you stay for an extra hour, for the next show? One of the cameramen for the night shift is running late. I asked Chill, but he has plans."

"For sure. I'm not in a rush." Alexandria was tired but accepted without hesitation. She was curious to see what went on during the nighttime shows.

"Thanks, I owe you," Nando said. "It's going to be filming in the other studio across the hallway. We just changed the setup and lights. Once you're done here, just join us over there. You have time when they break for commercial."

The women who worked the nighttime show were called "hot models," meaning their performances were more suggestive. They could take off their clothes, dance erotically, perform short, sensual scenes with each other, and engage in soft kissing—but never with tongues. That was forbidden. The women were allowed to be nude, but they could not broadcast any close-up shots of genitalia or penetration. Everything had to be gentle and presented beautifully. Viewers could send a text message and order up something that they wanted to see, which could be an erotic dance, a striptease, a woman playing with her feet or applying lotion on her body, someone getting tied up, and even models interacting sexually with other models. A lesbian show.

The moment when Alexandria heard her director say over the headset, "And we are out!" she left her camera and ran over to the other studio. The hot models began to enter at about the same time. They were dressed differently from the daytime show's women—those were the soft models. The hot models dressed much more extravagantly, their makeup was heavier, and each one of them entered with the confidence of a superstar. They took their positions.

The countdown began, the transmission was starting in *Three…two…one…*and the On Air signal lit up. Alexandria grabbed the headphones from the unstaffed camera, put them on, and took her first frame.

"Who is on Camera One?" she heard in her ears.

"It's Alexandria. I'm covering for someone—sorry, I'm not sure what his name is." For some reason, she could feel her heart suddenly, in her throat.

"Okay, Alexandria, zoom in on the girl with the microphone."

One of the women was holding a microphone, and when the red light came on to indicate that the mic was live, she introduced herself and then each of the other women individually. She promised the audience a very hot show that would not let them go to bed that night.

"Okay, boys," the director said from the control room. "Sorry—boy and girl. The phone lines are open. Give me some pretty frames…let's make the lines catch fire."

One of the monitors next to the cameras displayed a console of the studio phone lines. Lines lit up when calls came through from viewers. Alexandria noticed how, one by one, they all lit up red. Messages began to appear on the screen with various requests from the viewers. This show was much more dynamic and interactive than what Alexandria was used to filming, and that made her even more enthusiastic. In every corner of the studio, something was going on.

The director, on a video mixer, was yelling through the headset: "Show *her*! Give me a close-up of the other one—no, no, they're doing a lesbian show over there—two cameras right there!"

Each model was immersed in their own erotic storyline, and they all looked extremely sexy and stylish.

A message came in from some guy named Johan, asking for a striptease from the Top Model—that was

Aurora. She was the original model since the channel had first started, and she acted like she owned the whole production. A few months later Alexandria found out that she was dating Nando. Aurora had a perfect, slim body, slender ankles, well-shaped breasts, and a round butt. She walked with her nose held high and her every gesture or movement was extremely measured. She was black-haired and dark-eyed, and that night she wore a tight red dress, black heels, and a pearl necklace. There was a pole in one corner of the studio that hadn't yet been featured in a shot. Soon, all the cameras turned to focus there. A production assistant had already placed a smoke machine and two large fans nearby.

The moderator was announcing the next show from the control room. "Hey, everybody out there! This next show is a special request from Johan. How're you doing tonight, Johan? The top model on TV, the charming Aurora, will do a striptease just for you."

The lights dimmed and after a short pause, a slow, erotic song began. The smoke machine let out a stream of smoke. Aurora walked over to the pole and leaned her back against it. All the cameras were on her, and any woman there who wasn't in the frame was watching her show.

The technical director murmured into the headsets, "All cameras please, very slow motion."

One of the cameramen removed his camera from the tripod and approached her, moving his camera all over her body. Aurora stared straight into the lens, then slowly moved her gaze away, then playfully back at him again. She was flirting with him. This dance between the two of them, surrounded by smoke and red spotlights, was like an erotic dream. She turned her back and began to gently remove the straps of her dress. It was all very slow and measured.

Alexandria was filming on one of the cameras that was the furthest away, but despite the distance, she felt as though she were so close that she could feel Aurora's slow inhale and exhale on her own skin. The moment came when her dress fell on the ground. Aurora turned slowly towards the cameras. Her nipples were hard. She turned to the pole, slowly grabbed it with both hands, and began to spin around. A veil was tied to one side of the pole and it billowed in the wind created by the fans. Aurora grabbed it and covered part of her body. As the dance continued, she began a gentle game with her thong, pulling it and putting it back again. She repeated this gesture several times. Alexandria could easily see the outline of her pussy under the thin fabric of the thong. Aurora began to slowly tug at the only thing that separated her from the eager eyes of her viewers. She pulled down her thong, which slid to the ground, revealing everything that had been hiding beneath it.

There was the most beautiful pussy Alexandria had ever seen. Not like she'd seen many before now.

The dance continued, the top model slowly removing the pearl necklace from her neck. In perfect rhythm with the music, she took the unclasped string of pearls, one end in the fingertips of each hand, and brought the necklace between her legs. She began to slowly rub her perfect pussy with the string of pearls.

Alexandria held the camera, but her mind was somewhere, coming face to face with a world full of secret desires. She had seen movies, of course, but had never come into such close contact with these desires in real life.

She appreciated the beauty of the scene; it had felt soft and warm to her. The lights were low, the movements were elegant, and time moved so slowly that it felt like there was all the time in the world for this dance.

Suddenly the director at the console shouted, "Tell the other girls we're going back to them! Turn the cameras!"

Alexandria woke up from the dream she'd fallen into. The studio techs turned up the lights, while the other models jumped up and quickly assumed different positions than where they had been just seconds ago. The music changed too, and the host announced the call-in number of the request line.

"Hey, I'm here." Alexandria felt someone's hand on her shoulder. It was the cameraman who had been running late. "Thank you for covering for me," he said while Alexandria handed over the headset.

"No worries. I wasn't in a rush." It was after midnight and she'd been there for over ten hours, but she felt neither tired nor inclined to leave. On the contrary, she felt like she could have stayed until the end of the nighttime show. The dancing, the lighting, the smoke, the cameras, the passionate atmosphere had made the whole experience inspiring and stimulating.

~

Three months passed. It turned out that Alexandria was good at her job. She had an instinct for framing and composition, which quickly caught everyone's attention. She wasn't afraid of extra work and was eager to learn as much as she could about the intricacies of the profession.

Working at the studio was enjoyable and didn't wear her out. She didn't have many friends outside of work, so it wasn't a problem to stay late when she needed to. Slowly but surely, she came to know her colleagues better too.

Word of the talented new camera operator even reached the owner of the station, Mr. Lupan. He called her into his office.

"Come in, sit down. Do you want anything? Water?" he asked.

"No thanks, I don't need anything." Alexandria's mouth was parched from anxiety, and she actually needed the water she had just been offered, but she didn't want to inconvenience Mr. Lupan by asking. She was meeting him for the first time and she was nervous to be invited to his office.

"The chief cameraman has been very complimentary about you and your work." Mr. Lupan smiled at Alexandria and continued. "We've never had such a talented and hard-working assistant. Some of the directors also spoke very highly of you. And the girls feel comfortable when you're behind the camera."

"Thanks for the kind words. I try to do the best I can, and I really enjoy it. Videography has always been a passion of mine." Alexandria spoke calmly, but inside her heart was skipping. She was so proud to hear these words and realize that her work had been noticed.

"Starting next week, you won't be entering the schedule as an assistant, but as a regular cameraman. Of course, your pay will also increase. You'll be making the salary of a regular videographer. We'll add you to the schedule for both the day and night shifts. If you're serious about growing in this company, this is a big opportunity."

"I would like to grow, Mr. Lupan." Alexandria straightened a bit in her chair.

"I also like to keep my eyes open for people with growth potential who might do well as directors. That's a position that requires more creativity. Would that be something that might interest you, down the line?"

"Of course, that would be a huge professional goal for me. Plus, I'm about to finish my second major—directing. Thanks for the encouraging words."

"Okay then, I'll keep you in mind as soon as something comes up."

Chapter 3

May 2007

ALEXANDRIA WAS A BIG admirer of one of the models, Helena. She was a hot model, even though she worked the day shift a couple of times a week. Alexandria thought she was the epitome of beauty. She was a blonde with large breasts, a sculpted body, and silky skin. Alexandria liked to work on the same shows that Helena worked. Two or three times, Alexandria had touched her casually, feeling the softness of her skin, and noticing her lovely scent.

"No, I don't have a boyfriend, honey…yes, I like girls too, hun... Do you want me to tell you more about this, sweetheart?"

Helena was speaking with a caller, while Alexandria was filming her—close enough to hear every word. Helena was attracted to women! This revelation made Alexandria even more committed to filming her shows. Maybe this was the answer to the inexplicable chemistry that was emerging between them. Alexandria was afraid to admit this attraction, even to herself, so she watched Helena from behind her camera and tried to be as friendly as she could.

She had no expectations, let alone dreams, that

anything could happen between them. She simply liked being in the same room with her. She tried not to stare at her too much or draw her attention, but at the same time she hoped that Helena was watching and studying her in the same way. With Helena's beauty and sex appeal, she was one of the top models, and got her fair share of camera time. When filming her, Alexandria was at her creative best, feeling like Helena was a muse who could unleash the artist in her. Helena knew how to play with the camera, to communicate, to flirt, and when she was interacting with Alexandria's camera, the magic really happened. Helena, for her part, loved being filmed by Alexandria. Alexandria's camera angles and instincts proved that Helena was the prettiest and most desirable, and the narcissist in her loved having that proof. But on another level, she could admire Alexandria's talent and gift for capturing beautiful shots with her camera. She increasingly insisted that only Alexandria should shoot her close-ups. This had been going on for a few months. Off-air, when the lights went back on and everyone left the studio, the interactions between the two of them were reduced to collegial phrases like, "Great show—see you soon!" or "Next week we have another shift together, so you know the show's gonna be fantastic!"

Several months passed in which Alexandria worked almost without a break. She was covering for quite a few of her coworkers, who would call her to ask if she would take their shifts, since they had another commitment. She never refused because first, she loved her job, and second, the extra pay was decent.

Finally, she scheduled a few days off, a well-deserved break. One of her cousins was getting married, and she had plans to travel to her hometown, Constanța, where her family lived, to attend the wedding. Alexandria had moved to the capital for college. Before accepting the television job, she had traveled home more often to visit her family, but with her busy schedule, she hadn't done that in months.

On one of her last shows before this short vacation, she found herself working with Helena again. Halfway through the show, Alexandria stepped out for a short break in the breakroom. Helena came in shortly after her.

"Oh, I'm tired," Helena began casually. "I need rest." She took a small sip from a plastic cup of coffee.

"Tell me about it—I haven't had a day off in weeks! But I'll catch up on my rest next week; I'm going on a little vacation."

"So, what are your big plans?"

"Nothing too spectacular." Alexandria picked up her cup of coffee from the coffee machine in the corner. "A cousin of mine is getting married and I'll be traveling to Constanța for a couple of days for the occasion. We're actually not too close though," Alexandria added.

"Oh, I love weddings. I haven't gone to a wedding in so long. Do you have a plus one?"

"No, it's just me. And since I'm the best videographer in the family, I'm on duty, filming "backstage" at the wedding." Alexandria waved her hand somewhat descriptively.

"Why don't I come with you? I could be your plus one," Helena offered.

Silence followed. It was the last thing Alexandria expected to hear. They had almost never talked for longer than a few minutes—and always about trivial topics…the usual comments about the shows, the weather, whatever song was playing. Alexandria didn't know what to say.

Does Helena really want to go with me, and if she does, why? Was she joking? Or was that a rhetorical question to which the answer was: she wouldn't come? Alexandria silently ran through several possible options.

"Sure, I'd love for you to come. It's going to be a small wedding, nothing big. I have to drive a couple of hours anyway; the drive will be much more fun if I have company," replied Alexandria.

What am I doing, bringing a crush to a family event?

"Great!" Helena pulled out her phone, checking the calendar. "When exactly are you planning on leaving? I don't have much luggage to take; we're going only for a few days, aren't we?"

"Yeah, a couple days." Alexandria was getting more confused.

"It'll be fun, I haven't been to a wedding since…" she seemed to be counting, then interrupted herself. "Your family wouldn't mind if you brought a friend, would they?"

"Of course not." Alexandria wasn't sure if that was a joke, but she brushed it off. Helena sounded serious and determined to be a part of this adventure, and Alexandria wasn't sure yet how to explain this sudden plus one to her family. Alexandria concluded the deal by saying, "I'm planning to leave on Friday, after the day shift. You'll have to bring your bags with you so we can leave right from work."

She had her doubts about whether this would actually happen. Alexandria was the kind of person who became deeply disappointed by broken promises, so she tried to control her excitement.

~

Alexandria cornered Mel, one of the makeup artists from work who she'd gotten close to, and whispered, "You're the only lesbian that I know. What do you think about all this? Do you think Helena likes me?"

"But do *you* really like girls?"

"I thought you were going to tell me how to find out," Alexandria sighed, rubbing her forehead.

"Well, if you're planning to bring her to a family wedding just to explore your sexuality, honestly, Alex, I'm not sure that's a good idea," Mel said while organizing her makeup brushes. "Did you tell your family that you're planning to bring someone—a woman?"

"I haven't even thought what I'm going to tell them." Alexandria nervously twirled a strand of hair "How do I explain who this girl is, who's coming with me to a family wedding last minute, and I have never even mentioned her existence before!" Her family had no idea of the thrills and desires that raged within her. It was new to her too, and really still in the realm of fantasy, since she'd never acted on any of it before. "I've never been in a…real situation with a woman before, so I hadn't even gone that far in my thoughts—about what my parents might think, and if I'm even really into it."

Mel shook her head and laughed. "Yeah, that could make it very awkward. Coming out at the wedding—that'll be your wedding gift to everyone! But do you think you really like girls?" she added in a more serious tone.

"Well, I guess sometimes—you know, different

times and situations—I felt some girls and women were more special. And, when I watch movies and there are two women kissing, it makes me feel aroused. Sometimes I feel the world stop around me, and that scene lasts longer than anything else and I want to repeat it over and over again. Like I'm studying it."

"I thought you had more serious clues." Mel rolled her eyes.

"But, Mel, when that happens, I imagine what it would feel like if I was one of those characters. How exciting it would be to feel another woman's breath, her scent, her perfume so close…what it would be like to feel her lips on mine. All these questions keep popping into my head…I have dreams about it—dreams I didn't imagine would be possible until now."

"Then go to the wedding and let's see if you come back straight or gay," Mel laughed.

"I know it sounds crazy, but I recorded a CD just for the trip that I'll play in the car." Alexandria blushed. "I've strategically mixed 80 percent of her favorite songs, and a few of mine so it doesn't seem too obvious that this was made especially for her. I mean, I've got butterflies in my stomach. And the questions just keep coming…What would happen if we casually touched? Would that lead to something more? Why did she even want to come on this trip? Does she want something to happen, or is she just bored and looking to get out of town for a weekend?"

"Damn, girl, you *are* excited about this! I know you want to see this through, but you also have to be prepared that at the last minute, she might call it off and say she isn't coming. She might just want to go as a friend, so just stayed grounded. I don't want you to get hurt." A model in need of makeup walked into the room, and Mel had to end the conversation there.

~

Friday. Alexandria went to the studio with mixed feelings.

Is the bubble going to burst; is this too good to be true? Whatever is going to happen is going to happen— quit overthinking it.

But she kept thinking about it anyway. She walked into the studio and prepped her camera. She cleaned the lens, checked the lighting, inspected the set— all the time looking toward the makeup room, watching for Helena. She was right on time and came over to greet the team.

She approached Alexandria and asked, "Are you all packed? My suitcase is in the dressing room."

The great wave of worry subsided. She was going. Who knew what might happen, but the important thing was that they were going.

After the show, the two girls headed to Alexandria's car. It was freshly washed, and the sun reflected off the polished sheet metal. Inside was spotlessly clean too: it smelled of new car air freshener, and the collection of travel CDs was carefully arranged in its case. The adventure had begun.

Helena immediately recognized the first song that came on the stereo and called out.

"Hey, this is my favorite song! I can't believe it's your favorite too!" It was a popular French chanson. She adored classic Italian and French songs.

Alexandria answered casually, "Oh yeah, this song

has been a favorite of mine for a long time. I had almost forgotten I had it on this CD. I have a big collection here in the car when I travel. You need good music in the car."

"Yeah, music is one of the most important things for a road trip," said Helena, turning up the music. After a few more songs, she turned the volume down slightly again. "Alex, are you single?"

Alexandria wasn't expecting such a direct question, but answered casually, "Yes, I'm single at the moment."

"Guess you don't have much time because of work, huh? Tell me about yourself; we have time. What were you like as a kid?" asked Helena, looking at Alexandria expectantly.

"Haha, yeah, we have time." Alexandria activated the car's cruise control. "Okay, where do I start? When I was a kid, I loved playing with the boys, I loved boy toys. I loved playing soccer, watching martial arts movies, and imitating them. In most of my games with friends, I was the leader, the head of the gang. As a teenager, I was still into video games, sports, wrestling, and WWF. You know The Rock, right? I was a big fan of his. My classmates at the time were already going out on dates and had boyfriends."

"And didn't you want to have a boyfriend?"

"I honestly didn't want to be an outsider, so I felt like I had to start going out with guys. Finding a boyfriend was like a mission for me. It was harder than it is now. Back then, the internet and dating sites were still pretty new and not as common as they are today, you know."

"And did you manage to find a boyfriend?"

"It took me a long time, but yes, I did. He was the neighbor of one of my classmates—we met through her.

He was a little older than me. Tall, cute, with blond hair… I have a thing for blond hair." Alexandria smiled slightly.

"This sounds like first love. A schoolgirl crush. What happened?" Helena turned down the music two more ticks because she was intrigued by the teenage love story.

"I broke up with him after three months," Alexandria laughed. "He really liked me and wanted us to be together all the time. We had fun at first, but then I realized that something was missing for me. Still, it was important for me to be like everyone else, so I had to have a boyfriend. The search continued until I met my next boyfriend."

Alexandria looked over. Helena was listening intently.

"Well, things were better with him. He was older than me, much more mature. He had a job, he was an engineer, but also, he was a bit boring. His friends were boring, his sense of humor wasn't my type, and his interests weren't like mine either, but he fit the bill. I had a boyfriend at least. It was a small town; people thought you were weird if you were different."

"Don't tell me you dumped him just as quickly."

"Well, not exactly. I was a little bit bored, but I really didn't want to be alone. Unexpectedly, I met another guy. I started seeing him in secret, like an affair, or a love triangle, if that's what you want to call it. I'm not saying it was right, but that's what happened," laughed Alexandria.

"You were a naughty girl, weren't you!" Helena had been listening with interest.

"We're still friends, but of course, this whole love triangle didn't end well. The truth came out, but I was on the verge of moving to Bucharest for college, so I just ran away from the whole mess. And you, what's your story?"

"My first time was with a woman," said Helena.

Alexandria blushed and felt uncomfortable, but more than anything, she was curious.

"It just happened. We were very close, and that closeness escalated into something more one day. But nothing serious followed. Then I had a relationship with a guy who was bisexual. Sometimes when we had sex, he dressed in women's clothes, and we had sex for hours. I know it sounds weird, but I liked it a lot. It was super sexy. We were together for about two years. We loved each other a lot, but at some point, we both realized that this relationship wasn't exactly what we wanted. We were too young. After that, I mostly started going out with men who were older than me. Maybe I'm weird, but I'm attracted to the life experience and wisdom they have, the confidence, and generosity…and the financial stability. But right now, I'm single. I'm not with anyone."

Alexandria hadn't expected them to make such personal revelations, but the conversation had felt quite natural and simply something people did on road trips. But she wondered: was Helena trying to provoke a reaction with these stories, or was she just being more open in sharing? After these confessions, Alexandria really couldn't get away from the thought that something might happen between them.

Alexandria's phone rang. It was her mother. She picked up and said shortly, "I can't talk, I'm driving. Don't worry, we'll be there soon."

She had mentioned to her mother that she was bringing a friend, without giving any more detail. She was slightly uneasy about this, but she decided that she would deal with it when the time came.

Usually, Alexandria drove fast, without stopping, and made it home in no more than two and a half hours. This time, she drove at a much more leisurely pace, and stopped at a roadside gas station for coffee. She liked this drive, the feeling of being together in the car, the tickling tension in her stomach, Helena's energy with her in the car.

It was getting dark as they drove into the suburbs. Alexandria's mother had called a few more times to ask why they hadn't arrived yet. She knew Alexandria never took that much time to drive home. Alexandria, knowing her mother, thought, *Wouldn't she think something strange was going on?* She was coming with a friend she didn't know; she was over an hour late.

They arrived and entered the house.

"Hello!" Helena said warmly as she hugged Alexandria's mother. "It's such a pleasure to meet you. I'm Helena. I hope we didn't keep you up; we took our time on the drive."

"Likewise." Alexandria's mom smiled softly. "And no worries! Alexandria is a pretty fast driver, so we thought you'd be here earlier. I was just checking in to make sure everything was okay." She turned to hug Alexandria too, saying, "Your dad already went to bed. He was tired."

She led them into the house, explaining as they went, "After Alexandria moved out, we turned her childhood bedroom into a guest room. Helena, I hope you will feel comfortable there." At the bedroom door, she said, "Alexandria, you can sleep in the living room. Please, show Helena where everything is, get settled in, and we'll get to know each other better tomorrow."

Alexandria didn't feel like sleeping at all, and she

certainly didn't want to stay in the living room. She wanted more than anything in the world to spend more time with Helena, but there was no way she could argue with her mother's decision. It would have made her suspicious. Her mom had a rule for her daughter's teenage years: no boyfriends sleeping in the same bed while her daughter was under her roof. It was the law, and if Alexandria broke the rule—with a woman, no less—who knew what consequences she would bring upon herself? Of course, Alexandria's family had no idea of the naughty thoughts that were going through her head and her interest in women. Luckily, they didn't know about Helena's sexuality either.

Alexandria knew she would obey her mother but felt a deep disappointment that, after all this build-up, nothing had happened, and there was no sign of that changing. She went to the living room to drop her luggage, then she went to her mother's room to say goodnight.

"Tomorrow is going to be a long day. We have to get started in the morning. I want you to film every step, every detail, of your cousin's wedding."

"But they have a photographer, right? He'll document everything."

"Pictures aren't the same as video," she whispered so as not to wake her husband. "Don't forget to charge the camera batteries."

"I won't forget." Alexandria rolled her eyes. "I've got everything ready." She sensed that her mother had calmed herself. "I'll go see if Helena needs anything else, and go to bed. Good night." She left the room and headed to her old room. She knocked on the door to be respectful.

"We came all this way to go back in time! This

room has barely changed since I moved out. Do you need anything? Are you comfortable?"

"Don't worry, everything is just fine. You're providing five-star accommodation here," replied Helena.

Alexandria tried to think of another joke to prolong the last minutes of this day with Helena. She felt like she'd taken some strange drug. Nothing had happened between them, everything was innocent and friendly, but inside Alexandria felt like she was in another universe. She wanted to spend as much time as possible with Helena. She didn't have anything else to say, and there was nothing more to do except to shut the door on her way out and say, "Okay, I'll let you get some rest because tomorrow is going to be a long day. We have to get up early. Good night."

Alexandria was ready to turn and head out the door and do just that, when Helena walked toward her, and without saying a word, without making a sound, kissed Alexandria's lips softly.

At that moment everything stopped, as if someone pressed the pause button. Maybe Alexandria's heart even stopped for a moment. Her lips felt for the first time how soft and sweet another woman's kiss could be. It was the closest she had ever come to complete happiness. A cherished dream coming true. She was experiencing this not just on a physical level—the feeling was spiritual, absolute perfection.

Is this happening to me? It can't be true; I can't believe it. Helena's lips were so soft and gentle. Alexandria had never experienced these sensations before.

Growing up, it had somehow become trendy for two girls to kiss at a club or a party—not because they were interested in each other, necessarily, but to get attention from guys or to make the party more interesting. Alexandria hadn't tried even this before. And kissing guys was usually rough: their beards scratched her face, and even if they had just shaved, their skin could simply never be that delicate. Their lips had never been as soft or as full as Helena's. They melted into Alexandria's lips. Alexandria could feel her breath with Helena's, the slow inhale and exhale, the light movements, the sweetness. Helena inserted the tip of her tongue between Alexandria's lips, filling her with a new wave of passion, satisfaction, arousal, and desire. So many emotions passed through her, ranging from excitement to warmth and emotional connection. The kiss lasted seconds, but for Alexandria, time had nearly stopped. She was experiencing this moment in slow motion.

Afterward, neither of them said anything. They stood silently and looked at each other. Helena, the one who'd started the kiss, had a slight, satisfied smile on her face. Alexandria just blinked.

"I'd better go. I don't want my mother to come looking for me. Good night." She left the room. Helena kept smiling.

Alexandria went to the bathroom. Her underwear was wet. She couldn't believe what had just happened. She took a shower, then hurried to the living room. She didn't want to create the slightest suspicion. Lying on the couch that had been made up as a bed, she couldn't stop rewinding the tape and replaying in her mind every single detail of the last few minutes. She played that brief shot over and over, wanting to memorize every bit of it forever.

Did Helena feel the same way I did? Did she plan it? Had she been dreaming about it all the way down in the car too—wanting it, waiting for us to be alone?

So many questions, so many emotions, and so much desire were now in play. That kiss had unleashed an overwhelming sexual desire and passion in Alexandria. How could a short kiss have aroused her so much?

Alexandria woke up the next morning due to the buzzing of her phone's alarm next to her pillow. It was 8:30 a.m. and Alexandria felt she had fallen asleep only two hours ago. She tried to get her bearings, suddenly remembering everything, almost not believing what had happened. She couldn't wait to see Helena again. She needed to taste those lips again and feel the magic of her presence next to her.

She got up quickly, brushed her teeth, got dressed, and went into the kitchen. The enticing aroma of freshly made pancakes floated through the house, wrapping everything in a warm, nostalgic embrace. Her mother was made up and dressed and fussing about what a long day they had ahead of them. Her father had already gone, leaving for the carwash across the street to wash the car for the wedding.

Alexandria didn't know if Helena was awake, so she decided to send her a message.

Good morning, are you up yet? I hope I didn't wake you.

She didn't get a reply right away, but Helena walked into the kitchen a moment later. The two looked at each other and smiled. There was a slight tension because they were keeping a secret and weren't sure how to act.

Alexandria's mother asked Helena if she had slept well.

"I slept like a baby and had a very interesting

dream; it felt so real that I'm not even sure if it was a dream or if it really happened..."

Alexandria, who was sipping her coffee, almost choked. This playful provocation was clearly directed at her, but she didn't want to unlock the slightest suspicion in the others.

Alexandria nervously said, "I'll go check the camera."

~

Alexandria's family and Helena arrived at the small wedding venue a couple of hours early. Preparations for the ceremony were feverish. The hairdresser and makeup artist were finishing Alexandria's cousin's makeup and hair. Alexandria took the camera out of its bag and captured a few short clips of the bride. Her mother, who was so proud that Alexandria was graduating from one of the most elite universities of cinematography and directing in the country, had insisted that her daughter had to film the wedding.

"Hurry up, Alex." Her mom was directing the scene. "Take a shot of the decorations. Did you get the wedding cake?"

Filming was always a pleasure for Alexandria, but at that moment, she was in a different state of mind. She hadn't stopped thinking about what had happened the night before. She hadn't been able to be alone with Helena, which made her emotions even stronger. Impatience and desire grew in her like a climbing thermometer. Alexandria couldn't stop replaying every moment of that kiss over and over in her head—every movement, flicker, touch and look. She was floating on a pink cloud while everything around her passed by.

"Let me help you with these curls; I have a lot of experience with different hairstyles." Helena joined in the preparations, giving advice on the dress, how hair or makeup could look even better, introducing herself to any of the family members who had come over. When she had the chance, she chatted with Alexandria in a casual, friendly way. Alexandria worried that everyone would notice there was something more to their friendship.

Thankfully everyone is too busy to pay attention to us. Maybe it's all in my head. Stop overthinking.

Several times her mom reminded her that this needed to be filmed, or that some important moment had been missed. Alexandria would nod in agreement and pick up the camera, but her mind wasn't there. Her body and camera drifted around the reality of the wedding, while her mind remained in their parallel romantic universe. As a result, many important moments in one of her cousin's most important days weren't captured, and that would lead to more consequences.

~

The whole day, in the thick of the celebration, Alexandria and Helena had no time alone. At the end of the evening, Alexandria's parents were ready to head home.

"Well, that was a beautiful wedding, wasn't it?" Helena asked.

"Indeed," Alexandria's father nodded. "Are you coming with us, girls? Or will the party continue somewhere? There's room in the car." He looked at them expectantly.

Alexandria glanced at Helena and smiled before turning back to her parents. "Actually, Dad, we were thinking of checking out the after-party at that new club downtown. Don't worry, we'll call a cab to get back home later."

"Okay, have fun and be careful," her mom sighed, "And make sure to call us if you need anything, okay?" She opened the car door.

"We will, Mom," her daughter reassured her, giving her a quick hug.

"Have fun, girls," her father said as he started the ignition.

Alexandria and Helena found a high-top table in the middle of the club. A few of the wedding guests were already dancing on the dance floor. The music was blaring; everyone was dancing. Exquisite professional dancers twirled their bodies on high catwalks. Alexandria expected the newlyweds to show up at any moment.

"The music is great!" Helena was already swaying in rhythm.

Alexandria raised her hand to get the bartender's attention. "Two glasses of white wine, please," she shouted over the music. Just as she and Helena clinked glasses, a familiar voice called out from behind them.

"Hey, it's so cool that you could join the after-party!" The bride gave them both a big hug and the groom leaned in for hugs too.

"Cheers! To your happiness—again!" Alexandria shouted over the music.

Even after a couple of hours, Alexandria still couldn't relax with Helena, worried that someone might notice their closeness. But, as glasses of wine were drained, inhibitions began to loosen. She looked toward the newlyweds' table to make sure nobody was watching, took a sip from her sweaty glass of wine, leaned in toward Helena, and kissed her passionately. This was her reward for all that waiting and longing. A true, realized kiss, without questions or riddles. It went on and on, because neither of them wanted to stop, and the rest of the world didn't exist.

Alexandria's cousin happened to turn suddenly at just that moment. She watched in silence and confusion, then forced herself to look away, focusing on her husband, pretending that nothing had happened.

The night went on. The atmosphere was great, and Alexandria had surrendered to the moment.

"You know your cousin is at the next table, right?" Helena whispered in Alexandria's ear, trailing some kisses down her neck between words.

"I know, but I don't want that to spoil a great night." Her eyes were sparkling. "I hope she doesn't say anything to my parents but if she does, we'll just say we were drunk. Just a kiss between girlfriends who drank too much and partied like crazy. We wouldn't be the first, and that doesn't mean there's anything between us. Sounds plausible, doesn't it?"

Alexandria waited for Helena to confirm her theory. At that moment, everything seemed much easier to Alexandria. This potential problem seemed so small that it wasn't even worth thinking about. The night progressed and Alexandria went over to her cousin's table.

"Having fun?"

"Yeah, it's great! My first night in a club as a

married woman!"

"I'm so happy for you! We're pretty tired, so we're heading home. You're staying, right?" Alexandria asked, giving her a hug.

"The party is just beginning!" Her cousin was jumping around with a bottle of champagne in hand.

Alexandria and Helena left the club and waited for the cab Alexandria had called. The two stood at a slight distance from each other without betraying the sexual tension between them. Alexandria felt impatient but also unsure of what might happen next. She wanted more than anything to continue what they had started—to satisfy her curiosity, to explore this unknown and exciting territory—but she was also nervous about whether she would live up to Helena's expectations. Would she be able to give Helena what she wanted? Would she be good at it? Would she enjoy it as much as she hoped she would?

The taxi arrived and they got into the car. During the twenty-minute drive home, they couldn't keep their lips off each other. Those kisses were delicious, craving, burning, hot. The driver observed them in the mirror and joked, "You two having fun back there? Do you want me to take a few laps around the neighborhood?" His comment went unnoticed.

When they arrived at the house, they knew they had to be quiet as Alexandria's parents were asleep. Tiptoeing, they entered Alexandria's room and picked up where they had left off. Alexandria was enjoying all the kissing but was even more eager to take the next step to see what that felt like.

Helena had more experience than she did. She was in control. She had watched Alexandria in the studio, behind her camera, and thought she was sexy, authoritative, talented, attractive. She'd felt something special for her and that was exactly why she was there with her in her parents' home. She wanted to fully uncover the sexual energy that existed between them, but she also knew that Alexandria hadn't slept with another woman before. She felt there was a great responsibility in being her first.

"If you want, we can wait. We have all the time in the world," Helena said sincerely as she stopped for a moment.

"No, I don't want to wait anymore." Alexandria moaned, "I want it now."

Helena unbuttoned her own blouse and pulled it off. Alexandria ran a finger over Helena's bra strap, touching her shoulder and back with the tip of her two fingers. She reached behind her back to unfasten the clasp and slowly pulled the bra off. Alexandria began to gently touch and fondle Helena's breasts. It was her first time touching someone else's breasts. She gently kissed one of her nipples while lightly touching the other with her fingers. Helena breathed raggedly as she slowly ran her nails down Alexandria's back. If kissing had seemed magical to Alexandria, this moment was even more special. She inhaled the perfume of Helena's skin. It was transporting, intoxicating. She was surrounded by the feel of her body, her soft touch, and the soft moans she was making.

At that moment, something began to vibrate.

"Wait." Helena held Alexandria's hand. The buzzing continued. "That's my work phone."

"Your work phone?" Alexandria pulled back slightly.

"Yeah, they gave it to me last week. You didn't know?" Helena started looking for her purse that was somewhere on the floor. "It's a new project, for the hot models. If you're not in the studio, but want some extra money, some viewers can call you on these phones to talk. Only talking—they can't watch you." Helena finally found her purse.

"Oh, I see. So like your own after-hours line for people in need." Alexandria laughed a little while she fixed her messy hair.

"Can you hold on a second? I have to answer but I'll just tell him that I can't talk right now."

"Why do you even have to pick up?" Alexandria's patience wore thin. "Can't you just let it ring?"

"I can't. This is one of my regulars. If I don't pick up, he'll be upset, and I don't want to lose him." Helena answered the call and began whispering. Alexandria glanced at the clock on the nightstand. It was after 2 a.m. Maybe they should call it a night.

"Look, I'll let you have your conversation." Alexandria sat down on the corner of the bed. Helena nodded to her to wait one second.

"No worries…finish your call." Alexandria pressed a kiss on Helena's forehead.

"Are you sure?" Helena mouthed while signaling that she was going to hang up in just a minute.

"Yeah, let's save the moment for later. I can wait until next time." With a heavy sigh, Alexandria turned away and quietly exited the room.

~

The next day they had to travel back to the capital. They got up around noon, the hangover from the last night throbbing in both girls' heads. They had a real drive ahead of them and Alexandria wanted to leave as quickly as possible.

Her mom, who was making them food for the road, said, "Why do you always have to be in such a hurry? Why don't you stay for lunch? We could all eat together and watch the videos from yesterday."

In the clear light of day, Alexandria wasn't sure this was a good idea. She hoped that her cousin would be smart and tactful enough not to share anything with her mother about what had happened at the club. She also knew the videos of her cousin's wedding weren't her best work. She'd been distracted by her emotions, and hadn't even considered that the videos were evidence of that. She declined her mom's invitation and they waved to her parents as they drove away, down the driveway.

"This sounds bad, but I feel relieved to be leaving," Alexandria sighed to Helena.

"But you had a good time, right?" Helena smiled at Alexandria and turned on the CD Alexandria had made.

Alexandria felt safe in the car. She was finally alone with Helena.

"Oh yeah, for sure. And how did you like our little getaway?" Alexandria inquired with genuine curiosity.

"Yeah, I really enjoyed the city, the party, your family's vibe," Helena said, humming along to the chorus of the song.

As the car sped down the road, Alexandria felt a surge of courage and placed her palm on top of Helena's hand, feeling the touch of her warm skin. Helena smiled and turned up the music.

"Oh, I love this song!"

Alexandria decided to interrupt the French chanson.

"I just wanted to tell you how much I enjoyed what we started last night, and that I can't wait to continue it." She didn't want to give away all her feelings; she also wanted to know what Helena thought about last night, and about her feelings and plans for the future.

Helena was silent. Alexandria's mood and stomach turned upside down.

Feels like bad news. Did I do something wrong? Is it possible she didn't like what happened?

"You know, you're an amazing girl," Helena began, her voice soft but serious. "Very smart and talented. Anyone would be lucky to be here with you."

Alexandria could sense that a *BUT* was about to follow.

"I like you a lot and I would really like to spend more time with you and get to know you deeper, but...I'm not looking for anything serious."

Alexandria felt a sudden lurch in her stomach.

"Right now, I don't have time for a relationship, especially with a woman. Don't think I'm a gold digger or anything...but I can't be an erotic model forever. I need some stability, a man who can take care of me." Helena continued as her voice got colder. "I wish I could give you more of myself...I wish I could give you what you want, but I can't right now."

Alexandria's heart sank.

"I know I'm hurting you by telling you this, but I see the way you look at me. I don't want to lie to you, or give you hope that something else will happen back in our everyday lives. I've been thinking about this for the last few hours, and although I've had a lot of fun and I'm happy that I came with you on this trip, I feel that if I don't tell you this, it wouldn't be fair to you. And I want to be honest. You deserve to be very happy and loved, and to be with a person who will give you all of their time and attention."

Her words hit Alexandria like ice water, or a loud noise that woke her from a beautiful dream. And it hadn't even been a dream; it had really happened. The romantic fairy tale had evaporated, leaving a bitter emptiness in its place. Alexandria had hoped that the best was yet to come—dreaming of her first time with a woman…an intense and searing love that she knew she couldn't feel for any man. Helena had been like a gift that she was able to enjoy for only a very short time before it turned to mist and disappeared. She was shattered as Helena's words covered dream world in a dark shadow.

"Yeah, no problem. It's okay. I'm pretty busy too. I want to take as many shifts at the studio as possible, and also, I'm about to graduate, so I don't have too much free time either." Alexandria casually tried to cover up her hurricane of emotions. She didn't want to show Helena how disappointed and hurt she was, or how much she meant to her, and how she felt as though her dreams had been stolen and crushed. She listed several more daily tasks she had in her full schedule, in a desperate attempt to look as though she didn't mind at all.

She turned up the music, smiled like nothing had happened and said, "Do you like this song? I've been wanting to download it and burn it on this CD; it's my favorite." She held the steering wheel tight. It rained on and off throughout their drive, sometimes intensifying into a downpour. By the time they reached the city, the rain had become a steady drizzle, and that helped Alexandria to concentrate more on the road than on their earlier conversation. When they arrived in front of Helena's apartment, the drizzle had turned into more of a mist. The two women sat in the car looking at each other.

"Thank you for sharing this trip with me. I really had a great time." Helena's smile was soft but tinged with regret.

"Can I see you again?" asked Alexandria.

"Of course, I'll see you in the studio tomorrow. You're night shift, right? I'll be there. Hopefully, I'll get some extra time from the best camera," Helena laughed.

"I don't mean at work. Let's go out sometime, just you and me?"

"Yeah, why not. We can work something out," replied Helena as she started to gather her things from the back seat. "I'll tell you again: you're really great, and anyone would be lucky to be with you." She reached for the door. Alexandria hoped that after everything she might get one last kiss before the trip was truly over. She leaned forward, but Helena turned her head slightly and Alexandria's lips only found her cheek. Helena also kissed Alexandria's cheek and got out of the car.

It had stopped raining. The clouds were parting, and a few rays of sunlight were piercing through them. A pale rainbow appeared on the horizon. Alexandria moved through the CD, trying to find something that would make her feel better. She put on her sunglasses, tears falling behind the dark lenses.

Chapter 4

August 2010
Bucharest

"DO YOU HAVE a few minutes? I need to talk to you about something." Zara wasted no time this morning as she called her best childhood friend. "I found a very interesting job offer. Do you want to check it out with me? What could be better than working together?" Zara and Marilyn were almost inseparable. "They're looking for good-looking, English-speaking girls for a call center."

"Call center?" Marilyn scoffed. "If you're only talking on the phone, why do you have to be good-looking? It sounds a little strange." Clattering plates and commotion from the kitchen started to drown her out. "Wait until I get outside, I can't hear you very well. It's crazy here today!" Marilyn worked as a waitress in a popular restaurant. She was in her final year at college, studying dentistry.

"The money's good—way better than what you're making now. And if we work together, it would be so much fun." Zara could hear Marilyn pushing her way through the kitchen. "Come on, come with me to an interview! If we don't like it, we'll just tell them. Say yes and I'll call to ask when and where the interviews are happening." Zara sounded excited.

"Another one of your crazy ideas…well, you know it's not hard to convince me. Text me when the interview is." Zara could hear someone yelling at Marilyn in the kitchen.

"I have to go, I have a lot of work to do."

Three days later they met with Valentina, the manager, a former erotic model who had been promoted to a higher position. She was a tall, thin, dark-haired woman, with sharp cheekbones and a haughty look. Under her heavily made-up eyes, her gaze was stern, but she was actually quite pleased with these job candidates. They were both beautiful and showed potential—exactly the kind of faces the station needed.

"Working with us is entertaining," Valentina told them. "You get to talk to lots of new people from different countries. Our satellite covers Europe, parts of South and North America, and even Asia."

"So, they can watch it in Romania too? Marilyn asked with wide eyes.

"Don't worry, honey." Valentina shook her head. "The satellite is coded for Romania. Nobody here can watch you. We want to make sure the models feel safe, and they don't have to worry that their friends or family can see them on the screen." She grinned and continued. "The pay we offer is much better than at any other job you could get if you're still in school or just starting out in your career. And not only that…" She paused that thought as she led them around the studios, showing them what the work consisted of. "The channel is based on pay-per-view phone calls and on revenue from the cost per minute, per call. All of this raised everyone's pay on the show. When the show is really good, that means we get more calls and messages, and then everyone makes more money." Valentina, who had extensive experience in marketing, was great at selling. "If you speak more languages, that's also a bonus. Most of the girls communicate with the viewers in English, but if you speak a second or third language, the chances are higher that more people in different countries will call you, and again, that's more money."

She knew how to present a job as a dream opportunity. And when the interviewees were beautiful girls, her pitch became even more charming and convincing. The two women listened to her with open mouths.

"Just think about this—you'll be working in television, in front of cameras, a team of professionals behind them. Your audience, the people who watch you, will adore you. You'll be TV stars. Some girls start temporarily or as a side job, but once the checks start coming in, 90 percent of the girls come on full-time. We suggest all new girls start on daytime shows like this one here." She paused to let the girls look around the studio.

"The cameras and lights looked impressive," Marilyn said. "And everyone here is so pretty."

"Oh yeah. They're just having fun, listening to music. You can tell the sound director to play your favorite song or whatever music you like, and you can dance to it, and in the meantime have a casual conversation with someone on the other side of the earth."

"Looks cool," Zara said while looking at the models who were on air. "And that's what you're broadcasting all the time?"

"That's for the daytime shows; the nighttime shows have a little more erotic sensibility." Valentina cleared her throat and continued. "If at some point you feel ready to see how the nighttime shows go, well, give it a try. It's kind of the same, but the girls may have a more erotic attitude, be a bit more provocative, and have the option to remove some clothes. But nothing extreme. The night show is erotic, not porn." She folded her arms across her chest. "And it's totally up to the individual…what to do, what to reveal. It's also up to you what shifts to take, and how many days you want to work. We're pretty flexible. Both of you would be great additions to our team."

Marilyn and Zara were drawn in by Valentina's convincing words. After all, this was a job in television, it carried with it a sense of pride, satisfaction, adoration from viewers. Maybe a little fame. The studio was beautiful and glossy—all those cameras and spotlights, and most of all, the financial reward for a few hours of entertainment.

"What do you think? Do you want to try?" Zara looked at Marilyn. "I'm really impressed."

"For sure…it's interesting and the money will be good. We can try." Marilyn's eyes sparkled. "Temporarily. A few shows…just to see how it is. I told you, I never say no to your crazy ideas!" She tilted her head towards her friend.

~

When Marilyn and Zara entered the studio for their first show, the first person to greet them was the makeup artist, Mel.

"Welcome aboard," she said, and led them into the makeup room. It was a huge, bright room with good lighting and several makeup stations. Each station was equipped with a huge mirror and bright lights, as well as palettes of makeup, foundation, lipsticks, and all sorts of makeup applicators and tools. The chairs behind each station were soft and comfortable.

"Are you excited?" Mel saw Marilyn looking around like a child at a fair.

"Excited…and nervous."

"That's normal. After a few months here, you'll feel right at home."

"I'm not sure if we're going to stay for that long." Zara was watching herself in the big mirror.

"Okay, yeah, we'll see! Do either of you have any preference for makeup?"

"I don't think so," Zara said

"Are you open to experimenting with your style?"

"I am," Marilyn smiled.

The wardrobe stylist came in shortly after, carrying a couple of different dresses. After a while, the hair stylist came with questions about their hair.

"I feel like a real star," Zara giggled, posing in front of the mirror.

After about an hour, both women's beauty routines were complete and they looked stellar. The makeup highlighted their eyes and cheekbones, bringing out their best features without appearing overdone. Marilyn's hair was casually curly, while Zara's was straightened and silky. Their dresses were colorful and fresh with light floral accents and accessorized with matching earrings and necklaces. Other models arrived and took their places at the makeup station.

"Meet Marilyn and Zara," Mel said proudly, introducing them to the models who had just arrived. She loved how her makeup complemented the beautiful faces of the new girls.

"Raul, look at my masterpiece I created for your show," Mel called out to the director.

"Hello, girls! I'm Raul. Nice to meet you. Are you ready for a show?" he asked, offering his hand.

"You bet," Zara said, while smiling at Marilyn.

"Okay then, let me show you the studio." He led them out. The women were enthusiastic, curious, and wanted to meet everyone on the team.

"Nice to meet you." Marilyn shook hands with Chill, one of the cameramen.

"You too. If you need anything let me know. You can call me Chill." He was proud of his nickname, which had been given to him because he was a chill person. It wasn't that he didn't give a shit, just that he took everything in stride.

"Which one is the close-up camera? How should we stand to get the best angle?" Marilyn's eyes lit up with excitement.

"Just be yourself," Raul assured them. "This big screen here is the preview. You can see what we're broadcasting at any moment. Try not to look at it too often, but this is so you can be aware of what's in the frame. Every camera has a red light on top; when that camera is on air, the light is on." He pointed to the top of the cameras.

"I'm a little nervous about what I'm going to talk about with the people who call me." Zara's mind was racing as she thought about their upcoming performance.

"It's important to be nice, and polite. Ask questions that would keep the viewer engaged for longer, and find topics that would intrigue them—you know, make them want to call you again." Raul's voice was confident, each word carefully chosen to support the new models. "The rest is just dancing, smiling, posing for the camera. Just watch what the other girls do; they know what to do and can give you some tips. The best approach is just to make the person on the line feel that he is unique—that you picked him from all of the other viewers."

Octavia, a model who'd been with the channel for a couple of years, added, "Make him believe that you only want to talk to him."

When there were only a few seconds left until the start of the show, the control room crew started the countdown at ten. All cameras were focused on the models, the opening sequence was rolling.

"Three, two, one…on air!"

The music started and the red lights on each of the cameras turned on. The first wide shot of all the models appeared on the screen. They smiled and danced to the beat of the music. Octavia took the microphone and gave a sign to the cameraman. The sound technician pressed the red light to signal that the microphone was live, and the show began with one of the models on the microphone.

"Hello, everyone! I am thrilled to welcome you to our studio. I want to invite you to join us today. For the next five hours, you will be in the company of some of the most beautiful and attractive girls anywhere! You have the unique chance to dial the phone numbers that are listed at the bottom of the screen and talk to your favorite girl. Or, why not all of us? You can also send us text messages…maybe you want to pay a compliment—you know, say something nice— or you can say hello, or send in a request for what you'd like to see on-screen. And now it's time to introduce the rest of the girls who will put you in a good mood!"

Her voice was confident, each word was carefully chosen. She approached each one of the models individually and began to chat about their hobbies, the kinds of things that interested them, and how many languages they spoke. The beautiful emcee left the two new models for the end.

"And now," she continued, "I have a very special surprise for you all. Today we have two new girls joining our show for the very first time. This is their debut and I'm sure they'll entertain you, and you'll come to love them."

The cameras zoomed in on Marilyn and Zara. Marilyn immediately grabbed the microphone from the other model and continued.

"Hello everyone! I'm Marilyn and this is my best friend Zara. As you know, this is our first show and we are very excited about this new experience! We would love it if we made new friends here because we love to have the opportunity to talk on the phone with cool new people. We're just two crazy girls who love to have fun, meet new people, travel, and have parties. We love to chat, so give us a call and don't hold back."

After this, the sound technician turned off the emcee's microphone and cued the music. The girls danced while they waited for their first call. The cameras began to zoom in, to show each model in close-up, detailing each of their moves.

The phone lines quickly lit up. Marilyn and Zara immediately greeted callers on their headsets.

"Marilyn is busy right now; can you call back in a bit?" one of the models said into her headset.

Then another said, "Yes, I'll let Zara know that you want to talk to her."

A third model announced to the director, "I have a viewer who wants to talk to Marilyn."

The viewers were crazy about the two new models. Everyone wanted to talk to them, and they in turn were genuinely amused, and loved that they were so instantly popular. The number of text messages were much higher than usual. Most of them were simply compliments and greetings; others were wishes that were too provocative for the daytime show—a striptease or an erotic kiss—and still others were questions about how to contact the new models since the phone lines were busy.

Soon enough, the show was almost over. Marilyn had been busy and engaged with viewers during the entire shift. During that time she danced and responded on the microphone to the compliments sent her way. With five minutes to go, Raul asked her to close the show by thanking the viewers and callers and telling them that she and the other women would be back on the air in just two days.

"It was a huge success!" Raul said after the show. "You two girls broke all records for the last few months."

"Really?" Marilyn said.

"You two are solid gold. I'd love for you to join any show of mine, anytime."

"That was so fun! All my viewers were really nice and we talked about all sorts of things. Some called to tell me how beautiful I was; some wanted me to tell them about myself. I really made an impression on them." Marilyn's eyes were wide full of excitement. "I was worried at first that it might get weird, or someone would cross a line and say something I wouldn't like, but it all felt very normal."

"Normal!" Zara laughed. "Mine were normal too. Only one of my viewers asked if he could watch me on the nighttime show—so he could see me naked I guess—but otherwise, he was nice," Zara blushed. "See, that wasn't so scary; I'm glad you trusted me on this."

~

Marilyn sprang into her apartment feeling strangely energized after her first show, hoping to share her excitement with Felix, but he wasn't home. Her free-spirited, hippie-inspired boyfriend might be anywhere in town, doing anything from hiking a mountain to taking an odd job working for someone he'd met on the street.

It wasn't uncommon for Marilyn's friends to wonder what the attraction was. They wondered what she saw in him. Some noted in concern that he certainly wasn't much of a go-getter.

"Well, that's kind of what I like about him. He's sweet…he's cute…he's free." Marilyn's answer was wide-ranging, but not untrue. She never felt any pressure with Felix, and he was flexible, accommodating her in almost anything. She'd been the one to pursue him. On a camping trip, she'd been drawn to his laidback vibe and gentleness; it was a different feeling entirely from the nonstop stream of guys who always seemed to be chasing after her.

Chapter 5

June 2009
Eforie (near Constanţa), Romania

IN THE EVENING, they lit a campfire, and everyone gathered around in front of their tents. The beginning of the season was chilly, but it was nice near the fire. Everyone was enjoying the beautiful evening, with the sound of the waves of the Black Sea crashing a few feet away. Zara had had a few beers and was feeling a bit woozy. Cuddled up to her boyfriend, she noticed Marilyn standing slightly off to the side; she seemed bored. Zara walked over to the cooler that contained the ice and drinks and picked up two plastic cups. She filled them with ice, poured in vodka, then topped them off with soda and brought them to Marilyn.

"I brought a special cocktail," Zara said. "Why aren't you drinking anything?"

Marilyn smiled and took the cup. "I finished my beer a little while ago. I'm a bit sleepy."

"Is everything okay?" Zara asked, concerned. "You seem a bit out of it."

Marilyn sighed, glancing at the fire. "I'm just tired. Dentistry is so boring—and tough. I'm not even sure if that's what I want to do with my life, but I can't let my mom down."

"Why don't you tell her how you're feeling?" Zara suggested, sipping her drink.

"Oh, she really wants me to become a dentist because she thinks it's some kind of guarantee. Her biggest fear is that I'll always work in a restaurant."

"You don't want that, either. The tips might be good, but that's no dream job." Zara moved closer to Marilyn and put her hand on her shoulder. "Besides, you know your mom can be…overbearing. You need to start thinking of moving out, getting your own place, and start living your life on your own terms."

"I know. Let's not talk about this now, though; I want to have a good time tonight. This is my first time camping, you know."

After a couple more drinks, Marilyn felt much more relaxed, sociable, and adventurous. Their male friends had brought a large speaker, and the music was blaring under the night sky. Marilyn jumped up when "No One" by Alicia Keys started.

"Zara, that's my favorite song!" She grabbed her friend and belted out the song as the two danced on the sand. She knew all the lyrics. They moved to the rhythm, then hugged each other hard and leaned into each other as they danced. The guys who were sitting by the fire watched them playfully, clapping in rhythm; some of them even joined in the dance.

"Should we do something crazy?" Zara asked suddenly. "Would that be fun?"

Marilyn was nearly always ready, since her best friend was always full of crazy ideas. Zara walked over to

Marilyn, ran her hand through her hair, and slowly kissed her. Marilyn decided to go with the flow. As the gentle kiss began to get hotter and more passionate, the rest of the group became speechless. One of them mockingly told Zara's boyfriend, "I think you're going to sleep alone in your tent tonight."

For Marilyn, the kiss was surprising in several ways. She certainly wasn't expecting it, but she also found it arousing, even though Zara was her childhood friend. It was her first time kissing a woman, and it awakened a passion in her.

Zara slowly pulled away and said, "End of the show. Tips are optional but strongly appreciated."

They both walked over to the cooler and grabbed themselves beers without commenting any further on what had just happened. Zara's boyfriend walked over, grabbed Zara around the waist, and began to dance with her. She leaned her head on his shoulder and whispered, "Did you like what you saw?"

"It was unexpected, but yeah, I liked it," he replied.

Their relationship was great in many ways, but they'd been together a long time, and Zara was disappointed that there really wasn't any passion anymore between them. Forget passion—there wasn't really any sex, either. They loved and respected each other, and had been best friends for the last three years…but that was it. He wasn't interested in having sex. Zara, on the other hand, had tried everything to reignite the passion between them: lingerie, romantic dinners, erotic movies, role-playing, costumes. She even tried getting her needs met with other guys, but she always came back to her boyfriend.

The kiss with Marilyn had been another attempt to turn him on and spark something between them.

"The unexpected is exciting," she whispered in his ear and led him to their tent.

Marilyn sat by the fire, finishing her beer. Their friend Felix, who was staring off into the distance, was next to her. She moved closer to him and suggested they have some fun since it was still early.

"Nah, I'm high," Felix replied with half-closed eyes. He'd been smoking all day but he pulled out the small box he used to hold his marijuana and looked for his lighter again. He relit half of a joint that he found in there and held it out to Marilyn.

"No thanks, not my thing, but you enjoy. Do you want to go for a walk along the shore?" Marilyn asked him.

That was one of the last things Felix wanted to do at that moment. He'd rather just sit on the beach and watch the waves crash against the shore, but she talked him into it and they walked on the wet sand. The moon reflected in the water, forming a beautiful path. Marilyn had a romantic soul and moments like this always made her dreamy. They walked so far that they reached the rocks at the end of the beach. It was too dangerous to try to get over them, so they had no choice but to turn back. Felix wanted one more smoke before they left, so he reached for his little box again, but at that moment Marilyn kissed him.

This kiss was different from the one that had happened an hour ago. It was quick, instantaneous. There was almost no response from him—no chemistry either. It was more like a kiss between two strangers.

"Is there some kind of kissing contest tonight that I didn't know about? Not that I didn't like it, but what's going on?"

"My kiss with Zara was for fun. From you, I want something else…something not so…friendly."

Marilyn pressed her body closer to his and kissed his ear. He felt goosebumps on his entire body. Marilyn was determined, and she wasn't ready for the night to end there. She kept kissing and touching him and decided that she was going to have sex with him, right there on the rocks at the end of the beach. But when she started unbuttoning his pants, she realized he still wasn't ready.

"Is everything okay?"

"Yeah, it's just...I don't know what happened. I really want to sleep with you, I really do." Felix searched for the right words.

"It's okay," Marilyn said. "I guess I was off tonight too, maybe drank more than I should have. And all the emotions and the place here, the sea, the beach, the fire. Never mind. Let's get back to the campsite."

"I promise to make up for it," Felix said as he pulled the rest of the joint out of his pocket, lit it, and took a deep drag. He took Marilyn's hand as they walked across the wet sand back to the campsite.

Their friendship, and their not-so-successful first attempts at intimacy continued even after they went back to their regular lives in the city, and soon grew into something more. It wasn't the passion that Marilyn had dreamed of, but it more or less fulfilled her need to have a special person in her life.

~

September 2009
Bucharest

"It's too early to start living together!" Marilyn's mother was furious. "And Felix isn't the right one for you. No steady job and this hipster lifestyle? You're still in college—too young to be tied down like that!"

But for Marilyn, she felt tied down already, living under her mother's roof. When Marilyn had started dating, her mother had given her what she felt were unreasonable restrictions. Marilyn wanted to be more independent, and to be her own person. She wanted to enjoy a little adult freedom, to have fun, and what was so bad about that? She could feel herself rebelling against her mother's desire for control, and that made the idea of moving in with Felix seem even better.

"And where does he live now?"

"Mom, he's a free spirit, I already told you."

He had left home at a young age because he didn't have a good relationship with his parents. Their house didn't feel like home to him. Felix had lived with friends or a cousin for a few months, and sometimes traveled, or couch-surfed, or even spent time at cheap hostels. He didn't stay in one place for long.

Marilyn's mom didn't give up. "And what's with his look? Those Lennon glasses are a little dated. And what's the all the weed symbols?"

"I think he just admires that era, you know, the 1960s spirit."

They moved in together despite her mother's feelings. For Marilyn, it was a victory and even felt a little like a game, or like playing house. The first weeks of their life together were a new beginning for both of them, and they enjoyed nesting and making a home. They prepared meals together, decorated their place, watched television, and had their friends over. The problem with this relationship though—and as time went on this problem got worse—was the lack of intimacy. Marilyn had the same problem with Felix as Zara had with her boyfriend. He simply had no desire to have sex with her. He was kind, attentive and supportive, but when she started to hint or even be more direct about her desire for more physical intimacy, it simply didn't work. Felix would either change the subject, say he was tired, or promise that they would indulge in such activities over the weekend. This behavior was strange to Marilyn, who had somehow picked up the idea that men wanted sex, and asked for it, much more often than women did. She felt discouraged, and in time, she began to give up. No more attempts at seduction, or listening to girlfriends' advice, or reading magazine articles like "The Art of Flirting," "Understanding Male Psychology," or "Spicing Up Your Love Life." No more preparing romantic dinners with candles while he just wanted to watch National Geographic. It was all very frustrating and discouraging. She tried to accept that this was simply how their relationship was. They were a couple, they lived under the same roof, they were best friends, but it was all platonic, and they each had their own lives. Sometimes Felix would go away for a while to hike or go camping with friends, and Marilyn would enjoy this time without him.

It was during one of Felix's adventures that Marilyn had gone with Zara on the job interview and accepted their offer. That had marked the start of her own adventure in a way, and it was also a turning point in their relationship. The new job opened Marilyn's horizons and was a catalyst for change for her. She had taken the step of living with someone she had no real feelings for, just to escape her mother's control and in the hope that she would find freedom. Her romantic soul had dreamt of a great love, strong passions, and the wild sex that was supposed to happen when two people have chemistry with each other. And yet, this romance was anything but that.

"We need to talk," Marilyn said to Felix, a few days after he'd returned from his hike in the **Central Carpathians**. He'd been lounging in the hammock that hung on their balcony, taking deep drags from a marijuana cigarette.

"Sure. Hey, can you please bring me a beer from the fridge? Did I tell you that on the hike I met a guy who brews his own beer? He explained the whole process, and I wrote it all down on my phone. I'll show you. It's not very complicated; I think I'll give it a try. I need a huge pot, but I can do it in the bathroom. Do you want to help me?"

Marilyn went to the fridge, got two ice-cold beers, and sat down in the chair next to the hammock. She handed him his bottle and clinked hers against his. Felix went on and on about the technology of making home-brewed beer. Marilyn patiently listened until the end, when she hurried to interrupt him before he began another topic.

"I had a job interview the other day while you were gone," Marilyn said. "Zara and I both went."

"Really?" Felix took a sip from the bottle. "Nice. Did you decide to leave the restaurant? How much money are they going to pay you? Because you make good money at the restaurant, I don't know if it's worth it."

"The money *is* worth it, but that's not the most important thing. It's about television. Erotic satellite TV."

"Erotic television?" Felix struggled to sit upright in the hammock. "You mean porn. Are you going to shoot porn?"

"Yeah, I'm going to shoot porn," Marilyn said heatedly. "I'm going to blow other men and let them fuck me. Other men are going to lick me until I come." She never spoke this way, or used those kinds of words, but now she was mad.

"What's wrong with you?" Felix was shocked. "Why are you talking like that?"

"I don't know what is wrong with *you*, Felix! Sex is not part of our relationship. I suppose you won't mind if I do whatever I want to because realistically it's not cheating. Our relationship isn't sexual. We're friends. We've lived as roommates for a long time, but honestly, you've had no desire for me since the beginning."

"Wait one second—" Felix tried to protest, but she cut him off.

"I love sex. I love passion, I want to feel wanted, I want to do crazy things to each other. We're young, and— instead of having sex in unconventional places, trying new positions, experimenting—you just lie down next to me in bed every night and don't touch me!"

"That's not true…"

"I love you." Tears welled up in her eyes, but she pressed on, "You are the closest person to me, but I love you like a brother. Like a friend. The passion I had for you at the beginning of our relationship disappeared little by little each time you rejected me."

She fell silent and Felix did too. He hadn't expected

this. She didn't want him to make excuses, to try to explain himself, or even to try to understand why things were the way they were. He had no explanation anyway: it was how he felt, and he was a man who lived for the moment. He wouldn't change, and he couldn't change his sexual desire—or lack of it, anyway.

"I assume that what you're trying to tell me with all this is that you don't want to be with me anymore. You want to break up?"

"I just don't see the point of us continuing to try to act like a couple since we're basically not. I think we can continue living together, we can keep everything as it has been…we just won't sleep in the same bed. We have the guest room—you can move in there and I'll stay in the bedroom. Almost nothing will change, except the name of what we have will be a little different. I want us to stay friends. You're my best friend. We'll keep splitting the bills like we have been, so neither of us will have to look for a new apartment or worry about finances."

Felix was looking down, unable to meet her eyes.

"So, what do you think? I don't want to hurt you or make you feel bad, but it just doesn't make sense for us to be a couple since so many of the necessary requirements for a relationship—for me, at least—are missing."

"I hear what you're saying, and I know that maybe we both have different ideas about life, and about relationships. We don't have to lie or pretend with each other." He took another sip of his beer and looked in the bottle. "Whatever you say. I'll finish my beer and go move my stuff from your room to mine…roomie."

This shift prompted Marilyn to take a fresh look at her entire life. The constant attempts to transform this platonic relationship into something real had been draining for her. Now the air felt fresh, filled with great expectations, full of change and hope. She felt a weight fall from her shoulders. She knew Felix wouldn't dispute her decision or try to dissuade her. He was used to going with the flow. She had initiated this whole relationship. She had taken the first step. She had kept pushing to make things work between them. He'd just gone along with whatever she wanted. A small part of her wanted to see a little resistance from him. To show that he would fight for her, would stand up and tell her he disagreed.

Chapter 6

October 2010

"WHAT SHIFTS ARE we going to take next week?" Marilyn asked Zara on the phone impatiently. "I was wondering if we could try to get in some night shifts. Valentina told us that whenever we wanted, we could check it out, see what it's all about. Should we try it? We can tell them that there are lines we just won't cross, but that we can still put on a great show."

Marilyn waited nervously for Zara's reaction.

"Don't answer me right away. Think first. I've seen that they make a lot of money. There's a guy that I've talked to three times now, and he told me that if I take a shift on the nighttime show he would be on the phone with me the whole time because he won't let some horny guy call me up and ask for phone sex. Not that I'm worried…I'm actually kind of curious about what they do on the night shift. I mean, how obscene could it be?" She laughed.

"Are you really considering it?" Zara was surprised. "It seems like too much. I mean, most of the models will get naked at some point. Won't that be awkward for us?" Zara paused briefly. "I don't know…I'll think about it. We have to state our terms in advance…whether we'll strip, and we'd have to specify the things we don't want to do. Let's talk to them tomorrow." Zara yawned. "I'm going to go to bed. I'm very tired. We'll talk again later."

"Okay then...by the way, Felix and I broke up. But I'll tell you about it another time. I know you're tired." Marilyn was just about to hang up the phone.

"Broke up? What are you talking about? Why? How? Are you kidding me?"

"I'm not kidding. And I think this was a decision I should have made a long time ago. I didn't have the guts to do it before, but I think starting this job and with everything that's going on right now… well, I think it was meant to be. This job just helped me take the steps to make this change. I'll tell you everything tomorrow when I see you, but yeah, the fact is…I'm a single girl now and I like it."

The next day Marilyn walked into Valentina's office and asked to speak with her.

"Sure, go ahead. About the schedule?" She started clicking away on the computer. "Let me see which shifts we have we have to fill. Doesn't matter though—I can get you into any shift you want."

"Oh really?"

"The boss is very happy with your performance in the shows. We haven't hired such successful models in a long time. All the directors have been asking me if I can put you in their show." She continued to look intently at the schedule with a slightly satisfied smile.

"Yes, for the schedule, but not just that…I want to ask you something."

"Go ahead."

"I'd be interested in getting on the night shift, but you know, I'm not a hot model." Marilyn was tapping her foot rapidly. "I don't want to get naked or be made to do obscene things. I'd agree to be in a nighttime show, but I want to set the rules beforehand. Is that possible?"

"Don't worry about it. Friday and Saturday nights are our best shows. I've got a hole there. Alexandria is directing. I don't think you've been on her show yet."

"No, I haven't."

"The best hot models are there too." Valentina clicked a few times with the mouse.

"Is there any show that isn't that special? Something more laid back?"

"Well, if you want, we can start with something that's not so busy. Maybe Wednesday night. Do you want me to put you on the Wednesday schedule?"

"Yeah, I think the Wednesday night shift will be better. I think Zara might join too."

"The director on Wednesday is Raul—your first show was with him, right?"

"Yep," Marilyn said as she sent Zara a quick text.

"You can meet with him and explain to him what you'll do or what you don't want to do. Is that okay?"

"Sure. Sounds good to me."

"I'm adding you right now." Valentina hummed a simple melody while clicking on the screen. She was proud of her achievement on the schedule this week. It didn't matter that these two weren't hot models or doing erotic shows—they were setting the phone lines on fire. Viewers were calling in mostly to talk to them.

"Do you know if Raul's show will have a theme, or it will be a regular show?" Marilyn asked before leaving the office. Some directors had themed shows where the models performed simple etudes, requiring them to dress according to the theme. Sets were changed, and preparation was longer and more elaborate, but there was no strict script. Other directors had a more fluid style that was more about improvising. They decided in the moment how to run the show: which wishes would be fulfilled and when, how to move the camera around to get the best out of the models, what to do to change the pace.

"No, just regular. Nothing special." Valentina smiled and concentrated on the computer.

"Sorry to bother you—one last question. What exactly happens on Friday and Saturday night shows?"

"It's prime time. People are up late at night, in front of the TV, often in an erotic mood. Those are the two most-watched, most dynamic shows, which means we have to be at our best. To make the best show, we need our most in-demand girls and the best crew behind the camera. Sometimes those are themed shows. Those are also the shows that make the most money, and that means they pay the most. Everybody wants to be on for Friday and Saturday."

Alexandria had earned the privilege of being the director of the Friday and Saturday Night Show. It was a real struggle to get to that place, and it required sacrifice. Once you achieved that position, you had to be there every Friday and Saturday. If you missed one of them, you might as well miss all of them. Alexandria was there fifty-two Fridays and Saturdays a year. She loved what she did, she was a professional in the fullest sense of the word, and she dedicated all of her ambition, tenacity, and goal-setting completely to her work.

~

Marilyn met Raul in the break room as he was finishing the lunch that his wife had prepared for him. Raul was middle-aged, obese, and a father of three. He wasn't particularly ambitious and he'd become a director by accident. He wasn't particularly creative, approaching his job methodically, as a factory worker might. Usually, he was just trying to make it until the end of his shift so he could get home to his kids. He had gotten the Wednesday Night Show a long time ago, and since no one was clamoring for the position, he stayed there.

"Hey, Raul, I need to talk to you," Marilyn said.

"Sure, what's up?" Raul asked as he wiped his mouth with a napkin.

"But please…finish your lunch. I'll be in the makeup room—I'm running late."

Raul didn't like his job, and his shows weren't particularly interesting. The way he ran his shows was to closely adhere to the viewers' wishes so that he didn't have to think too much. With the models and crew, he was more of a logistics manager: timing who went on break and when, and making sure that the models responded to messages. Because he didn't really make creative contributions to the shows, some team members were annoyed that he made as much money as he did and even felt that he wasn't working as hard as the others. His style was to go with the flow, but if there was someone else there to nudge him along, it was even better.

"Hey Marilyn, you wanted to talk to me?" Raul asked when he showed up in the makeup room. "Do you want to be on my show again? Last Monday's daytime show was very successful. Let me get you on again next Monday—how about that?"

"Well, actually, I talked to Valentina, and I'll be coming on your show Wednesday night," Marilyn explained as Mel put eyeliner on her eyes.

He didn't know how to respond at first, and Mel was also staring. Wednesday night was a mediocre show, with a mediocre director, while Marilyn was the most desirable and successful model. The two things didn't go together. During her short time there, Marilyn's charisma had brought in more callers and viewers than some models who'd spent months there.

"I'd like to try the night shift, but I need to double-check something with you." She turned around on her chair. Mel leaned back on the makeup table, listening carefully. She liked gossip.

"Sure, what's up?"

"I will be a soft model. I won't undress, do stripteases, or fulfill overly erotic wishes. I know I'll bring in viewers and I'll be busy for maybe the whole show, which is good for everyone. Of course, if there's a wish I can do, then I will, but I don't want anyone to have different expectations about any of this. Can we make a deal on those terms? If not, I'll take another shift."

"No worries, there won't be any problem. Even as a soft model, you're equal to two hot models. No one will expect you to do anything that you don't want to do. I'd be very happy if you participated in my night show."

"So, we have a deal," Marilyn smiled. "Zara's interested in Wednesdays too, and it'll be nice if we can work it together. I'll let you know more after I talk to her."

"The night shift is where the money is," Mel said as she returned her attention to Marilyn's makeup, applying mascara on her lashes. "But Wednesdays…well, there's hardly anything going on. Prime time is something else. I don't know if you've stayed up later to watch. Alexandria, the director on those shows, is my best friend."

The directors always made a point to pass through the makeup room to make sure the models were there and would be ready on time. While they were there, they chatted with Mel. She knew everything about everyone. Mel was a butch lesbian who loved to have fun and experiment, avoided long relationships, and didn't want to lose her freedom for anything in the world. Her short blonde hair was shaved on one side, and one of her eyebrows was also shaved slightly in the middle. She was short and thin and usually wore wide pants that fell below her waist. She liked to wear big watches and various eye-popping accessories. Her sense of humor helped the models in her chair to relax before going on air. She frequently listened to Alexandria's confessions and gave the best advice. They'd been through a lot together over the years, and they knew each other inside and out.

"I haven't had a chance to meet Alexandria yet," Marilyn replied. "I've heard about her—that she's the best director, that her shows are the most interesting and profitable—but I'm nervous about the pressure of being on those shows. Maybe later on I'll feel ready, but for now I'd like to explore a more relaxed environment—on air, I mean."

"I'm sure you'll eventually end up on one of her shows, out there with the best models, the best director. Do you know that when I met Alexandria, she was just a videographer here?"

"No way!"

"Yeah, she paid her dues all these years and now she's the top director. But sometimes she still takes over a camera and films a scene. Just between us…" Mel whispered, "She could film you much better than any other cameraman who works here. I mean it!"

~

Marilyn convinced Zara to sign up with her on the nighttime show. They were both excited but a little worried about how it would go. On the day of their first shoot, they went to the mall to buy something elegant for their work that night. Although the studio provided a stylist and wardrobe, most of the models preferred to choose their own clothes for each show. The two models bought formal, glamorous dresses, with simple jewelry and stiletto heels. For the evening show, their makeup needs to be much more pronounced than on the daytime show. Mel applied a black smoky eye makeup on Marilyn to make her light blue eyes stand out. Her hair was pulled back into an elegant bun. She looked stunning. Even though the other models were also made up and dressed in beautiful clothes, Marilyn stood out.

"Marilyn, do you mind opening the show? Maybe Zara can join you at some point too?" Raul asked, passing the microphone to her.

"Sure! Do you want me to say something specific, or improvise?" She confidently grabbed the mic.

"I trust you. Improvise!" He winked at her.

The studio lighting was dimmed. The smoke

machine released wisps of smoke at regular intervals.

"Hello, everyone!" Marilyn began. "I'm Marilyn. Tonight's show will be special for me and for my friend Zara, and I hope for all of you in front of your screens. You haven't seen us here at the nighttime show yet." As she spoke, the console began to light up, indicating the first calls were coming in. "We'll do our best to fulfill your wishes, entertain you, and give you a great time. We are still a little bit shy, so please be patient with us and please understand if we can't do everything you want to see."

Zara signaled to Marilyn that she had a viewer on the line, waiting to talk to her. Raul started making signs to finish up her opening speech, pointing to the console to remind her about the calls.

"Call us, send us text messages, and tell us your fantasies," Marilyn continued with a smile. "We're here to make your night unforgettable. Let's have some fun together!"

The director nodded at her with a satisfied smile. All the phone lines were already full.

After midnight, they announced that the first dance would begin. The music was slow and erotic; the models all had experience on the night shift and knew how to get an audience aroused with just one move. The passion and sexual tension from the viewers could be felt in the studio too.

Marilyn was seated at the end of a red leather couch on set. She'd had a viewer on the line for the last hour.

"And what music do you like to listen to? Really? I love Rhianna too. What's your favorite song of hers?" As she spoke, she took in her surroundings. She'd never even been to a strip club, but she enjoyed the energy here, and wanted to be a part of it herself.

As two of the cameras filmed a striptease on the pole, she asked her caller, "Do you like to watch that kind of show?" Meanwhile, a new wish had come through: for two models to perform a lesbian scene. This wish was a viewer favorite, and it was automatically granted. Two models—who were not lesbian, or bisexual, or even attracted to each other at all—began touching, exchanging light kisses, and undressing each other. Kissing was allowed but only without tongue, due to industry regulations. A kiss with tongue would bring serious trouble, shutting down the whole production because the regulators would consider it as porn.

Raul handed the microphone to one of the other models and said, "Take the mic and respond about this message for the lesbian show, please. Some guy named Peter sent it. Tell him something nice. One camera here, please."

"Hey, Peter. You naughty boy!" The model began when the red light appeared. "Thank you for your message, because I like to play with these beautiful girls here. I promise you a very, very…" She paused, then exhaled, "…*hot* show! I hope you enjoy it as much as I do. Kisses, baby!" She sent a kiss to the camera.

One of the cameras moved to a large circular bed in the middle of the studio. A model who was clad only in revealing underwear was lying on it. Two fans gently blew a fairy-like veil behind the bed. The model with the microphone walked over slowly and was gently pulled down onto the bed by her partner. The erotic dance on the other side of the studio was coming to an end at the same time, and the director used the console to mix the last shots of the striptease with the beginning of the lesbian scene until all the cameras moved into place to film the two women in the new scene. The dancer from the pole was now free to gather her clothes from the floor, exit the area, and get dressed.

"Okay, let's watch it together." Marilyn whispered to her caller. "This is my first time."

On the bed, the two models were turning up the heat. One began slowly unhooking the other's bra, then removed the straps in slow motion. The bra slid down, revealing the other woman's breasts which were firm, tight, and almost perfectly round. Marilyn's attention was riveted, absorbed in the graceful movements, in the faces that showed they were enjoying themselves, and in the naked forms she hadn't looked at that way before. Then, it was the other model's turn; the nude model removed the other one's bra and began to gently touch her nipples.

"Raul, give me the bottle of massage oil!" one of the prop handlers called to the director. The director discreetly handed her a half-empty bottle, checking the preview screen to make sure he wasn't in the frame. The model doused her partner's breasts with the oil and began to spread the liquid all over her skin, massaging her nipples. All the cameras effortlessly floated around them, capturing their intimate expressions with a soft focus. One of the women started pulling on the other's panties, and Marilyn could see the shape of her pussy peeking out from under the lace. The two kept touching each other, and with light, dance-like moves, pulled down each other's panties. Both women were now completely naked; the only thing left on their bodies were their high heels and the massage oil. To finish the show, one of the models stood with her back to the camera and faced the other woman. She then slowly spread her legs towards her while her partner looked mischievously into her eyes and slowly crawled toward the space between her wide-open legs.

At this moment, Marilyn was right in front of her and the model's open pussy was revealed right before her eyes, in all its grandeur.

"And we are clear!" This was shouted from the control room as all the cameras turned in the opposite direction, where something new was about to happen.

"Yes, I'm here…did you like the show?" Marilyn hadn't heard a word of her phone conversation, as all her attention had been focused on what had just unfolded in front of her. It was the first time she had observed a woman's genitals like this—so open and close enough to see even the smallest details. The whole show had immersed her in another reality that she was curious to explore. She wanted to know what it felt like to be touched by another woman like that, and what she would experience if she were the one doing the touching. She wondered about the emotions too, and if she would experience a more intense arousal than what she had experienced before with a man. All these thoughts made her even more curious. She wanted it to happen to her too, and not for the cameras. Not for the show. She didn't want the professional experience; she wanted to experience it in real life, no cameras, no spectators, just her and another woman who would share those emotions with her.

The show was over and the whole team was happy.

"Thank you everyone, for the great job you did tonight," Raul said at the after-show meeting, with a broad smile on his face. "We got better ratings than last

Wednesday night's show. The lines were full most of the night, which doesn't happen often on Wednesdays. Special thanks to Marilyn and Zara who fielded some long calls. You all did a great job with most of the messages—I know some of them were too much and couldn't be fulfilled, but I think we responded to them well, and gave the viewers something else special to replace the original wishes. There are still things that could be improved, but we did a good job. Marilyn, Zara, how are you feeling after your first night show?"

"I imagined it would be scarier," Marilyn said. "I was worried that I might be uncomfortable or that some of the viewers might want things that were too raunchy, but it was the opposite. I enjoyed myself, and the time passed quickly. I was busy with a very sweet viewer who stayed on the line for three hours."

"Wait until he receives his phone bill!" Raul laughed and his face turned red.

"The show went very quickly," Zara agreed. "There was always something going on, and the crew was very professional. Thank you, guys!"

"And we'll get paid more than the crew on the daytime shows!" Raul was the happiest of all.

~

Marilyn updated Valentina and agreed to continue with the same working agreement for more nighttime shows. The manager was happy because this would help her balance the schedule, which was complicated by models' and directors' preferences, prime-time slots, and the distribution of both soft and hot models. In the break room, Marilyn started making a coffee at the espresso machine, her back to the door. She overheard a conversation at one of the tables.

"I need a specialist who deals with a device that emits fire. But it has to be safe for working in enclosed spaces—we don't want to set the studio on fire or get anyone hurt, you know? And the fire will burn while water is flowing from above, like rain. I know it sounds complicated, but it's not impossible; it's just something that hasn't been seen before. It'll be like an erotic Cirque Du Soleil."

Marilyn found this interesting; it sounded like an elaborate scene in a Hollywood production. She poured milk into her cup and turned to find a free table where she could sit. At one table were two men and a woman who was sitting with her back to Marilyn. She was the one who had been speaking. She had cascading, wavy hair the color of chestnuts, a straight posture, and was wearing a tight sweatshirt and light blue jeans.

"I want to know if it's technically possible to build, and then I'll talk to Mr. Lupan and see if he would agree to fund something like this. I know it hasn't been done before—that's why I want to do it." She was talking passionately. "Hold on a second. Let me make a coffee real quick. I have a show in an hour and I'm already late."

The woman stood up and headed for the espresso machine at the other end of the break room, continuing to talk to the men. Seeing Marilyn sipping her coffee, she was startled.

"Oh, hi. I didn't know there was anyone else in the room. I'm speaking a little louder because we're discussing a project." Alexandria smiled as she walked past Marilyn with a casual step.

"No problem. Nothing to apologize for. Super interesting. When's this all going to happen?"

"Not sure yet. Hopefully some Friday or Saturday night show." Alexandria was concentrating on the coffee coming out of the machine.

"So you're Alexandria? I heard your shows are the best and all the models want to be a part of them."

"Thanks." Alexandria was flattered. They shook hands and introduced themselves.

Marilyn said, "I hope we'll work together sometime."

"Oh, sure. I basically live here!" joked Alexandria. "Enjoy your coffee."

Back at her table, Alexandria was tempted to turn and look at her again. Marilyn was beautiful. Alexandria was used to seeing all sorts of women in the studio. Hundreds of models had passed through over the years, but Marilyn had a special aura; sunlight seemed to shine around her, and Alexandria almost felt like she knew her already. Mel had mentioned to her that there were two new models who had become very popular, and that one of them was very beautiful. She assumed that was one of the girls.

"Yes! That's her," Mel confirmed while she was lying down on the little grey couch in the makeup room. She just finished the last of the makeup for the shift and she was taking a break. "So what about her?"

"Nothing. I was just curious." Alexandria lay down on the other side of the soft couch. "You know me…that I'm an overthinker…I hope she didn't hear any rumors about me."

The station was a hotbed of gossip and intrigue.

Almost everyone was talking behind everyone else's back. Most people knew that Alexandria was attracted to women, and the juicier part—that she'd been involved with a few models.

"Mel, you know I always try to be professional…I just get paranoid in case any model would think that I have unprofessional thoughts about her. You know the stereotype that people sometimes have of queer women."

"Ha! What am I supposed to do then?" Mel laughed.

"Come on, I just don't want Marilyn to hear any of this. I wouldn't make a move in that direction at all."

"Yeah, you'd better not. She seems straight though, and you know you can trust my gaydar. I'm serious though—don't even think about it! Do you hear me?"

"Yes!" Alexandria rolled her eyes. "I know those previous relationships didn't end well, and I get that it's been a problem for management." The memories of those dramatic endings still haunted her.

"Of course it's a problem," Mel said seriously. "You have a pattern. You start relationships with the same toxic girls, who by no coincidence are always the best models, and in the end, they quit because you can't keep working together. Watch it, or they'll fire you."

Alexandria loved her job, and knew that she couldn't mix her personal and professional lives again. No more seductions at the studio.

~

Alexandria and Marilyn began to encounter each other at the television more often. Alexandria was happy to see her, but at the same time, Marilyn made her anxious. She felt vulnerable and uneasy, wondering what Marilyn might think of her. Sometimes she even tried to avoid her. Marilyn was always kind and expressive with everyone. When talking to Alexandria, she would smile and touch her lightly in a friendly way, but that made Alexandria feel awkward. Every interaction felt charged with a heightened awareness. In other circumstances, Alexandria would have insisted on having a model like Marilyn on her shows all the time, but the idea made Alexandria paranoid. Whenever they worked together, Alexandria was more than professional; she was cold.

Chapter 7

December 2010

"HEY ZARA, I won't be able to make it to our meeting today," Marilyn said, holding her phone to her ear while carrying different size bags in each hand.

"It's okay, we can postpone it. What are you doing?" Zara asked, even though she could hear what was clearly a saleswoman at a store speaking to Marilyn on the other end of the line.

"You won't believe where I am," Marilyn giggled, "I'm at a bridal shop!"

"Um, is there something you haven't told me?" Zara sounded confused.

"No, don't worry, you didn't miss anything. I'm on the night shift tonight with Alexandria. She told me the theme of the show..." Marilyn paused for dramatic effect. "'My Dream Girl' is the name of the show."

"Interesting…but I still don't understand what you are doing in the bridal shop?"

"Wait a minute…" Marilyn's voice trailed off for a moment. "No thank you, I'm just browsing for now…Sorry, here I am again. The idea of the show is that each girl represents a different type of woman, and of course, every viewer has some preference; some even have a fetish. I will be a bride."

"Wait, I still don't get it."

"Each girl is emphasizing something different and inviting the viewers to project their fantasies onto her. You know, they'll see their dream girl among all the different types of women that we'll show. Isn't that brilliant?'

"Yeah, I guess that's why Alexandria is so popular over there. I haven't seen the other directors do anything like that." Zara paused. "What are you doing—are you buying a dress or tasting wedding cakes?"

"No, no. They have all the props, and Alexandria told me that I didn't need to bring anything, but I wanted to bring something special. I want to find some accessories to complete the look...sexy lingerie, a wedding garter maybe...okay, I have to go...I want to take a look at what they have here. I'll see you soon."

"Okay, text later," Zara laughed as she hung up the phone.

~

Marilyn was the first to arrive at the studio for the next shift, besides Mel, who was organizing the makeup palettes when Marilyn burst into the makeup room.

"Am I the first? No one else has come yet?" Marilyn asked, panting.

"What are you in such a hurry for, girl? I usually fight with late models. You're kind of an exception, huh?"

"I want to show you what kind of wedding makeup I want you to do for me...look." Marilyn pulled out a wedding magazine and started flipping through the pages.

"Are you the bride?"

"Yes."

"Alexandria is in the studio with the crew, building the set. All morning, they've been bringing in wedding decorations, moving lighting around…as far as I understand, you will have an altar, with flowers and an arch over the top. It looks very pretty. There's also a pool table, an office desk, even a treadmill. A real Hollywood production."

"Really? I'm going to go look. I'm so excited for this show."

"Wait! Sit down first; let's decide how we're going to do your makeup. You wanted to be first, didn't you? Soon the other models will start coming and it's going to be crazy here."

Marilyn heard footsteps hurrying down the hallway. Alexandria rushed into the dressing room.

"Oh, I didn't know someone was already here." Alexandria smiled though she could barely catch her breath. "Hi Marilyn, how are you?"

"Hi—" Marilyn barely answered when Mel cut her off.

"She's excited about this spectacular production you're putting on tonight…she even came early."

Marilyn smiled, looking at Alexandria in the mirror.

"Great. Okay. Mel, first the girls sit down for makeup, then hair...where's the hairstylist at?'

"In the break room; I saw her when I came in," Marilyn said.

"Okay, everyone needs to be in the studio thirty minutes before the show so I can explain what we're doing, okay?" Alexandria didn't wait for an answer and walked out with the same hurried steps.

The studio was divided into different sets made to represent each dream girl's style and character. Each set also had individual spotlighting. For this show Alexandria had four cameramen on the three cameras, and one on a crane in order to pan out softly throughout the studio. The music playlist was prearranged in sync with the plans for the show.

Half an hour before the show, the crew and models stood in a circle, listening to Alexandria reveal the final details and instructions to the team, like a coach in a huddle. Marilyn was leaning on the white altar that was prepared for her scene and studying Alexandria's facial expression as she gave her instructions.

"The show is complicated," Alexandria said. "It's not like our usual shows. Each one of us has to be more focused and give even more than usual. Ladies, I know it won't be easy because besides all this complicated production, you still have to focus on the conversations with your viewers. But I believe that with what we have planned for tonight, there will be something for everyone."

"Sure," laughed Aurora, who was dressed like a 1950s housewife in a vintage dress and hairstyle.

"You're showcasing different types of women," Alexandria continued, "You're dream girls. We have everything—a successful businesswoman, exuding confidence in a suit...that one is especially for viewers who are submissive and admire dominant women." Alexandria turned and gestured to another model. "The mechanic, with her dirty overalls, for the viewers who like a woman who's not afraid to get her hands dirty." Alexandria turned to Marilyn. "The bride, for men who to find their perfect woman and make her their wife…the athlete, who spends all day getting toned at the gym, the bartender…this variety is designed to give something to everyone—all different tastes and preferences." Alexandria paused briefly and concluded, "If you don't have any questions, it's show time!"

The show got off to a dynamic start. One by one, the cameras revealed the heroines, in their sets, with theme music that set just the right mood. The girls performed short dance sketches, focusing on their characters and without looking at the camera, which made the scenes feel more realistic. The phone lines were flooded after the first shots that revealed the innovative show.

Marilyn was the last dream girl to be introduced. Her long white dress outlined her figure. A delicate floral crown fastened her veil of fine tulle which cascaded over her golden hair, styled in soft romantic curls. Her makeup accentuated her natural beauty. She looked at Alexandria, standing behind the cameras, gesturing and speaking via the headset. Marilyn felt Alexandria's gaze on her and shortly after, she gave the universal gesture for *You're Next*.

For a moment, Marilyn felt anxious, but quickly gained the confidence of an actress who has been on stage all her life. At that moment, she saw Alexandria speak to one of the cameramen, who handed the camera to her and as Marilyn managed to hear Alexandria speak through the headset.

"I'm on the second camera now, he said it was urgent and he had to go to the toilet...Is he new? At the most important moment!"

Marilyn's theme music began subtly. All the

cameras turned to her. Alexandria removed the camera from the tripod and walked over to Marilyn, who began to dance slowly and seductively. The crane made complex movements in several directions, while the other two cameras provided close-ups and tilt frames. Alexandria slowly walked around Marilyn with the camera on her shoulder, approaching and then receding as her dance partner.

Marilyn heard the orders Alexandria gave over the headset to the director on the mixer.

"After you switch my camera, keep me on. I'm going to get in close to her in a diagonal motion. Don't switch the camera until I am far enough away to get out of the frame of the other cameras."

Marilyn continued to move slowly and passionately as Alexandria approached her again. They were so close that Marilyn could smell Alexandria's perfume and hear the voices coming from her headset. They continued to move in sync like a couple dancing a waltz. Marilyn's song was coming to an end when she covered her headset with her hand.

Without stopping her dance, she whispered to Alexandria, "Can I do one more song?"

Alexandria looked away from the camera's viewfinder, directly at Marilyn.

"You can...what do you want to do?"

"Take the dress off."

Alexandria pushed her headset microphone away and looked at Marilyn. She knew about Marilyn's terms: she wasn't a hot model and the wishes she would fulfill were limited.

"Are you sure?"

"Yes…just the dress."

Alexandria brought the headset microphone to her mouth again and said, "Another song for Marilyn. All cameras stay here. We're moving on."

Marilyn changed her rhythm slightly to match the new song and continued to dance. Alexandria stayed with her, zooming slightly in and out. Marilyn turned her back to the camera, then approached and spun around the pillar of the wedding arch. Standing with her back to the camera again, she reached behind her back and pulled the zipper down. The dress slowly fell to the floor. Marilyn spun slowly back to Alexandria's camera and moved closer to her. She was wearing a tight lace bodice under her wedding dress. The floral motifs of the fine lace, along with the studio lighting, accentuated every movement. The narrow lace band of the garter on her right thigh completed her look. Marilyn looked at the preview monitor that was showing the broadcast, and began to dance even more confidently and passionately. She looked playfully into Alexandria's camera lens and winked. Alexandria responded to every flirtatious gesture with slow and masterful camera movements. Marilyn didn't want the dance to end. Everything around her had faded and she was dancing like she was alone with Alexandria and her camera.

As the final chords of the song played, Alexandria, who had been silent up to that moment, said into the microphone, "Prepare the wide shot. Everybody, ready to go back into the studio. I'm pulling out."

She smoothly took a few steps back until she stood behind the rest of the cameras and as the song changed, the director at the console switched to the wide shot from the crane.

~

"Are you up? I didn't want to wake you," Zara announced over the phone to Marilyn in the early afternoon.

"Yeah, I got up a while ago."

"I heard you guys were amazing last night—how was the show?"

"It was exciting, challenging—and tiring. I had viewers all night. I think they really liked the idea of different heroines," Marilyn said with a yawn.

"That's great. For me, shows where nothing happens are more tiring. At least it was fun."

"Yeah, it was…I have to tell you something. You're not going to believe this…but I did a striptease."

"What?" Zara shouted into the phone. "Are you kidding me?"

"Okay, not exactly a striptease, but it was an erotic and provocative dance. I finally took off my dress."

"No way! You're kidding!"

"I'm not kidding—I took it off, but I had another, sexy, lacy dress on underneath." Marilyn paused, waiting for another reaction from Zara.

"Did the director make you do it? Didn't you tell them you don't do that?"

"No, nobody made me do anything. I felt like it. Alexandria was filming at that moment, because one of the cameramen had to go to the bathroom." Marilyn was silent for a moment, "It was a strange feeling, but she made me feel comfortable, relaxed, safe. I knew she wouldn't show something that wasn't beautiful or that I didn't want her to show. There's a certain energy when she's on the camera…it's like everyone else disappears and what we do in that moment is just for us. I don't know how to explain it."

"I think you're very brave. I don't know if I could ever relax like that in front of the camera."

"I wasn't sure if I wanted to do it, but it just happened. That's how I felt in the moment and I don't regret it," Marilyn said as the coffee machine hummed and poured strong liquid into her cup.

"Tell me about Chill—what's happening there?"

"Nothing for now." Marilyn sipped her coffee and continued, "We're texting. It's sweet."

"Who knows, you might need those wedding decorations sooner than you think!" Zara laughed.

"Very funny. He's nice, and cute, but I don't know. I kind of want to be alone for a while. I want to enjoy myself…away from my mother, away from Felix… do what I want, you know, and not have to explain anything to anyone...just be free."

"Yeah, but you don't want to be alone either...you still dream about that great love, the passion, the strong feelings."

"I know…it's like I want everything all at once…"

Chapter 8

January 2011

"I DID THE makeup for your ex this morning," Mel said as she sipped a coffee in the break room.

"Who?"

"Yeah, sorry. I forgot to specify which one!" Mel's face lit up with a radiant smile, and she laughed. "Octavia."

Alexandra clenched her fists and her face flushed red. "I don't want to know anything. Well…did she ask about me?"

"No." Mel slurped her coffee, then exhaled and said, "Do you know what? I blame Helena. She started this pattern for you…after she broke your heart is when you started exploring your sexuality with all these models."

Soon after their affair, Helena had met a rich but jealous businessman who'd made her quit her job.

"I just wanted to build an emotional connection with a woman." Alexandria stared into the distance. "I wanted to be exclusive. I wanted the fairy tale, you know, be together and happy forever."

Alexandria had always suspected she was more attracted to women than to men, but after her experience with Helena, she was sure.

"You're looking in all the wrong places," Mel said. "Most of the time you're dating straight girls who just want to experiment. Or bisexuals who don't want to commit to a woman. Or girls who want to be polygamous but almost none of them wants to get into a serious lesbian relationship since society doesn't fully accept it either."

"Hey, it's not all my fault. Most of the time, they're the ones who are trying to start something with me."

"Of course. They're attracted to you—you're beautiful and feminine. You inspire respect. You're ambitious, smart, independent, and everyone knows you're the best at what you do."

"Wow, hold on, I'm blushing." Alexandria smiled.

"But you also have this strong, tough vibe, you know? You're a magnet for these straight girls who want to experiment. In the meantime, you like feminine and beautiful women. It's a recipe for disaster."

Alexandria knew that was true. She was surprised by how many women took the initiative to approach her. She couldn't resist them.

"I know all of this, and my other weakness is that I'm a hopeless romantic. At the beginning of every relationship, I believe that this time things will work out." Alexandria exhaled deeply. "And this has led only to disappointments, infidelities, and painful breakups."

"You have your traumas and issues, that's for sure. The disappointment had to show you that relationships with women are more difficult—even impossible," Mel said.

"After all that, I prefer not to commit."

Months ago, Alexandria ended a long, toxic relationship with Octavia, one of the most successful models. That relationship had featured a number of infidelities, as well as mental abuse, and permanent conflict. Alexandria had tried to end this relationship many times, but the hope that things would one day get better and that the girl she loved would change made her stay. Some of their drama had even become public in the studio. After that, Alexandria completely separated her personal life from work.

"And why are you wondering if Octavia asked about you?" Mel looked at Alexandria, searching for some hidden meaning.

"Habit." Alexandria waved her hand. "I spent months trying to recover from her but still…"

"Still what?"

"I haven't fully healed. Especially when I see her in the hallways, and we pass each other like strangers." Alexandria usually made sure her schedule didn't overlap with Octavia's, and her ex missed out on the high-salaried Friday and Saturday night shifts.

"Speaking of relationships at work…did you hear the latest?"

"You know I don't care. Especially in this place. Each person adds their own commentary, so it's probably not even true—we've been there," Alexandria sighed deeply.

"Yeah, but I'll tell you this one anyway: Marilyn is dating someone from the studio." Mel covered her mouth with her hand, whispering through her fingers "And you'll never guess who."

Alexandria was interested. "I don't know anyone who works there who could be worthy of Marilyn."

"Well, it looks like there is someone."

"I don't believe it. I told you, people there like to make things up, just to make their own lives more interesting. Marilyn wouldn't pay any attention to anyone here; she's too good for them. Someone was messing with you."

"Wow, you should hear yourself. Someone's got it bad!"

"Come on, you know she looks good, but it's not just that. She's so kind and empathetic. She makes everyone feel at ease with just a smile. I wondered what kind of a man Marilyn would fall for."

"Well, he's a colleague, and a friend of yours." Mel leaned in closer, her voice dropping to a whisper. "It's Chill."

"No way. I knew this was bullshit."

"Why?"

"Because Chill is mediocre in everything. He's a mediocre cameraman."

"She doesn't need a good cameraman for a boyfriend. And I thought you were friends with him."

"We were, at the beginning when we first started working here. We've been to a few parties. We did favors for each other when somebody needed something, but at some point, I started to move up and Chill just stayed put." Her brow furrowed in deep thought. "He just kind of settled…he takes the minimum number of shifts and still lives with roommates." Alexandria stayed silent for a second and continued, "I was always busy and I love my work, you know…and I think that was a factor—that Chill saw me as superior at work. A slight tension built up over time between us, with no one specifically to blame."

"I see…"

"Also his hobbies are going to the park with his buddies where they drink beer, smoke marijuana, and listen to rock music. Do you see Marilyn in that world?"

"Well, it's not our business; I'm just telling you. Marilyn mentioned it herself in the makeup room." Mel took a big sip of the almost empty cup of coffee. "And you already know my opinion about relationships here at work—Chill is making a big mistake, but anyway…don't say anything about this, okay? Sooner or later, it'll be public, but for now it's a secret." She put her finger against her lips.

"This is the most absurd thing I've ever heard. How could she pay attention to a guy like Chill? The two things don't go together." The news alone made Alexandria think less of Marilyn.

"I know it's a little weird, but I'm sure everybody will know soon enough."

"What are you talking about?" Nando entered the breakroom and started preparing a coffee.

"About how wrong is it to start a relationship in here. And since you, Nando, are one of these people who likes to screw up their life, I will leave you both to discuss. I have to start the makeup for the next shift. See ya!" Mel left the break room.

The months after Alexandria and Octavia broke up were hard and difficult. Alexandria was very lonely and unhappy and had become close with Nando during that time. She had shared a lot of what she'd gone through and he knew about most of the issues that had caused their breakup.

"I want to ask you something, but I'm not sure what you're going to say," Alexandria said.

"I'm listening." Nando leaned in closer, his eyes wide with curiosity.

"Well…I heard that Octavia has started seeing one of the video editors here at the station."

"Yeah?"

"I've seen you talking to him. The one with the beard."

"Petru? I didn't know. And?" Nando furrowed his brow, waiting for what would come next.

"Would you ask him if they're really together? I just want to know, that's all."

"Why would you want to know? Is it going to make you feel any better?"

"I just need to know," Alexandria's voice trembled with barely contained rage. "I think she's doing it on purpose! Do you know that I helped Petru get a promotion? Of all the people in the world, she wants to do this right under my nose, with someone from work!" Her lips pressed into a thin line. "I just want to know. Please just talk to him and see what you can find out—I know you're friends. I'm sure he already knows that we were together, so that's not too smart of him, either. Talk about biting the hand that feeds you."

"We're not buddies, but yeah, we chat sometimes. I know this isn't easy for you, but you're putting me in a tricky spot." Nando took a deep breath, feeling slightly angry at Alexandria's request. "You need to get over this already. Enough time has passed. Why continue to hurt yourself by digging that all up again? Pick yourself up and move on. I have to get into the studio." Nando took his cup of coffee and left Alexandria alone in the break room.

She looked out the window and thought about what

Mel had said.

Hearing about Marilyn and Chill definitely changed the way that Alexandria looked at Marilyn. Marilyn didn't seem so special anymore, since she'd been charmed by someone like Chill. But also, there couldn't be any tension related to Alexandria, since Marilyn was straight; it was better that way, and Alexandria didn't have to worry about her knowing that she'd dated models in the past. Alexandria felt like that problem had solved itself and she felt relieved.

For the next few days, Alexandria's mind was busy with thoughts of how beautiful women often end up with unsuitable men. And, about a parallel universe where she and Marilyn were in a harmonious and serious relationship, having found true happiness. And also, she found herself thinking about how unfair fate had been to her up until now…making her a lesbian but always sending her the most unreliable women.

~

"I did what you asked me to do," Nando said to Alexandria as they adjusted the white balance of the cameras in the studio. "I talked to your ex's new boyfriend."

"And?" Alexandria drummed her fingers on the top of the camera.

"I felt stupid to pretend like I really cared what was going on between him and Octavia."

"And???"

"You were wrong—she isn't with him just to hurt you. They really are together; it's not just sex."

"Sex? So she's having sex with him too?"

"Come on! What did you expect, that they just play chess? You know her, she likes cocks too. Remind me exactly how many times she cheated on you with a guy! Anyway, Petru told me he really likes her. Maybe this is good—everyone has moved on and she doesn't need to ruin your life anymore."

"You know what I would really like? Not to see her, or know anything about her. Because even when I take one step forward to get her out of my mind, the next thing I know, I hear something about her, or see her, and take two steps back." Alexandria's entire posture radiated hostility and she changed the subject. "Do you want me to go to the control room and check the cameras on the monitors?"

"No, I'll do it. Are you okay?"

"Yeah, I'm just tired; I haven't slept well."

"Do you sleep at all? Slow down with work. You don't even spend all that money you make."

"Oh, work distracts me. I don't want to be alone because when I'm alone I start remembering the good times we had together. And that torments me even more." Alexandria turned looked at the cameras again and left the studio saying, "I'm going to set the décor in the other studio for the night show."

While she crossed the hallway, she saw Petru giving Octavia a bouquet of flowers in the dressing room. He was just arriving at work and had thoughtfully brought her this little surprise. Alexandria wished she hadn't seen it. She went to the storage room to get the props she needed, grabbing a few accessories and thinking about the new couple. She was flooded with memories of her relationship with her ex—some happy, some sad—and all mixed up with her current exhaustion. With tears in her eyes, Alexandria headed to the studio and bumped into Petru at the door. She couldn't help herself.

"Those flowers you came in with—were they for one of the models?" she asked him unceremoniously through her teeth.

"I don't think it's any of your business. Can you move, please, so I can pass?"

"I know you know how long she was with me. I helped you get the promotion that you asked for. How can you be so ungrateful?" Alexandria balled her hands into fists.

"Whatever was between you two is over. Can you move?" He tried to get through again.

Alexandria's face turned a deep shade of red, the veins on her neck stood out, she threw the veils she was holding and jumped on Petru. She started hitting him and screamed, "I'll kill you if you touch her, I'll kill you!"

She felt like her body was working independently of her mind. Petru just stood there and tried to turn away her fists. Mel, Nando, and a cameraman who had all heard the commotion came running over. Nando grabbed Alexandria and pulled her away from Petru; Mel pulled her into the storage room with her and locked the door. Alexandria couldn't control herself, but her best friend was in damage-control mode.

"Are you out of your mind? What was that? Do you know what consequences this could have? If we can keep this quiet, you might get away with it. Hopefully Nando can talk to him, try to convince him not to take any action."

"I don't know what happened to me. Just all these emotions, all the built-up trauma, the exhaustion, and when

I saw how happy she was when he gave her the flowers…I guess that was the last straw. I don't know what happened." Alexandria was trying to steady her racing heart. "I couldn't control myself. I know it can have consequences."

"This has to stop!" Mel was beside herself. "If you don't get that woman out of your head…that was your wake-up call! Do you hear me?! You need to forget her. You don't listen to me! If you don't stop now, I'm done with you!"

"I know. I'm sorry." Every nerve in Alexandria's body was on high alert. "Give me a few minutes to calm down and I'll be back in the studio. I promise nothing will happen."

Nando came with a glass of water and knocked on the door. He handed her the glass and reported, "Surprisingly, almost no one heard what happened, just us and the cameraman, but he wouldn't say a word. I spoke to Petru...he's not going to take any action for now. Right now, he just wants to go home. You need to release him because you're in charge tonight."

"Leave? He's just going to go and see her," Alexandria muttered.

"You crazy bitch, what did I just say!" Mel hissed.

"I'll tell him he's free to go and if someone asks, tell them he went home sick." Nando looked at Alexandria "And he really doesn't feel well, you clawed half his face off with your nails. Listen: tomorrow after everyone's cooled off, I'll talk to him again. You calm down now and pretend nothing happened. And don't attack anyone else. Jesus. I really didn't expect that from you."

~

The next day, Alexandria called in sick because she wasn't feeling well. Even though she didn't like being home alone, she gave herself time over the next two days to process what had happened. She realized her love life—all those failed relationships and her attempts to find the right woman—had become like an obsession for her. Each new relationship somehow made her more insecure, more jealous, more distrustful. The seemingly unattainable goal of a happy relationship with a woman was eating away at her.

Mel called her to check how she was feeling. "I still can't believe what you did. But tell me, how do you feel?"

"Well, not great, but I'll get better. I think I hit rock bottom there. I'd like to just escape somewhere...pack two suitcases of clothes and leave. Maybe Thailand, maybe Bali...someplace warm with a change of scenery. Some faraway place where I don't know anyone and no one knows me."

"Escape is not a solution, or an option for you. Try to pull yourself together and start climbing out of this hole. You were lucky this time—thank goodness there weren't many witnesses. I heard Petru has given his two weeks' notice. He got another offer and he told Nando that he wants to stay away from this drama. I'm not even sure that things will continue between him and Octavia...you're both too unstable and crazy and Petru's obviously smart enough to run away. So I think you got what you wanted."

"I'll try to avoid her. I want to get rid of this nightmare I'm in because of her."

"Because of *her*? If she doesn't leave because of *you*, at least she's trying to avoid you, too. She's taking mostly early morning shifts and a lot less than before. You're killing the business with your drama, you know. Try to distract yourself. I'll come see you after work."

Alexandria had recently taken the step of purchasing her own place. At the right time, an offer had come up for an apartment five minutes away from the studio. She'd hoped she would be working in television for a long time, and even if something went wrong, she liked the neighborhood.

~

Alexandria was looking forward to hanging out with Mel. Having been in self-imposed isolation, she was craving company. Mel showed up with two bottles of fine white wine. One glass spilled into two, and eventually Alexandria's spirits lifted. Their conversation bounced from topic to topic.

"Oh, I almost forgot." Mel took a slow sip from her glass. "I heard something new: Marilyn has been approved for some program and she told Valentina that she'll be working for another four months, then she's leaving."

Alexandria exclaimed, leaping up from the comfy couch, "Where is she going? She's the most successful model right now! Are you sure? That would be a huge loss for the show."

"Yeah, she's going to New York on some student exchange program." Mel leaned back, cradling the wine glass in her hand. "She's supposed to go for a few months, but who knows if she'll come back at all. You're looking at it from the director's point of view, but the model side is different. Sure, she's a successful model, but for an erotic channel. If she can get things sorted out there, she'd better not come back."

"And what about Chill? He's staying, right?"

"He's not a student, so yeah, he's staying." Mel traced the rim of her glass with her finger. "He said he'd wait for her to come back, no matter how long that takes. I believe him, but the question is more like if *she* will come back to *him*. That's got to be hard for him. But I can't think about this anymore right now; enough of your love triangles and drama."

Alexandria was full of mixed feelings. The news that Marilyn was dating Chill had removed some of the anxiety she'd felt in her presence, but she didn't like that she might not see her again.

"Are you okay? Don't tell me you're thinking about Octavia again!"

"No, no. It's nothing important, I just thought of an interesting project to film."

Chapter 9

April 2011

HI, ALEX. I was wondering if you were free this Thursday to meet up and have a beer. There's a place downtown I really want to visit. They offer 100 kinds of beer. If Thursday doesn't work for you, we can make it Friday before your night show.

Alexandria received the Facebook message after coming home after a day show. It was about eleven o'clock in the evening and she was exhausted when she heard the message notification. She assumed it was Mel, but when she opened the page, she froze. How had Marilyn sent her a message?

She felt a wave of anxiety, and dozens of thoughts ran through her mind. Downtown? Beer? There was no context, but she didn't mention other people. Alexandria wondered if Chill knew about this. Alexandria's whole body was vibrating. It sounded like Marilyn was asking her out.

Hey, hi. I'm always up for a beer. My schedule's a little busy this week, I've got a double shift this Thursday. How about next Thursday?

Send. Alexandria pressed the button. It was immediately opened and read and Alexandria could see that Marilyn was typing a reply. She hadn't felt this excited in a long time. Excited and lucky, and not quite able to believe it.

Unfortunately, I can't next week. My flight is on Monday. I don't know if you heard, I'm going to New York for a few months. I'd like to do it while I'm still here, but no problem. If you have time and find someone to take your shift, text me.

Yeah, I'll let you know.

Have a good night and I'll see you in the studio tomorrow. Marilyn left the chat.

Alexandria wondered what was behind that invitation. It was very possible there was nothing behind it and Marilyn was just being nice. She worried what their coworkers would think if anyone overheard them talking about going out for beers. She thought it was possible that she could be fired but then realized that was probably extreme.

The next day Alexandria was working a double shift. For the first shift, she was directing a daytime show that Marilyn was starring in. Inwardly she was worried about how Marilyn would react when she saw her. She was always sweet and positive and worries over Marilyn innocently mentioning their Facebook conversation in front of everyone made Alexandria put off their meeting until the last minute. Minutes before show time she went to the makeup room, putting on a serious, hurried expression and quickening her stride.

"Is everyone ready? Do we have all the models here? Anyone still need makeup?"

"Everyone is on time, made up, ready, and looking like a million bucks." Mel said with her typical sense of humor. "Come on, get out of here and let me take a nap alone in my makeup room."

"We're ready and we're going to do a great show today. A few of my regulars will be calling me today and I'm sure I'll be busy with them throughout the show," Marilyn added cheerfully, fixing her lipstick, and heading to the studio followed by the rest of the girls.

Alexandria was relieved that everything had been completely normal with Marilyn. She felt she'd successfully cleared the first checkpoint. However, they were about to spend the next few hours together, so the danger had not passed.

"You look thoughtful. Are you going to do anything special on the show today?" Mel asked Alexandria after all the girls had left the dressing room.

"No, the usual. Nothing special. Did you know this is Marilyn's last week? She leaves for the USA next Monday."

"Yeah, I figured. We talked about it. I'm happy for her. It's a great opportunity."

"Yes, it is. Did she say anything else?" asked Alexandria.

"We talked about her flight, where she was going to stay, what she was going to do there, that kind of thing. What else would we talk about?"

"Nothing in particular, I was just curious." Alexandria walked over to one of the mirrors, looked at herself, straightened an unruly strand of hair, and headed toward the studio. The second checkpoint was cleared. She knew that if Marilyn had even hinted at anything to the others while they were getting their makeup done, Mel would have told her right away. She figured that if Mel didn't ask or know about anything, that meant there wasn't anything to know. She felt reassured.

The show began with the usual opening from the on-air host. Messages with the first requests poured in, and Marilyn, as expected, received her first call from one of her regular viewers. Alexandria thought that was a good sign; if Marilyn was busy with callers, she wouldn't be able to communicate with Alexandria, unless it was related to a caller request. Alexandria felt extremely tense. She nervously walked in and out of the control room.

"The lines are full, all the girls are on the phone. Just relax, we're going to make good money today," said the sound engineer.

"I know, but I don't want to lose the momentum" Alexandria replied as she checked the current call log, even though it was the last thing on her mind.

"Alex, Marilyn wants to talk to you," Chill, who was one of the cameramen on the show, announced over the intercom. "Can you come to the studio?"

Alexandria felt a new wave of adrenaline flowing through her body. She looked at the monitor and saw that Marilyn's line was busy. She knew that if Marilyn had a viewer on the line, she wouldn't say anything personal or inappropriate. However, her anxiety had reached a significant level. She put on an especially professional expression and entered the studio. She looked around to make sure everything was okay and signaled for Marilyn to step out of the frame and come over to her. Marilyn smiled and walked towards her. Alexandria counted the steps she took towards her with trepidation, but also with an inner elation. She liked it when Marilyn walked near her, when she could catch the scent of her fragrance, feel her energy. She felt a strange mix of fear and eagerness.

"Hey, it's my viewer's birthday. He would like all the girls to sing Happy Birthday to him on the microphone and give him a wish. Could we arrange it?" Marilyn covered her microphone with one hand and moved closer to Alexandria's ear to ask.

"Yeah, give me a second to warn the team and get the rest of the girls organized. Tell him we'll do it in a few minutes," Alexandria replied enthusiastically. Marilyn's perfume lingered and it enhanced her captivating presence.

~

At the end of the show, Alexandria gathered the entire team for a brief meeting.

"Good show today! Everyone gave their best and it shows in the ratings. Marilyn will get a little bonus for today's broadcast, since we passed last week's record and the call logs show that the longest conversation today was hers. Great job. One more thing…this is also the time to mention how sorry we all are that you're leaving us, Marilyn. I hope it's for a short time and that you'll be back soon on the small screen. Your coworkers and all your fans will miss you." Alexandria spared no praise for Marilyn.

"Friends, I'm going to miss you all so much!" Marilyn's voice rang out as usual, but it contained a slight sadness. "But it won't be for so long, just a few months. As soon as I get home, I'll call to get back on the schedule. The experience I've gained here has been so valuable to me, the friendships I've made, the people I've met, everyone behind the camera…you all have taught me so much. I don't want to give it all up, and I know there's a lot more I can contribute. Time will fly, I'll be back here soon, and we'll pick up where we left off."

Some of the models gave her a hug goodbye.

"That's it for today's show. You can all go," Alexandria said. "I have to get back in there for my next shift. Marilyn…good luck!"

Despite trying to play it cool, Alexandria spent the next day obsessed with Marilyn and her invitation. Sharing these feelings was out of the question, because Mel would just tell her to get her head out of her ass and stop entertaining fantasies about someone from work. She opened her laptop and typed a message that she would start, delete, restart, and delete again. This happened several times. She was ready to close the laptop again but finally decided to hit the Send button.

Hi, Marilyn. I tried to change my shift, but no one's available. I'm sorry, but I won't be able to come to have a beer with you. Maybe we can make it when you get back. She ended with a winking emoji.

Alexandria had, in fact, asked two of her colleagues to change their shifts but to no avail, so she took that as a sign of fate.

Marilyn's response was fast.

No problem. I understand. Maybe some other time. Good night. There was a smiley face at the end of the message.

Alexandria sighed, relieved and disappointed in equal measures.

Chapter 10

August 2011

ALEXANDRIA HAD LITTLE time to obsess about what might have been if she'd met Marilyn for a drink before she left. Between increasing hours and responsibility at work, she barely had time to think at all.

"Are you happy?" Mel asked Alexandria in the makeup room after all the models had left.

"You know I don't like that question."

"How long have you been single now? I don't think you've been single for this long the whole time I've known you!" Mel giggled, covering her mouth with her hand.

"Very funny."

"What are your plans for the future?"

"I think I gave up." Alexandria stared at the ground in silence. "No plans, I guess I've kind of lost hope that I'll ever find the love of my life. Maybe I should go back to guys. It's easier with them."

"You, straight? Girl, if you can't find happiness in a world full of amazing women, do you really think dealing with guys will be better? That's like giving up a gourmet meal for a microwave dinner!"

"Maybe it's better not to think that far ahead. For

now, I need to concentrate on myself and take a break from relationships."

"That works for me," Mel smirked, a playful glint in her eye. "Just don't forget we're going to a nightclub next Monday. We have a reservation."

"Your crush's club?" Alexandria winked.

"It's not hers, she's just a DJ. But yeah…there."

"Okay, let me know the details. I like going to clubs—the noise, and the people and the happiness in their eyes when they've had too much to drink and are genuinely enjoying themselves. At times like that, people are the most real because they've forgotten to pretend to be someone they're not."

Alexandria had started hanging out with Mel and a few of the models more often and she genuinely enjoyed herself with them. These clubbing nights always meant a lot of drinking, dancing, and exhaustion the following day. Mel was popular with the women they met at the clubs, but there was one in particular who she'd set her sights on.

"I talked to Miss DJ and there's going to be an after-party when she's done here." Mel was fixing her hair in front of the club's bathroom mirror. "We're invited. You'll come, right?"

"This after-party sounds like it might have a happy ending. Is tonight the night?"

"It might be...I'm really into her, and she always gives us a shout-out on the mic, so I know she likes me too," Mel replied. "So, are you coming? I'm sure there'll be somebody interesting for you there. What do you say?" Mel winked.

As much as Alexandria didn't want the evening to end, she also didn't want to be the third wheel for Mel and her new love interest. On the other hand, she was also tempted by the idea of meeting someone new, even though she also had really mixed feelings about that.

"Okay, I'll come. Just let me get my coat." Alexandria said as they walked out of the bathroom.

The after-party was in the large and spacious apartment of one of Miss DJ's friends. The host was serving only the best fine wine and exclusive spirits. The floor was marble, and the windows went from floor to ceiling. The furniture was new and expensive. A large black leather couch was set in the middle of the room, across from a beautiful electric fireplace. Stylish modern paintings added to the exquisite style. Crystal chandeliers cast a shimmering glow over the room. In one corner stood a shiny piano, across from a collection of rare artifacts showcased in glass cabinets.

"What are you going to drink?" Mel whispered in Alexandria's ear. "Pick something. See what expensive drinks there are, pick the most expensive one, and I'll bring it to you." Mel was unable to sit still "You know there's a jacuzzi in the other bedroom. This place is very cool, right?"

"I'll have some whiskey. But I might leave soon; I'm tired. Have fun. "

"You can't leave in the middle of the best party we've ever been to! Come with me so you can choose your whiskey…blue label, or green?"

Alexandria sat at the end of the couch, taking small sips from her drink; it was quality whiskey over two ice cubes. Mel was on the terrace, smoking with Miss DJ.

"I'm curious what you're thinking about when you're looking at your glass so intently." Alexandria looked up to see a beautiful dark-eyed woman who appeared as though she were about to sit down next to her.

"I imagine how those two perfectly shaped ice cubes floating in the exquisite crystal tumbler would look in the frame. If I had a camera right now, I'd take the shot of a lifetime." Alexandria sipped from the glass and smiled at the woman. She was tall and slim, with eyes like onyx. Her black hair fell below her shoulders in sleek waves. Her dress clung tightly to her and revealed the curves of her body. Her movements were slow and graceful.

"A photographer?" she asked.

"Director, but first and foremost, a videographer," Alexandria replied with pride.

"That sounds very interesting, I've never met such a beautiful director and cinematographer before. Do you shoot for films?"

"I wish, but no. Private production. Our work is shown overseas." Alexandria tried to give a roundabout answer that didn't invite follow-up questions.

"And why are you alone? Where's your friend?"

"I think she's currently smoking on the terrace, if she's not in the Jacuzzi in the bedroom. She's very impressed. And you? Have you been here before? Who are you here with?"

"Mutual friends. I love the music they play at these after-parties, and there aren't many places where you can do whatever you want and no one bothers you. Are you single?"

"Yes, I am." Alexandria noted that she got right to the point.

"Have you met anyone interesting here tonight?" The unknown woman moved slightly closer to Alexandria.

"Yes, there were a couple of very polite gentlemen who were sitting in your seat a few minutes ago. They wanted me to join them a little later in some foreplay. I had to disappoint them…but I would have accepted if they were female." Alexandria blushed slightly as she returned the flirtation.

"I see that I've come to the right place. You know, I've always dreamed of doing a professional nude photo shoot. I've taken a lot of selfies, but of course, it can't compare to the job you'd do, as a professional. Maybe one day when you have free time, we can arrange something? Or, I can show you the ones I have here on my phone, if you like."

"I'm sure you could make it as a professional nude model. You certainly have the figure for it." For a moment Alexandria imagined her in front of the cameras in the studio.

The woman took the glass from Alexandria's hand, sipped her whiskey, and handed the glass back to her. She came closer and kissed her, sending the whiskey into Alexandria's mouth while she felt for her tongue with her own. They lingered over the kiss, and Alexandria felt something stir in her. The high-quality alcohol had made her feel ready for anything.

"You're a very good kisser," the woman said after she had pulled away.

"You too," Alexandria replied.

"Would you like to come with me to see if anyone is in the Jacuzzi?"

Alexandria knew what to expect if she went with her. Her life lately had become more organized and harmonious. She was trying to maintain healthy habits, to take care of her physical and mental health, and to stay away from toxic people and patterns. This unexpected opportunity opened up new questions. This didn't have to be messy, did it? Could this proposal actually be simpler than she expected; maybe sex without strings could be an answer. It was helpful that the woman was a stranger, and not straight, or a model that she supervised on set.

At that moment, she saw Mel and Miss DJ emerge from the terrace and head for the bedroom, where the Jacuzzi was.

"I think we just missed our chance." Alexandria nodded towards the bedroom. Despite her words, she wasn't sure if she'd missed an unforgettable experience with a beautiful woman, or stayed true to her conscience. Her companion turned and saw Mel and Miss DJ close the door from the other side.

"I don't know what you'd say to this, but if you're adventurous enough, and if you really like me…we could join them. I guarantee you the DJ would be flattered, and I don't think your friend would mind either."

She took Alexandria's hand and looked at it as though she could find her answer there. Although the offer was tempting in some ways, Alexandria knew herself well enough to know that a one-night stand would leave her empty and sad.

"I'm normally quite adventurous and I like you a lot. I've had a few drinks and that's in your favor, but I just don't think I'm in the mood for group activities. You can join them if you want, but I think I'm heading out." Alexandria checked her watch to confirm her decision.

"Are you sure? Your lips are so delicious, they've made me want to taste other parts of you." The woman boldly put her cards on the table.

"I'm *not* totally sure, but maybe it's better to leave it for another time."

"What if we don't see each other another time?"

"Then this kiss between us will remain perfect forever, untouched by the uncertainties of what might have come next…"

"Hm, I see. Sometimes, perfection is better left undisturbed."

"If it's meant to be, we'll meet again." Alexandria took the last sip of whiskey. "Could you tell Mel I had to go? I don't want to interrupt her right now." She left and called a cab.

~

The next day Alexandria met Mel, who was lying on the couch in the makeup room. It was dark because the curtains were closed, and all the lights had been turned off.

"Hey, how are you doing? Are you alive?" Alexandria sat down on one of the chairs to get the gossip from the night before. "How did you make out last night?"

"Don't ask me." Mel groaned. Each movement was an effort. "My head is going to explode. When did you leave? Did you fuck any hot women last night?" Mel sounded congested and was clearly heavily hungover.

"Haha, no, I didn't do anything. I met a few people, had some conversations…when I saw you go try out the Jacuzzi, I headed out. I didn't want to get too late."

"Oh, that's a shame; you probably weren't even trying! That apartment is great. We have to do it again." Mel groaned. "I don't know how I'm gonna make it 'til the end of the day."

"I'll bring you some coffee."

"Did you see next week's schedule?"

"I haven't seen anything, I just got here. I slept all day long."

"Lucky you." Mel felt the faint taste of stale alcohol lingering on her tongue.

"What about the schedule? Any new models?"

"Yes, there is a new model," said Mel.

"That's good, we could use some fresh faces in here." Alexandria got up from the chair and went to start Mel's coffee.

"Marilyn!" Mel called out.

Alexandria sat back on her chair. "Marilyn? She's back?" She could barely hide her excitement. It had been four months since she had left.

"Yeah, you might see her name on next week's schedule. I was surprised too when I saw it. Zara also confirmed it this morning when she was here. I can just imagine all the directors fighting for her to be on their shows." said Mel, who was now trying to arrange the makeup palettes and brushes.

"Yeah, that's good news, we need models like her," Alexandria said casually.

"Next weekend, Nando's throwing a party at his place out of town. He invited everybody—you're coming, right?" asked Mel.

"No. You know I can't miss Friday and Saturday night. Any other day I can come up with something, but those shows are prime time." Alexandria was visibly disappointed though. "I wish he didn't schedule it on the weekend, I know it's going to be crazy."

"Why don't you give your show to someone else? The show won't die without you! Come on, it'll be really cool. Nando even invited Zara and Marilyn. C'mon, you're the only one who won't be there!"

"I told you—any other day would be a yes, but on the weekends I just can't. You know that." Everyone knew that Friday and Saturday night shows were sacred prime time. If you wanted to stay on top, you had to be there. She was proud to have the privilege of being the permanent and sole director of those shows, and there was no reason that would make her miss them.

Alexandria walked out of the makeup room, going to the schedule board to see with her own eyes whether Marilyn herself was listed for a shift. It was true. She walked into the studio in a good mood, smiling and greeting the models and crew. She walked into the control room and saw Nando checking the monitors.

"You look happy; you must've had sex!" he greeted her.

"I wish. I'm just in a good mood for the show. I hear you're throwing the party of the year."

"Will you be there?" asked Nando.

"I can't. I know everyone who isn't at work will be there. But as you know I'm one of the lucky ones—I've got the show."

"Yeah, you never take a night off. But if anything changes, you know where we'll be."

Nando was still chief cameraman. His girlfriend Aurora also was still a model; they'd been together already for several years. In the beginning, their relationship had been a secret, just like every other relationship between a model and someone from the crew. However, over the years, their relationship gradually came into the open, even though it wasn't exactly rock-steady. Aurora often lied to him and he pretended to believe her. He had caught her with other men several times, though she always had a brilliant explanation as to why it wasn't how it looked. Their drama seemed to confirm Mel's theory that all relationships started at the station were cursed.

"I guess Aurora will be at the party too," Alexandria said.

"She's a host. There's no way she's not going to be there."

"You're incredibly patient. Don't you think it's toxic, all the lies, cheating, and scandals? And when you try to break up with her, then she suddenly remembers she doesn't want to lose you, so she stalks you, chases you, or puts tracking devices in your car. You really must love her a lot to put up with all this!"

"Yeah, well, I don't know who's had bigger relationship drama—you or me. She loves me," Nando said.

"I'm not sure I understand the concept of loving someone and then cheating on them, do you? To me, when you love someone, you don't want to be with anyone else. When there is true love that person satisfies you; neither your soul nor your body craves anyone else. When you find your person, you lose your sensitivity to others. You exchange invisible particles, DNA, and energy so that you carry some of the other person inside you. You're happy to give up your freedom because you don't need anyone else. If you're lucky in this life, you'll get the same in return. If not, you may find out what hell on earth means."

"Is there anything else you want to share?" asked Nando.

Alexandria laughed and went back to the studio. The news that Marilyn was back made her dream again of great love, of true happiness. She really did want to go to Nando's party. She knew everyone would be there and it would be fun. She was curious to see Marilyn as well, but work was more important.

~

After Nando's party, Mel told Alexandria that she had to share something—but not at work. Alexandria had some free time before her show so they decided to meet at the café next door.

"Did you hear what happened at the party?" Mel began as she looked around the place for familiar faces.

"I haven't spoken to anyone. I assume you all got very drunk and are still recovering from the party of the season. What happened?"

"Well, Nando's guesthouse is great. We should go sometime. There's a big yard, a pool…never mind, I'll tell you about the house later." Mel settled comfortably in the chair and continued. "Everyone was there except you and anyone on your show. Any of course any of the losers who didn't get invited, haha. It was all great, there was lots of drinking and food, we were in the pool, the guys had brought two huge speakers, and the music was blaring."

"Okay, okay…and?"

"We all had a great time. Except about two in the morning, Aurora came up to me, crying." Alexandria didn't dare interrupt. "Wait, I'm skipping ahead. A little while earlier, Nando, who was drunk, gathered his courage and sent a message to Marilyn to come to the end of the backyard. There's a small grove there. She went, and he was waiting there for her with a rose. Get this—he told her he fell in love with her the moment he saw her, and that he wants to be with her. Later, he told Aurora that he wants to break up because he's madly in love with another woman."

"Oh, this sounds like alcohol was involved, huh. Of course, the next day when he sobers up, he doesn't dare look Marilyn in the eye out of shame and begs his girlfriend to take him back, like a kitten who ran away in a rainstorm," Alexandria guessed.

"That's what I thought. Because Nando was sleeping outside in the yard, Marilyn and Zara and a few other girls had left, and Aurora wanted to go outside and kill him, but I stopped her. In the morning, though, Nando said he didn't regret what had happened and stuck to his word. You can imagine what a shock that was, can't you? Everybody knows very well what his girlfriend was doing behind his back for so long and how she had him wrapped around her little finger. She was certain that *he* wouldn't do anything like that, and that the relationship would continue until *she* decided to end it. And now *BAM*! Expect the unexpected: a knife in the back from the person closest to you. Not that she doesn't deserve it."

"Wait a minute—what did Marilyn say to Nando? Isn't she still with Chill?" asked Alexandria.

"As far as I know they're *not* together. Even before she left for New York things had started to go downhill, and now that she's back, she's ended it. And he's been sitting and waiting for her all this time! That's why you have to be selfish and only look out for yourself, because as you can see, anyone is capable of hurting anyone else without even blinking an eye!" sputtered Mel. "I just think

Marilyn wasn't serious about their relationship from the beginning. And the poor guy was so in love with her, just like every other fool…"

"But what did Marilyn *say* to Nando?" Alexandria demanded an answer to her question.

"Well, the poor thing was in shock. She hadn't suspected that Nando might have feelings for her. She told him she didn't know what to say, and that she had to think. She tried to stop him from talking Aurora, but he was determined. That's why she left so quickly…I can imagine how embarrassed she felt. After all, he ended a long, serious relationship with her. And he and Aurora work together, and everybody knows them as a couple. What a mess. From what I heard, Marilyn has asked for time to think about what happened."

"How is this even possible? Nando has never been one to speak up to Aurora—he always just agreed with whatever she wanted. Where did he get this idea to just…break everything? I guess everything must've been building up for him, and he finally just had enough. Marilyn was the catalyst," Alexandria said.

"That's exactly what happened, but the question is—what comes next? Maybe Aurora won't let him go. You know when you lose something, you start to appreciate it more, and maybe she doesn't want to let him go."

"What if Marilyn decides to be with Nando? After she thinks about it, she might decide that she likes him too."

"Maybe…Nando is a good-looking guy…smart…with a good job. But she also knows that Nando's relationship was serious…she's unlikely to get involved in a love triangle or purposely hurt someone. We'll see."

What is it about Marilyn that makes everyone fall

in love with her? wondered Alexandria. She believed Nando would be much happier with someone like Marilyn, especially after enduring such a toxic relationship with Aurora.

~

A couple of weeks later, Nando and Marilyn went out on a date. Nando came to pick her up from the apartment where she was still living with Felix. She looked out her bedroom window and saw him in front of his car, shifting nervously from foot to foot, waiting for her with a huge bouquet of red roses. She grabbed her little purse and went downstairs. She hugged him, smelling the woody undertones and hints of leather from his expensive cologne.

"Thanks for the flowers; you shouldn't have," she said.

"I wouldn't think of coming without flowers!" He opened the car door and Marilyn slid into the passenger seat with a smile. "I hope you're hungry; I've made a reservation. I'm sure you'll like the restaurant I've chosen."

"Sounds perfect, let's go," said Marilyn.

The place was romantic and sophisticated, offering a stunning view of Bucharest. There was a piano in the middle of the room where a young woman was playing jazz music. They were seated at a table by the window where they could enjoy the view. Nando was a real gentleman, with great attention to detail and excellent manners. Marilyn had no experience with this type of date, since her previous partners were so immature and ill-mannered.

Nando was good at maintaining interesting conversations

on various topics. He didn't bring up what happened at the party because he didn't want Marilyn to feel pressured, or obligated to give him the answer he wanted to hear.

"About what happened the other night..." said Marilyn, sipping from her glass of wine as if she needed a little more courage. "What happened was very unexpected for me. I never suspected that you had feelings for me. I have a lot of respect for you and Aurora and your relationship, and the last thing I want is to be the cause of your breakup."

"We aren't splitting up because of you," he interrupted her. "My decision to break up with her had come long before that. I should have told her sooner, but I kept putting it off." He searched for the right way to express himself. "After the few drinks that I had that night, I mustered up the courage to tell you how I felt, and that's the most important thing right now."

A moment of silence hung between them.

"I know it came out badly; I know that discussing the two things together made the situation more confusing than it actually is, but...I really like you." Nando leaned in attentively. "From the first time I saw you in the studio I knew I wanted to be with you. I was on the verge of confessing my feelings to you earlier, but then I realized that you were with Chill so I decided to hold back. Since you're no longer together, and—as everyone already knows—I'm not committed anymore either...if you like me, I'd love it if you wanted to give it a try and see if there might be anything between us."

Marilyn remained silent, not sure how to respond.

"I'm not pressuring you. I don't need an answer now." The piano music faded into the background. "We can try hanging out together as friends, or just having fun to see if something might work out. Whatever your decision is, my feelings for you won't change."

She took a deep breath. "I'm not going to lie to you. I wasn't thinking of getting into another relationship after Chill. You know I just got back home and I haven't settled into my normal life here yet. I wanted some time to be by myself, devote more time to finishing my master's. I have to graduate this year. And the job…you know…I want to be free for a little while, and hang out at clubs and bars, with friends." Marilyn paused briefly. "I like you. I think you're a dream guy for a lot of women, and Aurora is losing a really valuable person in her life." She paused again and took a sip of wine, then continued. "Without making any promises or getting anyone's hopes up, we can keep seeing each other. We can go out together and see what happens. How does that sound?" asked Marilyn.

"We have a deal. Cheers!" Nando raised his glass.

After dinner, he drove her to her apartment and walked her to the door.

"Thanks for a great night. I really had a wonderful time," Marilyn said, but she didn't hurry inside. Nando wasn't sure if a kiss would be appropriate at this point so he just stood there.

"You can kiss me if you want," laughed Marilyn.

"Sorry," Nando blushed. "I feel like an idiot in a movie who had a chance to kiss the super cool girl but missed it."

Marilyn smiled. Nando ran his fingers through her hair. The light breeze brushed across her face. He leaned in slowly and pressed his lips to hers. After a few seconds she pulled back slightly and said, "Good night."

"See you soon," he said, and walked away.

Chapter 11

September 2011

"ARE YOU COMING to my place tonight?" Alexandria met Nando in the control room.

"Yes, I'll be there. And did you invite Marilyn?" Nando asked quietly.

"Well, no, I didn't. I've told a few people, but honestly, we're not that close. And I don't know if she'd be into that kind of partying. Camera One needs balance." Alexandria said, looking at the monitors.

"Why do you think she isn't into that kind of party?" Nando looked at Alexandria.

"No idea, I just don't think she'd come. But if you want, try inviting her. Do you see the colors of Cameras Two and Three?"

"I don't see anything. Can you ask her, please? I don't want to sound like I'm trying to arrange something between me and her. I'm sure she'd accept if you invited her," Nando said.

"Are you serious?"

"About the cameras or the party?"

"Okay, I'm doing this because I'm a good friend— I'll ask her if she wants to come when I see her in the makeup room." Alexandria sighed deeply. "Are you gonna fix Camera One?"

"I will! And thank you."

Now that everyone knew about what had happened between Marilyn and Nando, Alexandria felt more at ease talking to her. She felt empathy for Nando's attempts to win her over, and she was a supportive friend, so the friendship she felt for Nando had really quashed any romantic feelings she'd had for Marilyn.

"Is everyone ready?" she asked, entering the makeup room.

"Sir, yes sir!" joked Mel.

"Bravo! Let's do a good show, and then after the shift, we'll head to my place to toast a job well done. Marilyn, I don't know if I told you—if you have no other plans, you're welcome."

"Really? I hadn't heard about it. Yeah, I'll be there. What's the address?"

"It's super close. If you want, you can come with Nando, he's coming after work too," Alexandria replied, smiling and walked towards the studio.

~

After the show, a few of the models left with Alexandria to go to her house. Some of the crew went to a nearby store to buy alcohol. Nando and Marilyn left together, agreeing to stop first at Nando's apartment so that he could change his clothes. Alexandria was immediately suspicious that they wouldn't make it to the party. She was slightly disappointed, but also happy that a friend of hers had a chance with a woman like Marilyn.

Alexandria's apartment was spacious, with a large

terrace. Guests tended to spend more there since they could smoke. There was never a problem with noise, since none of her walls abutted the walls of any neighbors' apartments. This made it an even more convenient place for a party.

Almost everyone was there, and their glasses were full. One of the sound engineers adjusted the music, while Alexandria chatted with Mel and laughed uproariously at her jokes. Someone knocked on the door and Mel went to open it.

"Nando and Marilyn have arrived!" Mel called out.

"I lost the bet," Alexandria said, taking a sip from her whiskey glass. "We were betting you wouldn't come. Come on in. What would you like to drink?"

"I told you, I just needed to change. Marilyn was pissed because we were going to be late because of that," Nando said, examining the bottles of liquor.

"It's true—he's a bigger princess than me! He tried on three T-shirts because he couldn't decide," joked Marilyn. Nando poured a glass of wine and handed it to her.

"I'm glad you came. The drinks are here; help yourself. If you need anything, just let me know," Alexandria said, pouring more whiskey into her glass.

An hour later, the party was really rolling. All kinds of transgressive topics were on the table: everything imaginable about the body, sex, fetishes, and preferences were commented on freely and without inhibition. Nando and Alexandria shared past stories from the studio. It was the first time Alexandria felt so at ease in Marilyn's company. Whether it was because she'd had enough drinks, or because she was the host of the party, comfortable in her own territory, she felt a confidence she hadn't known before.

When Mel announced that she was leaving, Alexandria asked in frustration, "Why? It's the middle of the party!"

"My beloved DJ texted me. She's waiting for me. I love you very much, but duty calls." Mel winked mischievously at Alexandria and grabbed her jacket.

Alexandria approached the bar area and refilled her nearly empty glass. Nando walked over and said, "Where's the wine? Marilyn's ready to refuel."

"I put the bottle in the fridge to chill. I'll take care of it."

Marilyn walked over and held her glass out to Alexandria as she observed her opening the cold bottle. She held the bottle in one hand and reached for the glass with the other. Her fingers curled around the stem, and it was familiar to Marilyn. She'd observed her hands before when Alexandria held the camera and adjusted the lens left or right to find the focus. With a slow motion, Alexandria tilted the bottle, and the golden liquid began to fill the glass. There was a certain elegance in the way she moved her fingers and the delicate play of veins visible on the back of her hands. Marilyn watched her intently, her gaze moving from the precise movement of Alexandria's hands to her face. There was magnetism and tenderness in Alexandria's gaze. Marilyn's eyes traced the curve of her lips, where a slight smile played at the corners as she focused on her task. Her skin was porcelain smooth and kissed by the sun. The unruly curls that fell to her shoulders invited fingers to run through their gentle waves. Alexandria finished filling the glass as Marilyn continued to minutely study her every detail. Alexandria set the bottle aside and slowly handed the cool glass to Marilyn. In that brief moment, their fingers met and electricity crackled through the air. Time slowed its rhythm and their eyes met, locking in silent desire.

"Where's Mel? Did she leave?" Nando's voice cut through the air like a knife. It was a sudden intrusion, an unwelcome reminder of reality and the outside world. With a sigh, Alexandria tore her gaze away from Marilyn. Their connection was broken.

"Yes, she got an urgent call from Miss DJ so she rushed over. I think things might get serious there," Alexandria said. The conversation continued in a usual casual style, about mutual interests, interspersed with spicy stories from work. Glasses were emptied and refilled. Voices rose and fell, blending with the loud background music and the buzz of laughter filling the air.

"The music is very loud, but I know if I try to turn it down even slightly, someone will freak out. Do you want to go in the other room to talk because I can barely hear you!" Nando said.

"Yeah, forget it," Alexandria said while leading them to the bedroom. "I saw them arguing a little while ago about what the next song should be, so don't even bother!"

"So this is where the Roman Bacchanalia, famous since ancient Rome, takes place," joked Nando. "I hear that some of the hottest scenes in history, the hottest orgies, have happened here. Many of our own models have lost their virginity right here!"

Sheer curtains hung gracefully at the windows, swaying softly in the evening breeze. A large mirror in the corner reflected the whole room, creating an illusion of spaciousness. The bed was covered with satin sheets in light blue, with a few silky pillows thrown on top. A white plush area rug covered the floor and Marilyn felt its softness as soon as they walked in.

"You're exaggerating—but yes, this is the place," Alexandria laughed. "Here's the special lighting." Alexandria pressed a remote control and recessed lights in the ceiling dimmed to a pale orange glow.

"It's starting to feel like work!" Nando said. Marilyn chuckled lightly but said nothing.

"No! Enough with work! What were we talking about?" Alexandria sipped at her whiskey and set the glass on the nightstand.

"If I were the director and you two were the models, I would start the show right now," Nando said.

"Let's see you as a director. Direct us!" Marilyn unexpectedly jumped in. She took a sip of her wine and set it down next to the whiskey glass. Alexandria's eyes widened in surprise, and she shifted uncomfortably, then glanced away. Marilyn's boldness, combined with Nando's comments and the dimmed lights, stirred a mix of awkwardness, curiosity, and arousal in Alexandria.

"Alex, do you want to kiss Marilyn?" asked Nando.

Alexandria didn't know how to react because tons of thoughts quickly flew through her mind.

Of course I want to kiss her, but she's not into women! I don't think she'll say no, but what if she isn't into it? I bet this is Nando's plan to be left alone with her. I can't say I don't want to kiss her because that would offend her...

And lastly: *We've all had a lot to drink.*

She looked at Marilyn and their eyes met again. Marilyn wanted to hear her answer. Alexandria still held the small remote in her hand. She pressed the button and the lights dimmed even more. Alexandria moved closer and gently kissed Marilyn. Marilyn returned her kiss and the two remained pressed against each other as if unexplained magnetic forces had glued them that way. Marilyn kissed her even more passionately as if she had been waiting for this moment all her life. The gentle pressure of her lips against Alexandria's made her whole body tingle. Her sweet breath and the scent of Alexandria's skin intoxicated her and ignited a wild passion. All her senses felt heightened, and she wanted to take in as much of Alexandria as possible. Marilyn didn't pull away. She didn't want this kiss to stop.

Suddenly, Alexandria thought of Nando standing inches away from them. She knew that he liked what he saw, but more than that, he wanted to be in her place. She knew that he was in love with Marilyn and was willing to do anything to win her over. Alexandria was grateful that he had unknowingly given her that brief, passionate moment with Marilyn, though it had shaken her. She knew it was time to exit the scene and give the main character the moment he deserved. She didn't want to—Marilyn's gentle touch had shaken her more than any other—but she pulled away, looked at Nando, and gestured for him to come closer. Nando kissed Marilyn as well.

Knowing that the kiss was the most magical feeling she'd ever experienced, Alexandria wondered if Marilyn could possibly feel the same. She figured that no matter what, it was probably a one-time adventure for her. Maybe it had even been a way for her to seduce Nando, or to initiate a threesome.

Tomorrow I'll have to justify what happened by

saying I was drunk. I've used that before.

Hoping that Nando wouldn't expect a threesome because of what had just happened, Alexandria tiptoed toward the door. All she wanted was to retrieve her glass of whiskey and get out unnoticed. Alexandria closed the door behind her, proud of being a good friend to Nando, and sacrificing her own feelings to give him a chance with Marilyn. Trying to act casual in case anyone had noticed the three of them going into the bedroom together, she jumped into conversation with two of the cameramen while looking around the room and trying to guess if anyone had noticed her absence. She reassured herself that no one was suspicious and that everyone was having fun.

"Let me get you another beer," Alexandria told the cameramen and headed for the fridge.

"Alexandria!" She was startled by a shout behind her and turned around to see Nando standing in the hallway with his pants unbuttoned.

"Are you crazy? What are you doing?" Alexandria ran towards him.

"Go on, get in there," Nando said as he buttoned his pants. "Marilyn is crying…"

"Crying? How come she's crying; what happened?"

"She doesn't want me; she wants you," Nando said and walked past her, heading for the bar area.

Alexandria stood at the bedroom door. She knocked on the door and waited a few seconds. Slowly she opened the door and walked in. The lights were still dimmed. Marilyn sat on the edge of the bed, crying softly.

Alexandria sat next to her and asked, "Are you okay? Why are you crying? Please don't cry."

"Why don't you want me?" Marilyn looked at

Alexandria and her eyes were full of tears.

"How could I *not* want you? You're so beautiful and sweet, and everyone wants to be with you."

"Everyone but you," muttered Marilyn.

"That's not true. I want you. It's just all so messed up!" said Alexandria. "I didn't know you liked me that way. And Nando is so in love with you, I thought you wanted to be with him." She paused for a second and continued. "On top of that, you're the best—the top model of the whole station. I don't have a great reputation because of have gotten involved with models in the past. I got a warning from management to keep it professional with the models moving forward because it was interfering with the work. If I got involved in another relationship—let alone with their very best model—I could say goodbye to my job."

"That's not going to happen! I'll talk to them; I won't let them fire you because of me. You're the best director," said Marilyn.

Alexandria moved closer to her. "I don't want to see you cry; you're tearing my heart out." She gently wiped away the tears that left a trail under Marilyn's eyes. "We've all had enough to drink tonight. Let's get back to the others before they start looking for us. Tomorrow, after we've slept and sobered up, we'll talk again. I just want to make sure that none of this is affected by alcohol. I promise you that everything will be fine. I don't want you to think I don't want you. That's not true." Alexandria took Marilyn's hand and headed for the door.

"Wait," Marilyn said and gently pushed Alexandria against the wall. She stroked her face which reflected the warm, soft orange light. She looked her straight in the eyes, smiled, and kissed her softly. The kiss was slow and passionate. Alexandria didn't want this moment to end. She could have stayed there leaning against the wall, lost in Marilyn's lips for the rest of the night.

"Are you okay?" Alexandria asked her after the kiss ended. "Do you want to go back to the others?"

"Yeah, I'm fine." Marilyn kissed Alexandria on the forehead and they both reentered the party as if nothing had happened. Marilyn went to the restroom to freshen up her face and dry her eyes. Alexandria sat down next to Nando, who was on the couch holding a glass of whiskey.

"Did you fix it?" he asked.

"Yeah, it's fine."

"She's yours. I won't compete with you. I sincerely hope it works out for you," sighed Nando.

"I didn't know, I swear. I know that you really like her and I thought I was helping you." Alexandria exhaled sharply. "I had no idea something like this could happen,"

"I didn't know either," Nando said and sipped from his glass. "You have to be very careful from now on, you know. This time they won't forgive you at work."

"I know," Alexandria said and looked at Marilyn who was just coming out of the bathroom.

For the rest of the night, Alexandria and Marilyn tried very hard to appear as though nothing had happened. Alexandria, as host, was attentive to everyone, but when they could, they shared a glance or a smile. The feelings they'd just ignited were mixed with the tension of their secret, as well as a desire to continue.

Nando announced at the end of the night that they were ready to leave. To Alexandria, he whispered, "I'll drive Marilyn home so it doesn't look suspicious. We came together; everyone expects us to leave together."

Alexandria nodded in agreement.

"I'm glad you came," Alexandria said, hugging Nando. "Next week we can go to a bar or club." She hugged Marilyn as well.

"If you go to a club, give me a call. Thanks for inviting me tonight," Marilyn said and left with her arm slung around Nando's waist. The party was now officially over. Alexandria sent off the last guest and sat down on the couch. It was hard for her to analyze clearly what had happened, but she couldn't stop replaying the kisses with Marilyn, over and over again.

~

Alexandria woke up early the next morning and checked her phone for a message or call from Marilyn. The screen was blank. From her perspective, learning that Marilyn had feelings for her was too good to be true, but she was aware that alcohol was involved. She wondered if the delay in hearing from Marilyn was due to regret, or sleeping in after a late night. Either way, she didn't want to wait too long to reconnect.

Time passed and still not a word. After lunch, Alexandria sent a message, as Marilyn continued to remain silent.

Hey, how are you? I just want to say hi and see if you're still thinking like you did last night, or if it was because of the drinks... She ended with a smiley face emoji.

There was no reply in the next hour. Alexandria was nervous, anxious, impatient, and slightly frustrated. She tortured herself with the possibility that none of it had been real for Marilyn. She was considering her options—mostly that she would pretend nothing had happened—when the long-awaited text came.

None of what happened last night was the result of the drinks. I still feel the same way. Her closing emoji was the one that blew kisses.

The world changed, and Alexandria was flooded with a wave of feel-good hormones and happiness in its purest form.

Chapter 12

HEY, DO YOU have any plans for tomorrow night? Alexandria texted Marilyn.

It had been a few days since the party and communication between them was slow. Alexandria didn't want to appear pushy, but patience was not one of her virtues. She worried that Marilyn could change her mind, that their feelings from the party might cool off, or that she herself might lose her nerve. She really needed an outside opinion, even if she wasn't sure that she'd take their advice. There was Mel, of course, but she'd really have something something to say once she found out a model was involved again. Alexandria thought to herself that she simply couldn't handle one of her lectures right now.

Hey, something came up for tomorrow. What do you think about Sunday night?

Alexandria waited a few minutes before she texted back. *Sunday works, what time?*

I have to meet some friends and I'm not sure when I'll be done. I'm not sure about an exact time, it could be later. If you want, I can come to your apartment when I'm done with them?

Sounds like a plan. I'll wait for you at home Sunday

night.

Alexandria thought that a restaurant, maybe even a movie theater, would be the best first date option. Something casual, even cliché, without the pressure of being alone in her apartment. Alexandria herself was nervous about the date.

Sunday was taking a long time to arrive, and Alexandria had mixed feelings about it. She couldn't wait to see Marilyn, but the fear that she might be taking a step backwards worried her. She'd been proud of herself when she was single, feeling that she'd broken a destructive cycle within herself. She wanted to remember the lessons she'd learned, while trying not repeat her old patterns and mistakes.

Sunday

Alexandria had prepared everything by the time she got Marilyn's message saying that she was done and would be at her apartment in half an hour. She'd rearranged and cleaned the entire apartment. Fluffy towels were neatly arranged in the bathroom. She'd placed a vase of fresh flowers in the middle of the coffee table. She lit a scented candle, turned on some soft music, and chilled a bottle of expensive white wine.

"I hope you weren't waiting too long; I tried to finish quickly," Marilyn said, hugging Alexandria as she walked in. Alexandria hugged her tightly and inhaled the delicate fragrance of her hair. The familiar scent took her back to the night they'd first kissed.

"No, I wasn't even expecting you until later. Come on in." Alexandria took her coat. "Are you hungry? I can order something."

"No thanks, I ate with my friends." Marilyn noted the pleasant vanilla scent from the candle.

"Wine?" asked Alexandria, reaching for the chilled bottle.

The evening was spent getting to know each other better. Marilyn talked at length about her time in New York. Alexandria listened with interest, but what she really wanted to know was what Marilyn thought about their previous encounter, at the party. She hesitated to ask directly because she wanted the topic to come up naturally, but she needed to know if Marilyn was interested in experimenting with women, or if she was ready for something serious. Marilyn hadn't yet given any clear signals, so Alexandria was unsure what to expect from the evening. She hoped the wine would help them relax, but at the same time they needed to be sober enough to have an honest conversation. Alexandria started to gather the courage to begin that discussion, but at that moment Marilyn leaned in and kissed her—the same delicious, tender kiss she'd been dreaming about since the night of the party.

As much as she was enjoying it, she pulled back slightly and said, "I could kiss you all night long—I love your kisses and I don't want to stop for a second. But I want to talk with you for a minute."

"I feel like we've been talking all night," laughed Marilyn. "But okay, ask me anything; I'll tell you."

"I'm wondering…I don't think you've been with other women before; am I right?"

"No, I haven't been with other women. That doesn't mean anything, though."

"As I explained to you, my situation at work is quite specific," Alexandria said seriously. "Even the fact that you're here now is a professional risk for me. And that risk could be worth it, but I'd like to hear your perspective...you know, what do you want…what do you expect? I've mixed my personal life with my professional life before—which I'm not proud of, and it damaged my reputation at work—so if I were to get involved again with someone from the studio, I need to be sure. One thing I'm sure about is that I like you a lot, and I would love to be with a woman like you. I didn't realize that you had any interest in women and so I never thought that we'd ever be anything other than coworkers or friends."

"I haven't been with other women, and I can't put a label on myself…I don't know if I should say I'm straight, or bi, or lesbian, or what. I can't tell you for sure what might happen, but I know that I like you and want to be with you. I've heard rumors about you…that you had been involved in relationships at work, and that a lot of them weren't good…but I'm not like those other women." Marilyn's voice softened, reflecting the seriousness of the topic. "I will never hurt you in any way and I will not let you get fired because of me. They wouldn't dare do anything that would make me leave." A moment of silence hung between them. "I don't want to be with Nando. I don't want Chill. I don't feel the same way about them that I do about you."

"The week before you left for New York—when you texted me and asked me out for a beer—what exactly did you want then? We'd never spoken much before; we weren't close. Why did you text me? Did you have feelings for me then?"

"Yeah, I wanted to see you out of the studio."

Marilyn kept her gaze downcast. "I didn't have a clear plan, but I wanted you to think of me, somehow, while I was gone. I don't know what would have happened if we had met then…you know, would things have been different or not…but I believe everything happens for a reason. And I want to be here now. I'm not going anywhere. I want to see you, get to know you, and learn what the future might hold for us."

Marilyn paused briefly. She had taken Alexandria's hand and was gently touching it. "Ignoring the job situation for now…would you like to jump into this adventure with me?"

"It's not just an adventure for me. For me, it's not an experiment or satisfying my curiosity. I'm tired of that kind of thing. If I get into a relationship again, it needs to be serious, monogamous, sincere. My heart has been broken so many times that I wonder how I managed to put it back together and how I survived," said Alexandria.

"You're not an experiment for me." Marilyn said and was silent for a moment. Alexandria started to say something, but Marilyn cut her off.

"Can I kiss you?"

Alexandria looked Marilyn in the eye without saying a word. She moved a piece of her hair that had fallen in front of her face, stroked her gently, and kissed her. The kiss was soft and lingering. Alexandria wanted things to happen slowly, without her usual impatience. She wanted this time to be different, and to believe that she had learned from her mistakes. She felt sure that she needed to do things differently this time.

Marilyn continued to kiss her; she had never felt so desperate for this intimacy. She pulled Alexandria down onto the couch, tilting her head and trying to get closer to her. She unbuttoned her blouse while Alexandria caressed her back with her fingertips, gently tracing the contours of Marilyn's back, getting to know every curve and line. Marilyn rushed to remove her clothes as she continued to kiss Marilyn gently.

"Would you take this off?" said Marilyn, pointing to her own bra.

Alexandria popped the clasp with the fingers of one hand. She thought of Marilyn somehow as an innocent and gentle creature, and knowing that it was her first time, she was almost afraid to touch her. But Marilyn set the speed and the rules, and her speed was to hurry.

"Do you want to go to the bedroom? Marilyn whispered in Alexandria's ear. Despite some hesitation, Alexandria didn't want Marilyn to feel unwanted. Continuing to kiss her, she took her hand and led her towards the bedroom.

The moon cast a silver light through the curtains of the half-open window. In her attempts to make a fresh start, Alexandria hadn't turned on her special lighting because she wanted everything to be natural and different. As she continued to kiss her, she tangled her fingers in Marilyn's hair and gently pulled her hair back. Marilyn moaned in pleasure. Sometimes Alexandria liked to be a little rough in foreplay, but she wasn't sure if Marilyn would like it. With other women, Alexandria had felt that she could give in to the passion and do anything she wanted to do, without thinking. But with Marilyn, she had inhibitions.

"Do it again," Marilyn said. "*Loved* how you pulled my hair back."

"I'm scared to be rough with you," Alexandria said

while Marilyn bit her bottom lip.

The tension of anticipation was in the air; their built-up passion was about to erupt. Their breath mixed together as their bodies melded into each other, moving in the synchronized rhythm of an erotic dance. Marilyn slowly touched every part of Alexandria's body, discovering soft and gentle curves, nooks and shapes that she had never experienced before. She wanted to know everything about her, including her most private places, to feel her with all her senses…to taste her, smell her, hear her moans of pleasure…

That was the first night of five nights in a row that Marilyn spent in Alexandria's bedroom, enjoying the pleasure and passion that overtook them, a passion that was burning like wildfire.

Chapter 13

October 2011

FOR THE NEXT few weeks, Alexandria and Marilyn saw each other almost every day. Nando was understanding and accepting, and helped maintain the ruse that there might be something between him and Marilyn. When Marilyn and Nando worked the same shift, they left the studio together, though he dropped her off at Alexandria's apartment.

"Just to let you know, Mel asked me today if Marilyn and I were officially together," Nando told Alexandria through his car window on one of those days. "You know she sees everything. I'm not sure she's convinced; I feel like she might come to you about it, so be ready with an answer."

"I'm sure she'll ask me about it sooner or later. But for now, the less people know, the better."

"Why don't you just tell her? You're friends; she won't say anything," suggested Marilyn.

"Because she will be the first one to judge me for what is happening here. She always told me to never get involved with models from the station. She cares about me and wants to protect me. I just have to find a way to explain to her that everything is different this time."

"She's right, Marilyn, no offense. I got wrapped up

in this model culture, too, but I'm out of it now. Did you hear—Aurora quit yesterday? One more model gone because of a workplace romance," Nando said.

"Really?" Alexandria's eyes widened in surprise. "Damn, she was one of the first models at the station! That's not good." She paused, thinking how furious management would be to find out they'd lost another good model. "So, she finally gave up on you?"

"I guess."

"So you lost two girls in a couple of weeks, huh? Sorry to joke about it, you know that I love you!" Alexandra laughed.

"Don't be rude, babe!" Marilyn raised an eyebrow.

"Very funny. Okay, I'm leaving. If you throw any parties, give me a call—as you know, I'm single and ready to mingle."

"Yeah, next week! Mel is organizing some party at the club where Miss DJ plays. I'll keep you posted," Alexandria said.

"You'll be the first one we call," Marilyn added. "Thanks for the ride."

Nando turned back as he was about to exit the parking lot in front of the building and said, "I'm happy for you two…If it was someone else taking Marilyn away from me like that, I wouldn't have given up so easily, but because it's you, I forgive you. Kiss her tonight for me!" He winked playfully.

"Yeah, right, you perv—any kisses she gets will be from me!" Alexandria said, grinning.

Nando left and the two women went inside.

"I missed you," Marilyn said and kissed Alexandria. "I couldn't wait for the show to end so I could come home to you. I can't stop thinking about you. And when I see you in the studio, I just want to jump on you and cover you with hugs and kisses."

"I missed you too, babe."

"There's something I need to tell you." Marilyn looked guilty. "I did something, and I hope you won't be mad at me."

"What happened?"

"I told Zara about us. I couldn't hide it anymore—she's my best friend; I've always shared everything with her. All these emotions I have right now…I needed to talk to someone. What you and I have between us is so special that I want to tell someone how happy I am. How happy you make me. I want to scream to everyone that you're mine! I've never felt anything like this before. And Zara was very happy for me—for us. She knows how to keep a secret; she's never betrayed me before. Everything will be all right, my love."

"I know Zara won't say anything, but we need to keep the circle of people who know as small as possible." Alexandria's eyes filled with unease.

"Don't worry—nobody else will know. I promise." Marilyn kissed Alexandria's cheek.

"Why don't you invite Zara to Mel's party? There will be more people from work."

"I'll tell her," said Marilyn. "She could really stand to have some fun. Her relationship is kind of in the tank."

"Why, what's wrong?"

"Long story. I'll tell you later." Marilyn pushed Alexandria towards the wall. "Right now, can I show you how much I missed you today…?"

"Hell yeah."

This was the first time that either Alexandria or Marilyn had been in a relationship like this, so everything that was happening was new to both of them. For Marilyn, a relationship with a woman was uncharted territory on a physical and mental level. She was living an experience that she had never even conceived of. It was the first time Alexandria felt so calm, safe, and balanced—at peace with herself and the world around her. Her previous relationships had taught her to expect betrayal. In her experience, her happiest moments were also her most vulnerable, and were often followed by a catastrophe. But Marilyn made her feel like their love was so strong and mutual that there was no force that could stand between them. It seemed to Alexandria that this was the long-awaited true love. It was worth going through the toxic relationships because at the end, she'd found the grand prize.

~

"Where are you?" Mel called Alexandria as she waited in front of the club.

"Almost there!"

"How long is it almost? I'm freezing!" Mel's voice edged with irritation. "I'm waiting for you outside so you can skip the line."

"Okay, okay, I'm here," Alexandria said as Mel noticed the cab pulling up.

"That's the last time I'm freezing my ass for you," Mel said as Alexandria tipped the driver. "Nando, and a few people from the crew, and some of the models are already here. The party's already started!" Mel signaled to the bouncer and they passed by him. "Marilyn also told me she's coming with Zara."

"Oh really? Nice. We're gonna be a big group." Alexandria tried to sound casually surprised.

The rest of the group was already drawing attention at their VIP table, which was in the corner, with a view of the whole club. Just in front of them was the DJ booth. The models were attractive, seductive, of course, and the way they danced here was similar to the way they danced at the studio while they were on the clock. Their sexy vibe was enhanced by the closeness of the group; they all knew each other so well. The jokes flowed, and so did the drinks. Bottles and glasses ran out fast but were quickly replaced. Everyone was dancing and enjoying the night. Marilyn and Zara arrived together in the middle of the party and wasted no time in starting to enjoy themselves.

"You and Marilyn are together, aren't you?" said Mel in Alexandria's ear.

"Why would you think that?" Alexandria had been expecting that question.

"Because my radar is working, and I know something's going on. I know you're not going to listen to me." Mel rubbed her forehead. She grabbed Alexandria's hand and pulled her to the bathroom, where they could hear each other over the music. "Do you know what? Humans are curious creatures. They're willing to ignore any consequence just to do what they want." Mel looked around to make sure nobody from their group was there. "You've been glowing these last few weeks. I'm not stupid, I've noticed you're different. You seem to think no one would pay attention and see how you two look at each other, but I saw it. You should have told me right away.

How long have you been together?"

"Not long…a few months." Alexandria looked at the floor. She felt guilty; Mel was her best friend. "Are you sure it's noticeable? We tried to hide it, but I guess sometimes it's no use."

"Yeah, even a blind person would have noticed! I hope things are at least mutual this time?" Mel said suspiciously. "I see she's not taking her eyes off you, either. I never saw her look at Chill or Nando like that. Be careful, okay? You know that old Romanian saying—*Pretty woman and old car, only trouble.* You've got some baggage, and you need to control your jealousy."

"I trust her. She's so pure, so innocent, so in love with me. I don't think she would ever cheat on me. She's different, believe me." Alexandria said. "Let's get back to the party, and we'll talk more about it tomorrow."

They re-entered the dance floor to Mel's DJ playing Rhianna's "We Found Love." Marilyn, who loved this song, was dancing near Zara, and singing along with a smile on her face.

"We found love in a hopeless place, we found love in a hopeless place…"

Alexandria came closer and said in Marilyn's ear, "I can't stop looking at you…you're driving me crazy. Do you want to leave?"

"Let me ask Zara if she wants to stay longer, and what the plans are," Marilyn said. Alexandria nodded.

"Are you gonna leave with Miss DJ tonight?" Alexandria shouted at Mel.

"If you could shout that any louder, maybe she'd be able to hear you too!" Mel laughed. "Yeah, we're leaving together, once the party is over."

Marilyn came back and suggested, "Let's stay another twenty minutes or so. I'll tell everyone that I'm leaving with Zara and Nando. Then you come and ask if Nando could give you a ride because you'll be getting up early."

"Sounds perfect, just let me finish my drink." Alexandria raised her glass.

The plan worked perfectly.

~

"Can't you wait until we get there?" said Nando to Marilyn and Alexandria, who were almost tearing each other's clothes off in the back seat. He was driving with the music blaring, the windows wide open, and the wind rushing in from all sides. "Where do I leave you two lovebirds?" Nando called to the back seat. Zara was sitting in the front seat next to him.

"Bring us to my place. It's closer. We have urgent business!" Marilyn said. Her blouse was unbuttoned, and Alexandria was passionately kissing every exposed part of her body.

"Okay, we're almost there, keep your pants on!" Nando said, then winked at Zara.

"Girls, take it easy, or you're going to make us horny, too!" Zara laughed. "Nando, if you find a shoe print on the car's ceiling tomorrow, you'll know it's from Marilyn's high heels."

Nobody noticed their banter.

Nando dropped them off at Marilyn's apartment, where she still lived with her ex-boyfriend, Felix.

"Are you sure he isn't home?" whispered

Alexandria as they walked up the stairs. They continued to kiss, taking the steps one by one. "It'll be really awkward if he's home and we get stuck with him in the hallway."

"He isn't here. I saw that his room was dark. But it doesn't matter…why should it be awkward? We're just roommates; things between us ended a long time ago," Marilyn said, unlocking the front door. "See, there's no one."

Alexandria felt better. She grabbed Marilyn around the waist and lifted her gently, never taking her lips off hers.

"Wait until we get into my room," Marilyn said laughing.

"I can't wait!" Alexandria tried to undo the few remaining buttons.

They entered the room while trying to shed their clothes, never taking their lips off of each other. The tension of abstaining all night had built up and now they were both eager to get to it. Alexandria took a quick glance around the room in the soft light and saw a silk scarf hanging on the closet door. She reached for it, feeling its smooth fabric between her fingers.

"Trust me," Alexandria said, tying the scarf around Marilyn's head, her fingers passing through the soft strands of Marilyn's hair. She made sure the knot was secure but gentle. Depriving Marilyn of one of her senses would heighten the others, amplifying her arousal even more. Alexandria stepped back slightly.

"You're so beautiful," she said, and slowly began to remove Marilyn's remaining clothes, item by item. With the coolness of the silk against her eyelids, Marilyn could hear the soft rustle of fabric as Alexandria moved. The sound of each breath she took was deep and heavy. Every brush of Alexandria's fingers against her skin felt magnified.

Marilyn was wearing delicate stockings. Their fabric whispered against her skin as Alexandria gently pulled them off, then used them to tie Marilyn's hands together with a soft but secure knot. Marilyn could feel the gentle pressure around her wrists, knowing that she was unable to free herself. Aroused, she felt a mix of excitement and trust in Alexandria's hands. She hadn't experimented much when it came to sex, but she'd never felt this level of arousal before. Alexandria gently led her over to the dressing table where she kept her makeup. It was an example of organized chaos, though each product had been carefully selected. Marilyn heard the sound of something hitting the floor; a few lipsticks and makeup brushes had tumbled off the edge of the table.

"It's fine, please don't stop!" Marilyn whispered. Alexandria lifted one of her legs and set it on the plush chair next to her makeup table. She began to kiss Marilyn's ear, her lips tracking a path down her neck, and still going down. Marilyn could feel Alexandria's hot breath, lips, and tongue on her breast. Marilyn's breathing became more ragged, and she moaned, "Don't stop."

But Alexandria was just getting started. Her kisses continued, following the curve of Marilyn's body with a deliberate pace that teased and tantalized. Marilyn's skin tingled where Alexandria's mouth touched it. Her breath caught in her throat as Alexandria's lips moved further down, leaving a path of kisses along her abdomen. She continued her descent, trailing her tongue along the edge of Marilyn's underwear, teasing her. Her underwear was soaked.

"Please, eat me out!" Marilyn moaned. "I can't wait any longer!" While Alexandria slowly pulled her panties down, Marilyn felt the cool air against her skin, which heightened her desire for Alexandria's touch. Marilyn's heartbeat quickened as her body arched in the air. And once Marilyn was completely free from her underwear, Alexandria fulfilled her wish, giving her the best orgasm she'd ever experienced.

From the first night they'd spent together, Marilyn had discovered and experienced new and exciting delights. Alexandria revealed new pleasures to her every time and ignited her sexual curiosity. Everything Alexandria did to stimulate Marilyn's many different receptors was exciting, arousing, pleasurable. She couldn't get enough and wanted more and more.

The two girls lay on the bed in an embrace, after all their passion and desire had been consumed.

"Is that natural talent, or do you just have that much experience?" Marilyn asked.

"Maybe both."

Marilyn furrowed her brow and pouted slightly.

"Are you jealous?" asked Alexandria.

"Well, yeah, I wish I was the only one who knew you like this."

"If I'd known you were coming into my life, believe me, I wouldn't have touched anyone else. I would've waited for you to show up," Alexandria said and kissed Marilyn. "How's roommate's life going? I know there's nothing between you anymore, especially now that you have me, but still…isn't it a little weird living with your ex? "

"Are *you* jealous now?" asked Marilyn, returning the same question. "There's nothing to worry about. He doesn't look at me that way. He didn't even look at me like that when we were together, so why would he now? We almost never had sex. No matter what I tried, he just had no desire."

"Yeah, sure…" Alexandria rolled her eyes. "Like I believe that."

"I'm not kidding. I tried everything I could think of to get him going. Nothing worked, and I don't know why. And the weird thing is that Zara has the same problem with her boyfriend. But don't tell anyone, please."

"It's the first time I've heard anything like that. I can't believe there's a man on earth who doesn't want to rip your clothes off and want to have sex with you twenty-four-seven!" Alexandria's eyes widened in disbelief.

"I know, but I swear, you have nothing to worry about from my roommate. Oh! There's something I've found out, but it's a huge secret. You can't tell anyone."

"What is it?"

"Zara and Nando have something going on."

"Wait, what? Nando and Zara?" Alexandria sat up. "Are you sure?" Alexandria's hands flew to cover her mouth.

"Well, that's what happens when your boyfriend has no interest in you. As far as I know, not much has happened yet, but they've definitely kissed. He gave her a ride home from work a few times. Zara told me because she wanted to know if I'd mind if they started something. I don't know what might've happened after they dropped us off tonight, but she'll give me the details tomorrow," Marilyn said and winked.

"Wow. Well, that's a surprise." Alexandria paused briefly and then continued. "Still, what are your plans? You know, how long are you thinking of living with Felix?"

"Is there some reason why you're asking?"

"Maybe…" Alexandria smiled slightly. "I know it's a little early to talk about this, but if things between us continue to be as great as they have been, do you think you might want to move in with me?"

"Of course I would." Marilyn laid down on Alexandria's shoulder. "I already spend so much time at your place…I'm sure Felix is starting to notice that I don't come home."

Chapter 14

THE OWNER OF the station, Mr. Lupan, called Alexandria into his office for a chat. She didn't know the reason for the meeting, but her stomach curled into a ball. Her first guess was that someone had opened their mouth about Marilyn. She secretly hoped there'd been praise for one of her shows and he just had to share it with her, but part of her was already considering her option, in case she was out of a job.

"Come in; sit down." the owner said, his eyes fixed on the computer screen, his face serious. Alexandria sat down in the chair across from him, her leg wobbling nervously. Sunlight from the big windows lit the spacious office.

"Sorry, I was focused on something here," he said, leaning back in his chair. "How are you? How are your shows—I see the results are good."

"Yeah, they are good. Last week we set a record for wishes received. I've got a few new ideas for themed shows I'd like to discuss."

"We will get to that. But I've asked you here because there is something more important right now." Alexandria felt her heart race. She was expecting the worst.

"We've entered into a contract with another studio that does similar things to us, but broadcasts over the internet. They have interesting virtual studios, diverse girls, but we have better technical capabilities. We want to use our equipment and know-how there to do live broadcasts together. Their models will talk to ours live, and the phone lines will also be merged, so viewers will be able to talk to twice as many girls and have even more choices. Their studio is in Germany. It's a new and experimental project, so I don't have a huge budget right now. I need someone who can do everything—lighting, filming, sound check, directing…everything. Will you be able to handle that?"

"Sure thing. For how many shows?" asked Alexandria. Her anxiety and nervousness had turned to pride and excitement.

"Two weeks. We will broadcast for two weeks, several shows per day. I'll arrange for your plane ticket; you'll leave in ten days," Mr. Lupan said and signaled to his assistant.

This was unexpected. Alexandria went through three different moods in five minutes: fear, excitement, and disappointment. Under different circumstances, she would have been thrilled to have been chosen for this project… but not right now, and not for two whole weeks. Right now, her life was perfect. Her relationship with Marilyn was going so well. They were so in love. Everything was like a fairy tale. Two weeks was a long time to put the fairy tale on pause.

Maybe I should say I can't do it, or that I have other plans?

"I'm glad I can count on you to take on this

responsibility," Said Mr. Lupan as he stood up and patted Alexandria's shoulder. "I can't think of anyone else who could have handled it. Let me show you the transmission equipment I've bought." The two of them headed down the hall, speaking in detail about the future project.

~

Alexandria had decided to tell Marilyn after dinner. She knew there was nothing else she could do, other than to go on the trip.

"I have something I need to tell you," Alexandria began.

"Me too. Who's first?"

"Um, why don't you start, I want to hear you first."

"You might think I'm crazy, and I don't even know if you'd want to do it, but I thought I'd ask you what you think. I really, really want to be with you. There are so many things I want to do together. I want to try everything with you, to travel, to discover new places, to share the little things and the big moments. I want to be with you forever." Marilyn said, pausing briefly.

Alexandria's worry grew during the silence, anticipating a "but" that might follow.

"I know we've been together for a relatively short time…a few months isn't enough, but I'm sure that I want to spend my life with you. I know you're the one I've been looking for and waiting for. This relationship is new to me, but I adore every moment we have, everything I have because of you. I would like us to get married one day. I want to make our relationship official and for the whole world to know that you are mine and no one can ever separate us."

"You can't believe how happy you've just made me," Alexandria said. "I would want all of that too, but you know it's impossible. I don't believe Romania will legalize gay marriage—ever. Our society is still so conservative and resistant to change. It feels like we're constantly fighting." Despite how perfect their own relationship was, Alexandria still felt like their community was not completely accepted by society, on that didn't want to see them as legal families or deserving of equal rights. She gave Marilyn's hand a reassuring squeeze, trying to think of the right thing to say.

"Maybe we can get married in a country where gay marriage is already legalized. I don't know if we have to have citizenship, but…it's been legal in the Netherlands since 2001…we can check there."

"Wait, babe…here's what I wanted to talk to you about. I know it's early in our relationship, but this is our opportunity. A friend of mine is studying theatre, and she told me that they're having a special event on the eleventh of December, where they're going to perform marriage ceremonies. The event is called "Marriages of Love." They will be performing wedding ceremonies and then giving out marriage certificates with the names and signatures of the newlyweds. It's not traditional or official; it's an alternative marriage ceremony that the professor and some students created. I still don't know what it is exactly! The people doing it are taking it seriously though, and that's the important thing. It's a symbolic wedding, but I think that might be the closest we can come to getting married."

Alexandria listened intently, not wanting to interrupt.

"I don't care that the laws of Romania or the politicians who are in power don't recognize our relationship—I don't need to get married in front of them! This will be *our* way, our wedding, our exchanging of vows. To me, that's as real as signing any documents in court, in front of everybody. We can invite a small circle of people—the ones who know about us—and celebrate our love with a reception after the ceremony. We will make it real, and it *will* be real! What do you think? Am I crazy?"

"Crazy? I can't even believe they do things like that! When can we do it?" said Alexandria, smiling from ear to ear.

"It's like a performance that they do every year on the same date. There's one in just a couple of weeks. The next one will be next year, at the University of Theatre and Art, in of their performance halls. "

Alexandria jumped in. "I don't want to wait a year; why don't we do it now?! There's one little detail I have to tell you. In fact, it's the thing I wanted to talk to you about." Alexandria got serious.

"Don't tell me you have another girlfriend?" Marilyn said, arching her eyebrows.

"Never! I'm going on a business trip."

"That's great! Where?" asked Marilyn.

"Germany…for two weeks. Two weeks is a long time, and I don't want to be away from you for that long, but I couldn't refuse."

"But you'll be back for the wedding, right?"

"Yeah, I'll be back a couple of days before the wedding. I was hoping there would be other dates because I don't think those few days will be enough time to get ready," Alexandria said.

"That's okay; I'll take care of everything! You just do your job, leave everything to me. It would be nice if we could do it together, but I'll handle it. You're getting a real powerhouse for a wife!" Marilyn laughed and kissed Alexandria. "It all happened so fast and I'm not prepared. I don't have an engagement ring and I didn't formally propose to you…wait!" Marilyn grabbed her purse and started digging into it.

"What are you looking for? What do you need?"

Marilyn finally found it. She pulled a pink plastic Hello Kitty ring out of her purse.

She took Alexandria's hand and said formally, "Will you do me the honor of becoming my wife? Will you marry me?"

"Of course. Yes! Yes! Yes!" Alexandria hugged Marilyn tightly and they kissed.

~

The two weeks of the business trip passed slowly for Alexandria. Every day she looked forward to the end of the show so that she could call Marilyn.

"I'm trying your dress on myself; we're almost the same size," said Marilyn over the speakerphone as she measured the wedding dresses. It was Marilyn's idea that she, Mel, and Zara would make the wedding dresses, to complement the unusual ceremony. Mel had a sewing machine and magazines filled with dress patterns, and even though the project was complicated, they had enjoyed every moment of it during the last ten days. "I hope the dress will suit you. If something goes wrong, we'll fix it on the spot when you come back. We'll still have two days after you arrive home. If not, you'll be naked—I prefer you that way," Marilyn laughed. "How's work going? Did you find a German girlfriend yet?"

"There might be this one girl…I'm kidding! Just kidding," Alexandria laughed.

"It's not funny."

"Sorry, love. Today was pretty busy. Hardly any wishes here are too provocative, and the team here is very professional. They laugh at me that we're too soft. Tonight, they're going to take me out to see the city and the sights."

"That's great, I wish we could explore the city together!"

"Me too. It's pretty chilly here though. I really can't wait to get home. I feel bad that you have to do everything by yourself—leave some things for me to do when I get back. What else do we need to do?"

"We need to get the wedding rings. I've had them put our initials and wedding dates on the inside. We need to buy food and drinks for the party afterward, make the decorations and the wedding bouquets, pick the wedding glasses. Zara and Mel are helping me a lot. Nando has agreed to take photos. Everyone I've sent invitations to has confirmed they're coming. Oh, and Mel will bring a plus one…you know who it is, right?"

"Miss DJ!" Alexandria laughed.

"Yep. Mel and Nando will come by your apartment in the morning. They'll help you with your makeup, your hair, your dress. I'll stay in my apartment with Zara the last night before the wedding and you guys will come to pick us up. We'll go to the ceremony together. And after that, when I officially become your wife, I won't live in my apartment ever again! I'm moving—I talked to Felix."

"And what did he say?"

"I told him I'm getting married, and he couldn't believe it. He wasn't too happy that I'm moving out so quickly, but there was nothing he could do. He said he would stay there for now until he finds something new, or maybe a new roommate."

"I like the plan so far. Do you want to do that shoe-and-money tradition that we were talking about?" asked Alexandria. The fun ritual had been a long-standing tradition for generations in some places in the Balkans. The groom's party goes to the bride's house to pick her up for the wedding, but finds the door locked. In order to agree to open the door, the bridesmaids demand a ransom from the groom, which is paid by stuffing the bride's shoe with money. All this is meant to promise good fortune, luck and love.

"Yes, we will keep all the traditions we want; everything will be according to our rules in our own style. I can't wait for our wedding day! It will be the happiest day of my life."

"I still can't believe it's happening..."

Alexandria couldn't stop thinking about the upcoming wedding. Everything had moved so fast. It seemed like only a day ago that Marilyn had been just a dream and then, in a matter of months her whole life had been turned upside down. Alexandria loved Marilyn more than anything, but she hadn't told her "I love you" yet. She'd said those words often in her previous relationships, but she'd deliberately avoided saying these words to Marilyn. She wanted it to be special, at the right time—or to hear them from Marilyn first. Despite her impatient nature and the way she always forced things, Alexandria had waited patiently for this important declaration. In just a few days, she would be marrying the woman of her dreams, but she hadn't even said the most important words yet. She'd wanted to say them when Marilyn proposed to her, but she thought it felt too predictable, just for the sake of the proposal. Over the phone wasn't right either.

December 11, 2011

The long-awaited day finally arrived. Mel and Miss DJ, who were Alexandria's bridesmaids, came to her place at 9 a.m. Nando brought a friend who had a luxury car and had agreed to chauffeur the two brides on their special day.

"Aren't we going to drink anything at this wedding?" said Nando, looking around at the bottles on the counter. "Whiskey! I'm pouring for everyone—especially the bride. Relax a little! I can see you're stressed…do you have any doubts? If so, I can cover for you at the altar."

"Very funny," Alexandria said. "You're right about the whiskey; let's all have some."

"Stop moving all over the place! I smudged your eyeliner!" Mel was applying the bridal makeup.

"Sorry, I won't move anymore," Alexandria said, trying to not move a muscle. "You know what I was thinking…we didn't have time for a bachelor party," Alexandria said.

"Didn't you have enough bachelor parties? How many parties have we been to? Enough parties—by tomorrow you'll be a married woman!" Mel said, then continued with the makeup. "Nando, you take the ribbons from my bag and blow up the balloons; you need to decorate the car. You have to help me with the flowers as well."

"Jeez, hang on—wait 'til I pour your whiskey," said Nando, searching the cabinet for glasses.

Soon enough, Alexandria's hair was done, makeup too. All that was left was the dress. She went to change and when she came back, her friends couldn't take their eyes off her.

The dress was so well made that no one could tell that three women without experience in dress design had made it all by themselves. The gown was delicate and airy, with a plunging, feminine neckline. The bodice gently hugged her body, and the thin straps added another delightful complement to Alexandria's beauty, drawing the eye upward and highlighting her smile. The tulle skirt made her look like a princess. It was exactly Alexandria's size. Mel placed a delicate pearl bracelet with a little blue flower on Alexandria's hand and carefully arranged the gold tiara with tiny beads on her head, to secure her veil. Alexandria looked at herself in the mirror and couldn't believe what she saw.

"Oh…this is…this is beyond my wildest dreams. I almost can't believe it. Is all this really happening?" Alexandria said.

By that time, Nando had finished decorating the car. Everybody got in and drove to Marilyn's apartment.

Zara had stayed over at Marilyn's the night before, and they had started their day early. Two other friends had also arrived, and the frantic preparations were in full swing. Felix had been woken up by the voices and commotion and come over to Marilyn's room to see what was going on.

"Wow, you girls look so beautiful—especially you, Marilyn," he said. He couldn't take his eyes off her.

"Sorry we woke you up," said Marilyn.

"Don't worry, I have to get up anyway. I wasn't planning to be here today…well, congratulations and best of luck to you, Marilyn. I hope you'll be happy." He walked over to her, kissed her forehead, then left.

"He didn't look too happy about the fact that you're getting married," Zara said, looking out the window.

"Oh, he's fine. What time is it?" Marilyn's voice was tinged with a mix of excitement and anxiety.

"Here they are!" Zara began to fuss around Marilyn. "The car just stopped out front, and we're not ready yet. Hurry up, girls!"

Marilyn glanced at the mirror, her heart pounding. Zara took her hand and assured her, "Everything will be perfect!"

There was a loud rapping on the door.

"Quick—where's the shoe?" said Zara as she put the final touches on Marilyn's hair.

"Catch!" Marilyn threw the shoe toward Zara.

The tapping on the door was repeated.

"Who is it?" Zara breathlessly called from inside.

"We've come for a bride!" the group shouted laughingly from outside.

"You'll have to pay a ransom!" Zara playfully returned. She opened the door slightly, keeping the chain on, and handed one wedding shoe to Alexandria. "Here, put the money in here and we'll decide if it's enough."

Nando handed a roll of bills to Alexandria, and she put a few inside, then handed the shoe to Zara.

"Oh, that's not enough—our bride is expensive," Zara said and handed the shoe back outside. They put in more bills and passed them back through the door.

"Okay, Marilyn is going to try on the shoe, and then we'll decide." After a moment Zara opened the door again and announced, "The shoe is still big on her…we need to put more bills in, and fill it up so her shoe doesn't fall off."

They kept putting in more bills until there was no more room. "This bride is very expensive, we give up…we're leaving," said the voices from outside.

"Don't give up," Zara replied. "We'll try the shoe again." After a short pause, she said, "That's it, she stood up in the shoe, and it's not too big anymore. You can come in."

Zara opened the door, and Alexandria saw Marilyn waiting for her. It was like seeing her for the first time. She was struck by her beauty and for a second found herself unable to move. She couldn't believe this was the beginning of their life together…their new family. She was filled with gratitude for this moment and knew she would remember this day forever.

"Incredible, isn't she?" Zara whispered to Alexandria.

"You're incredibly beautiful," Alexandria murmured quietly. She slowly walked over to Marilyn and hugged her.

"*You* are incredibly beautiful," Marilyn whispered, reaching out to take Alexandria's hand. "I love you."

"I love you," Alexandria replied. The words came at the perfect time. They kissed, and their friends, who had just witnessed this moving scene, applauded.

"You made me tear up—my mascara is going to

smudge now," Mel said as she gently dabbed at her moistened eyes with a tissue.

"Let's go, love. I can't wait," Marilyn said, and they all headed for the University of Theatre and Arts, where the Marriages of Love ceremonies were being held.

Chapter 15

March 2012
Bucharest, Romania

"WHEN ARE YOU thinking of telling your family you're a married woman?" Marilyn asked Alexandria one morning as they lay in their newlywed bed. The sun was shining its first rays all over the room. They always enjoyed mornings because they loved waking up next to each other. Marilyn held Alexandria's hand in hers and looked at their wedding rings.

"What about you? When are *you* going to tell *your* mom that you married a woman?" Alexandria asked. "You're right. It's time to tell our families about us. It's been more than three months since the wedding. I know everything has happened so fast between us, and our whole lives have been on fast forward the last few months, but at some point, we're going to have to come out of the closet to our families. I want the whole world to know about us—how much we love each other, how happy we are."

"I adore *this*, I adore *you*, and I adore *us*." Marilyn covered Alexandria's entire face in kisses. "Why don't you tell your parents before your family vacation next month? That way they'll know who I am, why I'm living in your apartment…and I won't have to hide."

Alexandria had planned a family trip to Italy. These annual vacations were a special time to bond and create cherished memories. She didn't have time to travel to Constanta often, so she was overdue to spend time with her family.

"I don't know how they're going to take it." Alexandria took a deep breath. "I don't want to spoil everyone's mood and then have the whole vacation be awkward."

"Do you think they won't accept it?"

"I know they will. Just…" Alexandria sat upright in bed. "A few years ago, I brought my first crush home to my parents' house. I didn't tell them we were kind of together, and my cousin saw us making out in a nightclub. She told my mother. My mom did not take it well! She was angry when she found out, and angry that I had lied to them that the girl was just a friend. Anyway, it was my cousin's wedding—that was why we went home to my parents' place to begin with—and I was supposed to film it. As a result of my being so wrapped up in this crush and all that craziness, I filmed almost nothing of the wedding, and that was my job. My family didn't talk to me for over a month! I lied to them and told them that I was drunk at the club, and it was a one-time thing, that there was nothing between us."

"Jeez. Did they believe you?"

"Well…I think so. I felt like I had to deny everything because I didn't want to disappoint them. Maybe if I had explained it to them at the time, they would have understood and accepted it, but I just…didn't. I couldn't find the right moment." Alexandria stayed quiet for a second. "I'm going to have this conversation with them, but I don't want to do it right before the vacation."

"How long are they going to stay here?" Marilyn

asked.

"It's just one night. Our flight back from Italy is late in the evening, so they'll have to stay overnight here, and leave for Constanta early in the morning. That's the only time you might have to go to Zara's place. You two could do something fun, couldn't you?"

"I'll talk to Zara. I'm sure she won't mind if I stay with her for the night," Marilyn said.

"Believe me, I want to tell them more than anything. They're probably the only people who don't know yet." Alexandria rubbed her temples with weary fingers. "You know I don't see them often. And the life I have here doesn't really intersect with theirs; all this time it's been easier to let them stay in the bubble they've been living in. Also, I didn't want them to know about all the nightmare relationships I had! A lot of times when I was getting into a new relationship, I told myself that this time I would introduce my girlfriend to them and confess everything…but every time something happened, and I realized that would be a terrible mistake. But it's different now. I've finally found the person who makes me proud to have her by my side and I want to share that with my family. I want them to know who I am and what my real life is like here. I'll find a good moment after the vacation to tell them everything." Alexandria hugged Marilyn.

"And didn't they ever ask you the usual questions…why you didn't bring a boyfriend home, or when you were going to get married, or start a family?"

"My answer was always that I was very busy with my work and building a career, and that was enough."

"I see…" Marilyn kissed Alexandria and got up from the bed. "I'm going to take a shower."

"And you?" Alexandria held out her hand. "Have you thought about when you're going to tell your mother?"

"You know my mother is different." Marilyn sat down on the corner of the bed and looked out the window. "She has a hard time accepting things. It was very hard for her to accept when I moved out. She didn't want to accept that I was an adult, and she didn't want to let me go to New York. I know this is going to be a big shock for her. For your family, there might be some logic to it because you've already had that situation in the past…but for my mom, it will be out of the blue. She might expect a lot of things from me—but not that I like women, much less that I'm already married to one! Besides, she wouldn't look at our wedding the way we do; she'll say that it's a joke, or at least not real. I'm sure in her eyes it's just a phase I'm going through that will wear off in time, or that I haven't found my way…or I'm confused, blah, blah, blah. I know her very well."

"That's so sad, honey. Do you think she believes you, that I'm just your roommate?"

"I'm sure. For her, no other option would make sense," Marilyn said.

"I'm going to miss you while I'm in Italy." Alexandria came closer and hugged Marilyn. "I promise, the next vacation you will officially come with me as my wife. By then everyone will know—even at work."

"I'll miss you too, but I want you to have fun. When you get back, we'll do our trip together."

"Wherever you want. We could travel all over the world together."

"Promise me!" Marilyn pressed a kiss to Alexandria's forehead. "By the way, more and more people in the studio know we're together. I haven't sensed any negativity or noticed anyone talking behind our backs. People are happy for us." Marilyn laughed contentedly. "And I'm sure a lot of people have noticed our wedding rings."

"You don't have to be very smart to notice, do you?"

"I told you, we need to stop being afraid people will find out because when they do, no one will mind. I love you so much." Marilyn kissed Alexandria again and ran into the bathroom.

~

Alexandria went on her family vacation but spent most of her time texting with Marilyn. Although she loved traveling, and her family, she couldn't fully enjoy herself because she was constantly thinking about her wife. Their relationship was so wonderful, and the marriage ceremony seemed to add to their happiness, with the certainty that it really would be forever. To Alexandria, the symbolic marriage certificate from the ceremony had more value than any actual legal document. They'd framed it and hung it right next to a boudoir portrait of Marilyn that Alexandria had taken.

The day had come; the family vacation was over, and they were returning home. Alexandria, who was tired, nervous, impatient, and bored from the flight, was looking forward to landing.

"I'll go to the bathroom before we land," Alexandria told her mother. "I don't want to waste time while we're getting out of the gate. By the time we get our bags, it'll be midnight."

"What is this rush? We're on time," her mom replied. Alexandria couldn't wait to get back to her happy family life with Marilyn. The moment the plane touched the ground, she turned on her phone to send a message.

We just landed. Can't wait to see you. Love you!

Marilyn immediately replied: *I can't wait to see you either, when you get off the plane go to the bathroom.*

Alexandria didn't understand what Marilyn meant. *Why would I go to the bathroom? What do you mean?*

I want to see you right now. I miss you so much. I love you.

Alexandria wanted more than anything to see Marilyn, but she'd already announced to her family that she didn't want to waste any time, and this change of plans made her feel pressured. She was stressed.

I don't think that's a good idea. Don't tell me you're at the airport. I'll see you tomorrow morning when my parents leave.

Marilyn immediately replied: *No one will suspect anything. It'll be a quickie. I wanted to surprise you.*

As much as Alexandria couldn't wait to see Marilyn, her surprise was having the opposite effect. *That's really not a good idea. Please go to Zara's and I'll text you when we get home. It's just one night. In the morning when they leave I'll call you to come over.*

Marilyn didn't reply. Alexandria lined up at baggage claim, looking around nervously to see if Marilyn was among the crowd. Once they collected all their suitcases, she called a cab, and everyone headed to her apartment. Alexandria kept glancing at her phone all the way home, but there were no new messages from Marilyn.

Alexandria sent another message: *What are you doing? I love you.*

She could see that the message had been sent, but it didn't seem to have been read.

They arrived at the apartment, and Alexandria waited impatiently for her parents to go to bed. She kept opening and closing her messaging app. The moment she was alone, she grabbed the phone and dialed Marilyn.

What she heard was, "The person you are trying to reach is not available." She tried again, but the answer was the same.

Alexandria went into a slight panic. She was finally home, just hours away from seeing her beloved, and something unexpected was happening. She sent her a message on Facebook, and on all their social media, but the messages remained unseen. All kinds of thoughts went through her head.

Her last hope was that Zara would respond. She didn't like to involve other people because that always led to more complications in her experience, but felt like she didn't have a choice. Zara replied almost immediately that she had just arrived at the studio because she had taken an extra shift at the last minute. Long story short: she didn't know where Marilyn was. Alexandria was desperate. She paced nervously around the entire room. If at first, she had tried to write off the delay, saying that it had a simple explanation, by this time she felt desperate and powerless. She sat down on the couch and looked at the blank wall where the marriage certificate and Marilyn's picture had been. She'd taken them down a week ago so her parents wouldn't see them and now the wall was empty, as if it held an omen. She covered her face with her hands and wept.

~

"Where are you? What's going on? Are you okay?" Alexandria called Marilyn's phone right after her parents left in the morning. The messages she had sent the night before had been read. At least she knew her phone was on, and that she was alive.

"I'm fine. Are you okay?" asked Marilyn with a slight chill in her voice.

"I'm fine. Tell me where you are. When are you coming home? My parents just left."

"Soon...I'll be home soon. See you in a bit." Marilyn hung up.

After about half an hour, Alexandria heard the key slowly unlocking the front door. She jumped off the couch and went to meet Marilyn.

"Where were you? Do you know what I went through all night?" Alexandria's whole body was shaking with worry. "I called you a million times. I texted you. I even texted Zara. Why was your phone off?"

"I'm sorry I made you feel that way." Marilyn hugged Alexandria tightly. "That wasn't my intention. I'm sorry. I'm here now."

"Sit down and tell me what happened. Where were you all night?" Alexandria continued to nervously ask questions. She took Marilyn's hand and looked into her eyes, trying to decipher the emotions behind her gaze.

"I was mad at you last night. I wanted to meet you at the airport. I bought you flowers." Marilyn's voice wavered as she struggled to keep her emotions. "I just wanted to see you for a minute. But the way you answered me…you never spoke to me like that before. Do you know how that felt—I'm standing there at the airport, waiting for you to land, and I get the message that you were already here?"

"I know... I'm sorry. I'm sorry I acted that way. I was nervous about the whole situation, and a lot of stuff had built up. I wanted to see you more than anything, but…not like that. I wanted to stick to our plan and be patient just a little longer." Alexandria hugged Marilyn tightly. "Do you want me to show you something?"

"I don't know. What do you want to show me?"

"I brought some presents for you. Every place I went, I thought of you, and I wanted to bring you back something special from each of those places, so that way you could be a part of this trip in some way, too."

Alexandria opened the suitcase and began taking out a variety of souvenirs, showing them to Marilyn one by one, and telling her about the places where she'd bought them.

"Do you like them?"

"Yes, they're all very beautiful," Marilyn said.

"Are you tired? You look a little…I don't know…worn out?"

"Yes, I'm tired. I'm sorry about last night; let's forget everything. Let's erase this moment and move on."

"I agree...are you going to tell me where you slept last night?" asked Alexandria

"I went to my mom's. I stayed at her place."

"Didn't she realize something was going on? You haven't stayed there in a long time."

"No," Marilyn answered shortly. "Listen, I'm going to take a shower and then let's just stay home—I

want to stay in bed and cuddle all day. I've missed it."
Marilyn headed to the bathroom.

Alexandria was relieved that Marilyn was home and her trip was over. She was looking forward to returning to their happy newlywed life. Still, she couldn't shake the worry of having their first real fight.

Is Marilyn really capable of turning off her phone and letting me worry all night? After one little disagreement? What would happen if we had a big argument? My love for her is so big that I could never do anything like that to her.

Alexandria couldn't stop thinking while listening to the sound of the running water of the shower.

"Okay, I feel better." Marilyn said coming out of the bathroom, a cloud of steam trailing after her. "I really needed that shower. Come on, tell me all about the trip."

"I will, but I want to apologize one more time for my reaction at the airport. I was wrong. I know you wanted to surprise me and I wanted to see you too, as soon as possible. I made a big deal out of it but maybe my family wouldn't have cared that I took a detour in the airport…or maybe I should have just introduced you to my parents. All these secrets make me nervous, and that's why I reacted that way. Please forgive me," said Alexandria.

"Everything is fine. Let's forget it. Can you help me to put some lotion on my back?" Marilyn said as her towel fell on the floor. It was clear to Alexandria that this request had another meaning.

"I also have a little surprise for you. Marilyn gestured toward the nightstand and the scented candle on top of it.

"A candle? Thank you, you know I love candles,"

Alexandria said as she massaged the lotion into Marilyn's damp skin with slow, deep movements.

"This candle is special. You'll see…light it and let it burn for a while."

"Then maybe I'll take a shower too," Alexandria said, smoothing the last traces of lotion into the delicate skin on Marilyn's shoulders.

When Alexandria came out of the bathroom wrapped in a plush bath towel, she heard music coming from the bedroom. Opening the door, she saw the curtains were drawn and the soft glow of candlelight lent a flickering warmth to the walls. Madonna's song "Secret" was playing.

Marilyn stood in the corner of the room behind a chair. She was wearing a red lace bra; its fine material revealed her nipples quite clearly. She also wore a red lace garter belt that was decorated with little white ribbons and attached to black silk stockings with a seam running all the way up her leg. A sheer lace thong with floral patterns clung tightly to her skin, highlighting her most intimate curves. High black heels completed her look, and it was hot. One look filled Alexandria with mind-blowing desire and passion. Marilyn reached out one finger to Alexandria, crooked it at her in a classic beckoning gesture, and motioned for her to come closer.

Alexandria moved in and tried to kiss her, but Marilyn placed her finger on her lips to stop her.

"Just sit," she whispered in her ear and walked her over to the chair.

Marilyn turned up the volume of the music, then turned her back to Alexandria and began to dance slowly. With graceful movements, she skillfully followed the rhythm of the music. She moved her hands along the curves of her body, sometimes slowly caressing what was underneath the transparent fabric. Marilyn spun her head around, allowing her hair to fall over Alexandria's face while she inhaled deeply of her scent. Marilyn was beautiful, and the performance was captivatingly sensual. As the tempo began to increase, Alexandria could hardly contain her desire; all she wanted to do was to touch her. Marilyn's hips continued to sway in mesmerizing circles, making her even more intoxicating to Alexandria. She struggled to hold back and to sit still, yearning for more. Marilyn stood turned her back to her and slowly undid the tiny buttons of the garter belt, releasing the silk stockings.

"Good?" Marilyn whispered in Alexandria's ear. She nodded in response.

Marilyn spun around, expertly placed her leg on the chair between Alexandria's legs, and gracefully slid one stocking off her foot. Then the other. As a new song began to play, Marilyn gently took both of Alexandria's hands and ran the stocking around them. She pulled sharply and tightened, and Alexandria felt her hands being tied behind the chair she was sitting on. Marilyn slowly opened the towel that still covered part of Alexandria's body. Her skin was flushed with arousal.

"Let's try your gift," Marilyn breathed deeply into Alexandria's ear, sending shivers through her entire body. Marilyn picked up the candle from the nightstand; it had already burned enough to form a layer of melted wax. She ran her fingers through Alexandria's hair and tugged with one hand, pulling her head back. Alexandria closed her eyes, feeling even more aroused at the way that Marilyn had taken control over her and this encounter of theirs. The way that she was making the rules, and completing dictating the terms had absolutely set Alexandria on fire. She literally felt waves of arousal run through her naked body, until the next moment, when she felt a sharp—yet delicious—pain on her chest. She moaned softly.

"Is it that good?" whispered Marilyn quietly. "Do you like it?"

Alexandria nodded her approval, and a new stream of hot wax spilled from the candle in Marilyn's hand, trickling down her belly. Alexandria let out another moan, smelling the pleasant scents of vanilla and sandalwood that wafted from the wax that had spread over her body. Marilyn continued to move the candle along Alexandria's body as the wax continued to melt. Marilyn trickled fresh, hot wax onto her lower abdomen as Alexandria's body shuddered and bristled. Marilyn finally released the hair she still held in her hand, and set the candle down on the nightstand. Slowly, she began to lightly buff the traces of wax on Alexandria's body, and they transformed into oil that glistened in the candlelight. Marilyn's fingers gently massaged the oil, which soaked into Alexandria's heated skin.

"Would you like to move this over to the bed?" Marilyn asked as she untied Alexandria's hands.

"You're driving me crazy!" Alexandria grabbed Marilyn and moved her expertly onto the bed. "God, you can arouse me with just one look—I can barely handle a performance like this!"

Alexandria and Marilyn spent the whole day making love. Time had stopped for them and the world outside the bedroom simply didn't exist. With every kiss, they became emotionally and spiritually stronger, and felt even more connected and in love.

Chapter 16

April 2012
Bucharest, Romania

THE HONEYMOON PHASE continued. A month had passed since the incident at the airport and they felt again like they were living a fairy tale. The rumor that the two women were together had reached the station executives, but—certainly to Alexandria's surprise—no negative response followed. On the contrary, their collaborative work continued to garner praise and boost ratings. There was no doubt that Alexandria and Marilyn were an excellent team, at work and at home. For Alexandria, the dark clouds of her anxieties and fears had lifted. She felt that nothing could stand in the way of her happiness.

A distinctive *ding* rang out one day, the sound of a new message arriving on Skype. Alexandria, making coffee and getting ready to go to the studio for her Friday Night show, wondered what the sound could be. It couldn't be Skype, since neither she nor Marilyn used it. Alexandria herself didn't even have the app downloaded.

Marilyn had gone to see her mother. Alexandria was expecting her home shortly before she had to leave for work so they could see each other for a few minutes.

After a moment, there was another *ding*, followed

by another, and then another. Ten messages in a row. Alexandria inhaled from her cup of strong espresso, willing herself to ignore the stream of messages.

Alexandria went into the other room to change. From there, she could still hear the sounds of messages continuing to come in. The thought crossed her mind to open Marilyn's laptop, but she rejected it.

That would mean I don't trust her.

Alexandria had previous experience with this, and each time it had blown up in her face. Whenever she'd doubted a previous girlfriend, she'd decided to check up on her, and had ended up opening a Pandora's box. She knew that Marilyn was different and that their relationship was trusting and completely full of love—nothing like the ones that had come before. She decided again to ignore it until she could ask Marilyn about it later.

Alexandria continued to ponder as she moved from room to room in an attempt to distract her thoughts and unconsciously move away from the laptop. Marilyn was already running late, and that added to Alexandria's sense of unease. She continued to wrestle with herself over opening Marilyn's laptop, desperate to confirm her belief that she was *not* hiding anything.

Alexandria slowly opened the laptop, but her inner self was struggling over the decision. She closed it again and looked at Marilyn's photo on the wall. She knew she wouldn't have any peace until she knew. She opened the laptop again and clicked on the Skype icon, which announced fifteen unread messages.

The app opened and Alexandria saw the sender's name. It was Felix. She was surprised, since she'd thought that Marilyn and Felix weren't in communication anymore, and hadn't been in touch since the morning of the wedding. Cold sweat broke out on her forehead.

Alexandria hated herself for what she was about to do, but she reasoned that she'd already opened the computer, and seen who texted. She had to finish what she'd started. She decided to read the messages.

Alexandria clicked her mouse once more and Pandora's box flew open.

She saw a series of messages, an entire conversation that went back and forth between Felix and Marilyn. The first thing she saw was the large number of emojis—mainly hearts and kisses. Alexandria was desperate to answer her questions, calm down, and trust again. She scrolled furiously and words and phrases jumped out at her, words that had no business being in a conversation between friends: *I want you too*, and *I can't stop thinking about that night*.

Her heartbeat loudly, and her hands shook.

Felix: *I want to do it again.*
Marilyn: *Me too.*
Felix: *When can we see each other again?*
Marilyn: *I don't know, I can't promise anything.*
Felix: *I want to cuddle with you like that morning* (heart emoji)
Marilyn: *I want it too, a lot...* (heart, kiss, heart emojis)

Alexandria thought to herself that the chat must be at least a year old. She checked the dates a few times; the date was a week ago. Then she verified the date on the computer in case a bug had somehow glitched the dates.

She scrolled further back.

Marilyn: *Please don't call or text me unless I do it first.*
Felix: *Don't worry I won't bother you.*
Marilyn: *Maybe next week I'll call you.*
Felix: *Can't wait to see you again. Last night was the best.*
Marilyn: *I liked it too. I missed you, bear* (heart, kiss, bear, kiss emoji)

There was no mistake about the date. It was the night Alexandria came home from her family vacation. Tears rolled down her cheeks as her heartbeat wildly, and a cold wave washed over her entire body. She thought that it couldn't possibly be true, so there must be a logical explanation…maybe a joke, either on her or on another friend. She told herself that Marilyn would explain it and they'd have a good laugh—after she apologized and dealt with Marilyn's anger over checking her messages, of course. But she felt that Marilyn's outrage would be nothing compared to the feeling of dread that gripped her at this moment. Alexandria waited on the couch for Marilyn while her tears flowed with no end in sight.

Alexandria finally heard the sound of the door opening and wiped her tears away. Despite what she'd read, she was hopeful, and she trusted Marilyn like no one else. No matter how crazy the explanation, Alexandria knew she would believe it, because she felt that a love as strong as theirs would not allow anyone else between them.

"Hey, love!" Marilyn's voice echoed through the hallway. "Sorry, I'm a little late! I had to help Mom with the bags of clothes she's going to donate—all that stuff from cleaning out her closet. I think I even scored some interesting pieces for myself!" She balanced several bags in her arms. "Are you about to leave for work yet? Is it time?"

"I have a little more time," Alexandria replied coldly. Marilyn quickly came over and kissed her. She noticed that her eyes were red.

"Is everything okay? Have you been crying? What, were you missing me already, love?" Marilyn joked as she gently touched Alexandria's cheek.

Alexandria was silent. She wanted to know the truth, but fear kept her from asking her wife about the messages. She felt in that moment that ignorance was bliss, and that she might prefer to stay in this dimension between happiness and grief. There would be no turning back and what she learned could define the rest of her life. What if everything collapsed; wasn't it better to not know than to spend her whole life in anguish?

Finally, she asked, "Is there something you need to tell me?" Cold sweat drenched her entire body. Every muscle had clenched, and she could feel herself breathing hard.

"Sweetheart, what's going on? Has something happened?" Marilyn put everything else aside, focusing solely on Alexandria. "Tell me, I'm getting worried!"

"Is there anything I need to know?"

"I don't think so, but if you tell me what it's about, I'll tell you. "

"While I was waiting for you to come back, you got a few messages on your laptop…on Skype."

"Hm, okay, thanks, I'll take a look; I very rarely use

Skype," said Marilyn.

"I need to ask you something about the messages."

"I need to open them and see what this is about. I told you, I hardly use Skype. Is that why you're upset? Because someone texted me?"

"I opened your messages," Alexandria said, expecting Marilyn to be angry that she had invaded her personal space and gone through her private communications.

Marilyn stayed silent. Alexandria had braced herself for the explosion that might follow and stood waiting for Marilyn's reaction. She continued to remain silent.

"I'm asking you again—is there anything I need to know?" Alexandria persisted.

Marilyn stood looking at her, without saying a word. Her silence continued until her blue eyes started to water. One tear rolled down her cheek and made room for the next. Marilyn continued to look Alexandria straight in the eye. Alexandria hadn't been ready for that reaction.

A thousand thoughts and assumptions flew through her mind: maybe Marilyn was sad because she'd caused this terrible misunderstanding or made a shitty joke that wasn't funny at all. All Alexandria knew for sure was that she would believe anything Marilyn told her, and would never ask about it again. She knew that Marilyn loved her, and that what they had was real. She knew that Marilyn couldn't have done anything with Felix or anyone else. Yet panic continued to overwhelm Alexandria as Marilyn remained speechless.

"Why aren't you saying anything? Why are you crying? Please tell me what's going on because I'm going crazy!" said Alexandria, keeping the distance between them.

"I'm sorry," Marilyn said, as more tears spilled from her eyes. She took a step toward Alexandria, but Alexandria stopped her.

"Don't come any closer. I want to hear everything. What are you sorry about? I want to know everything that happened. Tell me!" croaked Alexandria. Her belief that Marilyn was innocent began to grow weaker and weaker, as the truth began to reveal itself from behind the veil of Marilyn's lies.

"I'm sorry. I know whatever I say will be pointless," Marilyn cried. "I don't know why I did it…I just don't." She sat down on the couch and covered her face with her hands.

"What did you do? Did you sleep with him?"

"Yes."

That one word was a deadly blast to Alexandria. Destruction. Utter ruin. A sense of profound doom flooded through her. Physically, a sharp pain pierced her stomach, her chest tightened, and her breath left her. Wrenching pain, anger and disgust poured into Alexandria's heart. Tears gushed from her eyes. She'd gotten the answer she asked for, and the mystery was solved. There was no more guesswork, and yet Alexandria wasn't ready to believe it. There was no way it could be true.

"Do you want to be with him?" asked Alexandria through her tears. "How long has this been going on? Do you love him?" She barely paused between questions.

"No, no! I don't love him, and I don't want to be with him! You're the only person I want to be with. I love you more than anything and I wish I could turn back time!"

Alexandria continued to pepper her with one question after another. "Why did you sleep with him then?

When? How many times? I want you to tell me everything, all the details! I want to know *exactly* how he fucked you! Did you suck his dick? Did you come?" Alexandria had a masochistic desire to put salt into the gaping wound, to burn everything to the ground, to self-destruct. Somehow, she needed the most painful and detailed descriptions to fully believe what had happened.

"Please stop!" Marilyn cried.

"I won't stop! You need to tell me everything! How many times did you fuck him?" Alexandria shouted through her tears.

"Once! It only happened once…the night you came back from Italy. You were awful to me; you didn't have to push me away! I only wanted to see you, and you hurt me…you were so cold and there I was, waiting for you, bringing you flowers!"

"Oh, so it's my fault? I made you go out and fuck your ex? Are you kidding me with this—you're really blaming *me* for what *you* did?" said Alexandria. She couldn't believe it, and she kept pushing.

"Where did you spend the night? Did you really go to your mother's, or did you stay with him?"

"Why are you doing this? Why do you keep wanting to know more, after I already told you?" asked Marilyn. She sat on the edge of the couch, choking through her tears. "Yes, I stayed with him, okay! I lied to you! I didn't go to my mother's at all! I don't know why I did it…I needed to talk to someone. I was so upset, sad, and *angry*! Zara didn't pick up the phone and Felix was the next one I called, okay? I didn't plan to do anything with him. We were just supposed to meet for a drink."

"Oh, really? How do you get from a drink to the bed?"

"I don't know! I was angry with you and needed to relax. I drank a little more and somehow…it happened. I really don't know how, but trust me, it was the biggest mistake of my life. I would do anything to turn the time back. I don't know if you'll ever forgive me...I don't know if you'll ever trust me again…but you're the only person I want to be with."

"If all that's true, then what are these messages between you two after that? For *weeks* you've kept up communication with him! Those chats sure sound like you have something else going on with him…how you miss him, how you want to see him and cuddle again. I don't understand! So did you see each other after that, or are these plans for future encounters!?"

"We haven't seen each other again, and I didn't plan for anything more to happen. We just kept texting…I don't know; it was all just *words*. I know you don't believe me, and I know what I'm telling you doesn't make sense to you, but I really was planning on ending these stupid chats. That's why he texted me today—because I hadn't replied to him in a long time. You've seen the dates, right? I didn't text him." Marilyn pressed her hands to her face, trying to stifle her tears.

"I want to understand you… I want to know what made you do it. How could what happened at the airport— and come on, that was a minor thing! How could something as minimal as *that* provoke you to do the worst? How could you sleep with the man who didn't even want to touch you when you were together? Huh? While you were together you didn't have sex, but now that we're married, you're gonna cheat on me with him? Everything between us was so pure and beautiful…immaculate. I've never trusted anyone more than I trusted you. Now you broke it and we can't glue it back together! This can't be fixed, Marilyn…or forgotten, or erased. Why did you do this to me?" Alexandria slumped to the ground, drenched in tears.

Marilyn knelt beside her and hugged her tightly. They were both crying inconsolably. Marilyn tried to kiss Alexandria. She pulled away, but the salty taste of her tears stayed on Marilyn's lips.

"I'll do whatever you want. If you want me to, I'll pack my bags and move out. I know you hate me right now. Just tell me what you want me to do, and I'll do it," Marilyn said.

"Is it that easy for you?" Alexandria's voice cracked with shock and hurt. "You can just pack up your stuff and leave, like that?" She took a deep breath, struggling to keep whatever composure she had left. "We're married, for God's sake! This marriage is *real* to me! It's not a game. It's not theater. You're my wife!" Alexandria slammed her fist on the floor.

"Do you want me here?" Marilyn whispered, her voice trembling. "Will you be able to look at me again?"

"Before you came home and admitted it, I believed there was a logical explanation. I wish you'd tell me something to erase this pain. Tell me it's *not* true! Tell me anything, please! A few minutes ago, I was the happiest woman in the world, and now we're standing over the wreckage of the greatest love in the world!" Alexandria grabbed her coat and headed for the door.

"Where are you going? Please don't leave. Tell me where you're going!" Marilyn sobbed as the door slammed in her face.

Chapter 17

May 2012

ALEXANDRIA SECLUDED HERSELF at Mel's apartment, craving solitude for her grief. She needed time for the shock to fade, the stress to ease, and to gain a new perspective. Mel knocked on the door of the guest room where Alexandria was staying. She knocked once more, a little louder this time, before cautiously pushing the door open. Inside, she found Alexandria lying on the bed, her eyes fixed on the wall opposite her. The room was softly lit by the afternoon sun that filtered through the curtains, lending the room a tranquil, yet somewhat solemn, atmosphere.

"Do you want something to eat?" Mel said, walking in with slow steps, almost on tiptoe. "You haven't eaten anything in two days." Small rays of sunlight streamed through the cracks between the curtains. A half-empty bottle of whiskey lay beside Alexandria's bed.

"I'm not hungry. I can't put anything in my mouth." Alexandria's face was marked by fatigue and weariness.

"You need to eat something. I'll make you a sandwich," Mel said and sat on the bed. "They asked about you at work today—I told them you were sick and that's why you weren't coming in…except they know that even if you were on your deathbed, you'd never miss the Friday or Saturday night show." She noted the clothes scattered across the floor, and the untouched plate of food on the nightstand.

"Everyone there probably knows what happened," Alexandria mumbled as her eyes filled with tears. Her gaze remained fixed on a distant point on the wall.

"Nobody knows, but they're assuming that something really serious is going on with you. In all the years you've been working there, you've never missed one of your night shows."

"She sent me several messages," Alexandria said, shifting the subject.

"Who? Marilyn?"

"Yes."

"Well, you can stay here as long as you want. If you want, we can both live here together. We can be a couple." Mel tried to cheer Alexandria up. "I like that you're here. But…do you have any idea what you're going to do?" Mel took the liquor bottle out of her hands.

"I want to see her more than anything!" The tears streamed down her face and soaked into the pillow. "Why did this have to happen to me? This time, I really thought it would be different. I just have to accept that love isn't for me. It's mostly pain…long, deep, constant pain that you have to endure with infinite humility and patience. It's much more suffering than pleasure."

"Don't talk like that! If it makes you feel any better, I also believed this time would be different…and you *know* my opinions of relationships that start in the studio. I truly believed Marilyn was different. I still can't quite believe what you told me." Mel said while her fingers curled around the neck of the whiskey bottle. "I've never seen a couple love each other as much as you two do...did. She always looked at you the way I dream of a woman looking at me someday. So much love in her eyes, you know? She never took her eyes off you. I really can't believe it..."

"Ugh...I want to take some pill that will help me forget her. I want to erase everything from the moment I first met her. I can't accept the reality." Alexandria's voice sounded desperate, and her gaze was distant, lost in memories that haunted her every waking moment. "I can't get used to her not being here, you know? Every morning when I wake up, I have to relive the shock all over again because I'm still not used to being alone. In the brief moments that I manage to fall asleep, I forget…but every time I wake up, I'm reminded all over again that things are not the same…and never will be. I can't stop loving her, but you…I don't hate her. When you love someone so much that you fall apart in pain because they're gone, you don't have the strength to hate. You don't have the strength for anything. I can't stop thinking about the pain she caused me. I just want to forget everything!" Each syllable dripped with pain and longing. "How do I tell her to leave our home, then watch her pack her things? Watch her leave the place where we were happiest? I want to be with her. Everything was just beginning for us! This is so wrong. Why did she have to do this?"

"There are people who go through this and somehow find a way to forgive and move on. I couldn't…I mean, for me, cheating is the end. You have to think if that's an option for you…if you could let go of those feelings that you have inside of you right now, and do it sincerely. If you really wanted to be together, you just can't hold onto this pain…or it could end up even worse."

Mel punctuated this by walking through the room toward the window. She pulled open the curtains, and a strong beam of light flooded the entire room. Alexandria squinted her eyes, which were swollen and red.

"I want to see her more than anything." Alexandria's gaze drifted towards the window and the sun's warm light. "Maybe I'll go to the apartment tonight."

"Are you sure?" Mel's brow furrowed with concern. "Let's just think about it first." Her eyes met Alexandria's briefly, searching, silently pleading with her to consider the consequences…to understand the difference between longing and reality.

"I'm not…"

"Whatever you decide, you're always welcome here. I'm here for you if you need to talk, or just need someone to lean on."

~

Alexandria found herself sitting on the couch in her apartment. Everything was the same, just as she'd left it before slamming the door behind her. She looked at the wedding certificate on the wall and Marilyn's picture next to it, just like always. It still showed her stunning, nude body, covered only slightly by a flowing pink veil that cascaded gracefully over her breasts and fell downward. These two framed artifacts anchored to the past, bringing her back to warm memories of her previously happy marriage. Alexandria noticed that a huge piece of her heart seemed to be stuck in her throat.

"I'm happy you came home," said Marilyn, who was sitting across from her. Alexandria noted that she was still wearing her wedding ring.

"Well, yeah, I still live here," Alexandria replied coldly.

"I'll accept any decision you make. But above all, I want you to know that I love you and I want you to be happy. If being around me hurts you, I'll leave. But if you decide to forgive me, I will love you forever, and what happened will never happen again."

"I've been doing a lot of thinking," Alexandria began, her voice firm. "In fact, I can't do anything but think about what happened. And I still can't believe it. I have never felt so broken in my life." Alexandria's eyes filled with tears again, but she took a deep breath and managed to get herself under control.

"I know…" Marilyn whispered, her gaze directed downward.

"Worst of all—I can't stop loving you." Alexandria's voice was a mixture of anguish and longing. She paused, while her words hung heavy in the air, then continued. "As much as it hurts, I don't want to let you go. I don't know how we're going to continue, but I want us to find some way."

Marilyn burst into tears.

"I don't want you to cry. And I'm not saying I'm forgiving you—I don't know if I can do that right now. It's all too fresh. I just don't want to end it now; I don't want the relationship we had to be just a memory. I don't know how I'm going to keep living with this, but I want to try."

"I understand, and I won't pressure you. I'll give you the time and space you need."

Marilyn wanted Alexandria to know she was willing to make any sacrifice, even if it meant distancing herself physically.

"If you want, I could sleep on the couch?"

"I don't want you sleeping on the couch, but I don't know when I'll be able to touch you again. I still can't stop thinking about how *he* touched you, and that's very hard to swallow. It's something that can't be erased."

"I know; it's all my fault." Tears silently flowed down Marilyn's face, and her voice was barely above a whisper. "I know I hurt you, and I'm truly sorry." Marilyn removed a tissue from the box next to her and wiped at her tears. "Nothing I can say can change what I did, but I want you to know that I'm very hurt too. I've never loved someone as much as you before, and I've never had such a beautiful relationship with anyone. The thought that I hurt the most important person in my life is killing me. I hate myself for what I did! It's so hard for me to know that I'm the cause of all this pain and that I'm the one who broke our marriage. I've never cheated on anyone in my life. Just..." Marilyn glanced out the window briefly before returning her gaze to Alexandria. "The disappointment of your reaction at the airport...the tension of the secrets we're still hiding…not being able to tell my mom…the fact that I have to hide when your parents come to town…"

Alexandria got up from the couch and walked over to Marilyn.

"I told you this was the last time we'd ever run into this issue—I had planned to talk to my parents soon. But what's happened makes me wonder whether it's worth it. *This* is the reason I haven't come out of the closet to my family—because everything always ends up like this!

Because I don't want to sit in front of them and tell them that all my relationships with women have been disastrous and have brought me so much pain! What parent wants to know that their child is unhappy? And what am I—am I happy?!"

"I know. But you have the option to tell your family…and I know you would do it at some point. In my case, I don't know if I can *ever* do it. My mother won't take it well—the thought of telling her I'm attracted to a woman scares me…and at the same time, I don't know how long I can lead this double life—we live in the same city! Someone will see us someday…a friend of my mom's…or she'll see us herself. It's hard to live in this dual world where I want to scream to the whole world how much I love you, but I always have to look behind me to see if my mom is there! When I met Felix that last time…it was just so easy. I know that was far from what I wanted, but all this tension was nonexistent. Can you understand that? I sort of felt safe for a moment, being with him again."

"Then what are you and I even doing?" Alexandria's eyes searched Marilyn's face for answers. "Why did you make any move on me at all? Why did we start all this if you weren't ready to come out? If you'd always be afraid your mother would see you? Is this how you want to spend your life—being with someone who would make your *mother* happy? Is that why you cheated on me, to clear your conscience?" The tone of Alexandria's voice was pure fury.

"No! I'm trying to find an explanation for what happened to us." Marilyn sat down and stayed quiet for a moment. "Why don't we just go somewhere? Why not move out of this town, maybe even out of the country?

Why don't we start all over, from scratch, in a place where the memories, the people, everything around us will be different? A place where gay relationships are normal and accepted, and nobody is judging who you love?"

"Come on. You know my career is here. You know that I can't just walk away from everything I've accomplished here. Everything we have is here—I have a home; we both have jobs. You haven't finished your master's yet. We can't throw everything away and start from scratch! At least I can't."

The two of them sat in silence without looking at each other.

"There's one more thing: I want you to text him and tell him to never come near you again. In any way—text you, call you, whatever. I want you to delete his phone number, Skype, social media, wherever you have contact with him—I want it all deleted."

"Okay. I will."

~

In the weeks that followed, Alexandria tried to return to a normal routine. Working hard had helped her before, so she took extra shifts to make up for the days she'd taken off. At least it distracted her. She threw herself into different projects—the more complex, the better—that required more concentration and creativity, so she had no room to think about anything else. Often, she stayed late at the studio, if only to rearrange the lighting, try different perspectives, or swap sets.

Will you be home for dinner, love? Marilyn messaged her.

Yeah, I'm leaving the studio in a bit. Do you want me to pick something up on the way home?

No. I'm just checking when you're coming. Waiting for you. Love you.

A few minutes later, Alexandria entered the apartment and heard unfamiliar music from the doorway.

"What are you listening to? What is this music—Japanese?" called Alexandria as she hung her coat.

"Correct," Marilyn replied from the kitchen and went to greet her wife.

"Wow, what's going on here?" said Alexandria as she looked at Marilyn over from head to toe. She was wearing a kimono, and her hair was gathered into a bun that was secured with ornaments and hairpins. She'd done her makeup specially, to complement her look. She had layered on a light foundation and given her cheekbones a soft, pink blush. She'd defined her eyes with soft, neutral eyeshadows along with a thin line of black eyeliner. Bright red lipstick completed her look.

She bowed and said, somewhat hesitatingly, "*Konbanwa.* That means *good evening* in Japanese."

"I don't know what to say." There appeared to be a geisha in her home.

"I hope you're hungry. I made sushi today. I wanted to serve it to you properly," said Marilyn as she accompanied Alexandria to the middle of the room. She had set up a small, low table and arranged cushions around it for them to sit on. Chopsticks and small bowls of soy sauce were already waiting on the table.

"Make yourself comfortable. You can sit on your knees, but if you're not comfortable, you can sit cross-legged."

"I see you've taken care of all the details," Alexandria laughed as she sat down on the ground.

"Yeah, I wanted it to be perfect. Making sushi isn't as easy as I thought, but I really hope you like it," said Marilyn as she carried in the tray of food. She loved surprising her wife like this. Alexandria thought back to the beginning of their relationship, when they sometimes competed over who could surprise the other the most…it was often themed dinners, just for the two of them, that was extraordinarily elaborate.

"I'm sure I'll like it. I can't believe you did all this. It's great!"

"I was debating whether to wait for you like this, or surprise you with body sushi....you know, arranging the sushi on my naked body and serving it to you like that. I decided to stick with the traditional. Maybe later you'll get dessert that way," suggested Marilyn with a wink.

"I can't wait to try everything…it looks even better than that fancy restaurant downtown!" Alexandria said while dipping her first bite of sushi into the soy sauce.

"How was your day? Did you get good ratings on the day show?" asked Marilyn.

"Yeah, not too bad," Alexandria replied with her mouth full. "Mmm, this is great. Is this really your first time preparing sushi?" Alexandria dipped the next piece into the sauce just as the sound of a buzzing phone interrupted the dinner. Alexandria looked at her phone, but the screen was blank.

"Yeah, I was about to give up…the rice was falling apart, nothing was working, and I was almost panicking about what I was going to do with all these ingredients!" As Marilyn explained, her phone vibrated again.

"Something important?" Alexandria nodded at Marilyn's phone, which was face down on the table.

"I don't think so. I'm not expecting anything important. Maybe it's Zara."

"Aren't you going to look who it is?" asked Alexandria.

"Nah, I'll take a look after we finish dinner. I want us to enjoy our Japanese evening. Tell me, do you really like it?"

"Yeah, I like it…checking who texted you won't end our Japanese night, will it?" insisted Alexandria.

"No, it won't, but everything else can wait. Our time together is what's important now."

"Who's texting you?" demanded Alexandria. She'd put her food aside and focused her eyes on Marilyn's phone.

Marilyn picked it up, looked at it, and replied, "Like I told you, it's Zara. She wants to know what shifts I'm working next week. Do you want to see with your own eyes?" She turned the screen toward Alexandria and moved it closer to her. "I know trust takes years to build but is lost in a second, so I really have no expectations about being entitled to your trust…but do you really think I'd be doing something behind your back at the same as I'm preparing all this for you?"

"No, I don't. Sorry."

"I'll go change. We can watch a movie," Marilyn said and got up from the ground.

"Wait—sorry. Please come back, I don't want you to change." Alexandria grabbed Marilyn's arm and guided her back to the low table. She had entered the familiar, vicious cycle again: jealousy was taking over her life.

Chapter 18

July 2012
Bucharest, Romania

MARILYN HAD JUST finished her shift at the station when she arranged to meet Zara at a fun café that they both liked, and that was near the studio. They wanted to talk privately, so they found a quiet corner table. They settled in for a chat, surrounded by the aroma of freshly brewed coffee.

"How are things at home?" Zara leaned in slightly with a serious expression.

"Oh, we're trying to get back to normal life. It's not easy." Marilyn sipped her cappuccino thoughtfully. "I know it's going to be a slow process, but it is what it is, you know."

"Have you heard from Felix?"

"I texted him and told him very clearly not to text me anymore. That it was all a huge mistake and that I was going to try to fix my marriage. Alexandria wanted me to be very clear with him about that, and to delete all his contacts, so that's what I did."

"How did he react?"

"Normal, I guess. He said he understands. You know him, he won't do anything, just like he won't do anything with his life. He's always been like that—kind of passive, content with whatever you give him. I really don't know how I let all this happen…"

"Do you think Alexandria can forgive you?" asked Zara.

"I don't know. I know I lost all her trust…I feel like she doubts me even when I go to the bathroom. She probably doubts I'm with you right now! Who knows what kind of things she thinks."

"I mean, really, can you blame her? You wouldn't trust her if your positions were reversed, would you?"

"I know…I get it, but things are starting to get out of hand. Every time she hears a text come through, she jumps. I can see the tension in her—she can't calm down until she knows who texted me, what they want, where I'm going. One night we were out at a bar and some random guy sent me a rose, you know how sometimes they sell roses in bars? Well, it made Alexandria so furious I could barely recognize her! We fought all night. We fought at the bar, we kept fighting at home, and we went to bed angry and upset again. It's my fault for getting us here, I know. But I'm having a hard time too. I know I hurt her, but she needs to get over it. Let it go! She's making this whole situation even more intense."

"I don't know how long you can keep this up. I mean, I still can't believe what happened—I never would've thought you'd cheat," said Zara.

"Are *you* judging *me*—what about you and Nando? And where exactly do you want to take this affair when you have a serious boyfriend you've supposedly been committed to for years?"

"I'm not judging you. First, you know that no matter

what happens—even when you're wrong—I'll always be on your side. Second, I'm not saying it's right…I love my boyfriend and I wouldn't leave him for the world, but I miss the adrenaline and the thrill that Nando is giving me right now. We just have fun and enjoy the moment. So when the time comes, I'll end it, but I'm not going to destroy my relationship over it."

"What about Nando?" Marilyn furrowed her brow slightly and tapped her fingers on the edge of the table. "Does he know that he's just an affair? That he'll always be in second place for you...you know, good enough to entertain you when you're bored, but you're always going to go home to your boyfriend."

"I think he's okay with that for now. After the long relationship, he just came out of—and after *you* broke his heart too, I might add—our arrangement works for him."

Zara's phone buzzed. She picked it up from the table, typed a quick reply, and said, "By the way, he doesn't know about what happened between you and Alexandria. I haven't told him."

"Yeah, don't tell him. I don't want anyone to know, especially at work. I know some people get suspicious after Alexandria didn't go to work for a few days, but I don't think anyone realizes what's behind that," Marilyn said as Zara's eyes flicked between her and the phone as it buzzed again.

Marilyn took a sip of her cappuccino, feeling the conversation slipping away.

"Any plans for tonight?" Zara asked, holding her phone in her hand.

"Nothing special, why?"

"Friends of mine are in town. They just texted me.

Do you want to join us for a drink? I think you met some of them when we went camping."

"That could be fun." Marilyn smiled. She had fond memories of that trip, which had been so filled with laughter and seaside adventures. "Let me text Alex that I'll be a little late."

Zara's smile widened. "Great! I'll text them and let them know we're in. It'll be just like old times!"

Alexandria sat in the control room, staring at the monitors. This particular show was slow and monotonous. Work usually distracted her, but when she was alone with her thoughts everything turned back to anger and pain. The buzzing of her phone brought her out of her hypnosis.

Alexandria opened Marilyn's text.

I might be a little late tonight, don't worry

This short message instantly activated a volcanic eruption of fear and jealousy. Having once lost trust, she found herself always on the edge of paranoia. She didn't answer immediately, trying to control herself, and not say or do anything that she might regret later. She put her phone down, walked into the studio, gave her team their assignments, and walked out. She returned to the control room, sat back down in her chair, and stared at her phone where it lay on her desk. After a few seconds, she picked it up again, unable to contain herself any longer.

Who are you with?

Friends.

Which friends? Alexandria could feel that her jealousy was a live grenade and knew she had to defuse it before it detonated over both of them.

Mutual friends of mine, and Zara's

Alexandria's imagination ran wild; she knew

Marilyn had met Felix through friends of Zara's.

Will HE be there?

Don't start again. No one who would bother you will be there.

I don't like this. Are you sure you're not hiding something?

Marilyn didn't reply. This provoked Alexandria, and she sent another message: *Are you going to turn your phone off again?*

No response. Alexandria left the control room to call Marilyn, who declined her call. After a few minutes, Alexandria finally got her reply: *When you come home, you won't find me there. I can't live like this anymore.*

Alexandria's heart raced. She felt awful about what she'd written. She went straight to the control room and told the video mixer director that something urgent had come up and that she had to leave. It was the middle of the show, and she knew what she was doing was unprofessional and irresponsible, but at that moment nothing else mattered.

She flew out of the studio, jumped in her car and peeled out of the parking lot, tires screeching. The short distance to her apartment seemed like dozens of miles. She hoped she wasn't too late. She prayed that Marilyn was bluffing, that she wouldn't have time to leave so quickly, that she would accept her apology, and that somehow, things would work out. She pulled up in front of the apartment building and leaped out of the car, leaving the door open and the engine running. She fumbled with the keys to the front door because her hand was shaking so badly. She finally burst into the apartment, calling out for Marilyn. Nobody responded. She looked around;

everything seemed the same. Marilyn's clothes, toiletries, and personal items were still there.

Alexandria considered her options. She knew that Marilyn wouldn't want to talk to her when they were both so angry. She didn't want to push her and reasoned that if she tried to call her again, she'd only turn her phone off. She thought her best course of action was to give her some time to calm down, to realize that she was being impulsive. She felt pretty sure that she'd come around, and either call Alexandria or simply come home.

Several days passed and still no word from Marilyn.

She had canceled all her shifts at work, telling Valentina that she had to study for final exams. She hadn't put herself on the schedule for the following week, nor had she said when she'd be back.

The days went by and still no word from her. Alexandria was hardly eating and had clearly lost weight. Her gaze was perpetually blank as if a ghost were walking the halls in her body. Marilyn's belongings were still in the apartment, and Alexandria took hope from the fact that she wouldn't leave these things behind. Marilyn would have to come and get them if her decision was final. Every time Alexandria came home, she rushed through the door to make sure they were still there. These left-behind items were Alexandria's last hope.

~

Alexandria was sitting on the couch in the television's break room when she saw Zara crossing the hallway. Alexandria jumped up and ran after her.

"Zara! Wait a second!" Alexandria called as she ran after her. Zara stopped and turned around. "Please—hang on. Do you have a few minutes?"

"Just a couple of minutes." said Zara.

"Okay, thanks, let's go outside. We can talk in my car; it's parked around the corner. I need to talk to you alone."

The two walked out of the building and got into Alexandria's car.

"I'm sure Marilyn has told you what's been going on with us, right?"

"Look, I don't want to get involved in this. I feel for you and I'm sad about all of this, but Marilyn is my best friend and I need to be there for her when she needs me. Please don't put me in a tough spot here. The situation is even more complicated by the fact that we all work together. You didn't ask me for advice but you want my two cents? I think you have to move on with your life. What happened was a terrible mistake, and all this is sad, but she's made up her mind."

"Is she with him?" asked Alexandria, her eyes moistening. "Do you know where she is now? At least tell me that."

After a few seconds, Zara said, "She isn't with him. She hasn't heard from him or seen him. She doesn't want to be with him."

"Where is she then? All her things are still at home." The weight of the question hung in the tiny space in the car. The tension stretched out farther with each second that passed. Zara looked out the window for a few seconds, then turned back to Alexandria.

"She's at my place." Zara rubbed her forehead,

regretting her words. "Please don't try to come after her—it's not easy for her either, you know. It's best to just move on. And don't worry about her things. When she feels ready, she'll come get them. If they bother you, just bring them to work. I'll pick them up."

"Zara, I can't just move on!" Alexandria's voice wavered and nearly broke. "We are married. I know our wedding means as much to all of you who were there with us, as it does to us. She is my wife…I can't and don't want things to end here. I know she feels the same. I made the mistake of being blinded by jealousy, but you have to agree that it didn't come out of nowhere. I know I should have trusted her more! I know I overreacted, and I couldn't control my jealousy. I made her leave—I know that—but I want to fix it."

Alexandria's eyes filled with tears, and she wiped at her cheeks. Her breath came in shaky gasps as she tried to keep her composure. "All I'm asking is that you talk to her and ask her to meet with me. I really can't move on with things the way they are. Look at me—I can't eat, I haven't slept. If I do fall asleep, nightmares wake me up anyway, so why bother? I beg you— just try to get her to see me. Nothing more, I promise."

"No, I can't promise you anything. I honestly don't know if she'd be willing to talk to you." Zara squeezed Alexandria's hand, making physical contact for the first time. "I can see that you don't look well. You should try to start eating and taking care of yourself. I'll talk to her, but I can't really promise anything."

"That's all I can ask for, thank you," Alexandria said and hugged her.

After the conversation with Zara, Alexandria was

hopeful that Marilyn might change her mind. Yet, every day that passed widened the gap between them. While Marilyn became more convinced that the decision to separate might have been the right one, Alexandria woke in the morning and went to bed at night with only one thought: would Zara be able to get Marilyn to see her?

Chapter 19

August 2012

ARRIVING EARLY AT the small place downtown where they serve one hundred kinds of beer, the same place Marilyn had invited her to over a year and a half ago—Alexandria couldn't contain her nerves. Time passed slowly as she anxiously awaited Marilyn's arrival. She looked again at her phone and reviewed the message that had arrived a few nights ago.

Hello. If you're free tonight, I can see you at the place that serves 100 kinds of beer, downtown, at 7 pm.

Since Marilyn had left, Alexandria always kept her phone close to her pillow, even waking many times in the night, just to check if Marilyn had texted her. The long-awaited message finally came.

Hi. I'll be there at 7 o'clock. Thank you.

Alexandria checked her watch again. Still a few minutes before seven o'clock. Her heart was beating madly again, but this time it was filled with hope. She knew there wouldn't be another opportunity. She was sure that if she got a second chance, she wouldn't let anything come between them again. She was willing to do whatever it took: eradicate her jealousy, forget Marilyn's infidelity…change. She didn't want to even consider the possibility of going home again without Marilyn. It would destroy her.

The waitress arrived. "Are you ready to order?"

"Just a glass of water for now, thank you." It was the first time Alexandria had been there. She imagined what she would have felt if she'd come to the original date, a year ago.

Chaos theory." Alexandria thought, *a small change at the beginning can lead to big changes at the end.* She wondered where they might be if she hadn't turned down that first date. She was seated at a table that faced the entrance. She was fidgeting with a small box, moving it from one hand to the other without realizing what she was doing. She had bought a gold necklace, a thin chain with a delicate heart dangling from it. She was going to give it to Marilyn, no matter what her answer was, as a symbol of their love.

Alexandria stared at the door, adrenaline pumping through her whole body. Finally, Marilyn walked in. She looked around and quickly located Alexandria. She approached with a slow step, and without looking Alexandria in the eye. Alexandria wanted more than anything to hug her, but she didn't dare. Even the smallest mistake could reduce her chance of success. Marilyn took a seat across Alexandria and got right to the point.

"I'm here because Zara convinced me to come."

"I know, and I'm grateful...to you, and to her," Alexandria said, glancing at Marilyn's hand. She was still wearing her wedding ring.

"You've lost weight. You aren't eating?" asked Marilyn in an even tone.

"I don't have much of an appetite these days."

The waitress approached and asked if they were ready to order.

"Give us two minutes, please." Marilyn smiled at the waitress with the gentle smile that Alexandria adored. Marilyn turned back to Alexandria and the smile was gone. "Well, at least you'll have something to eat now. What are you having? You'll drink beer, won't you?" Marilyn began to thumb through the menu.

"Yes, I'll have whatever you're having."

"So, I'm listening. What do you want to talk about?" she said, still with her attention on the menu.

"About what happened in the last two months," Alexandria said. "About how we both made mistakes, but I'd like to fix them as adults. I don't want to talk about the night at the airport again—we've discussed it enough and there's nothing new to say. The mistake I made later was that I couldn't forgive you, even though I decided to stay together. I was jealous and hurt and couldn't see how hard you were trying. But the pain I felt when I came home to the empty apartment and you were gone…that completely destroyed me. What I went through after that completely changed me—changed my whole inner self. I wish you could come home. You have my forgiveness for everything." Alexandria paused in an attempt to lend more weight to her words. "I forgive you. If you love me too, if you still want to be with me, let's fix what we did."

"It's not as easy as you think," Marilyn said and made a sign to the waitress that they were ready. She smiled again as she interacted with their server.

"I love you without a doubt," Marilyn continued, returning to the conversation. "But this mess we've made is awful. We got other people involved…Zara, my mother.

They're asking questions at work. We can't keep playing games." Marilyn was silent for a moment then continued. "I'm not coming back to work."

"Why? Because of me?"

"Because of *us*. Because I don't want you to lose your job because of what's going on between us. Because I want to change my life. I knew from the beginning that this job was temporary for me. But you, you're a director, you have the career you studied for and dreamed of your whole life. Do you think my dream was to be an erotic model? And I'm tired of all the secrets, and the fear that someone will find out. Everything has to be kept secret…what I do, who I live with…things I'll never be able to admit to my family."

"I understand. Are you planning to look for a job as a dentist when you graduate?"

"I'm not sure yet. You know that's never been my passion. I might have something else in mind…"

Alexandria waited while the waitress served the food and drinks, then she continued. "You wanted us to leave, remember? To pick up and move somewhere else? Let's do it. I know I turned you down last time, but things are different now. Let's leave town—let's leave the whole country. We could travel, go to different places. We have savings; we can afford it. And we always wanted to travel the world."

"You're just saying that because you want to convince me to come back, but you don't want to move."

"That's not true. I was planning on making the trip we talked about—I was thinking of booking a trip to Amsterdam. I found a couple of good prices. You've been talking about it for a long time; we might start with that, then travel to other places. We can see if we could live somewhere else. And the Netherlands is a liberal and LGBTQIA-friendly country—we wouldn't need to hide from anyone there. And we'd never run into your mother."

" Alex…it's not that simple," Marilyn said.

"I kind of think it is, though. I'll give my notice at work right away. I'm tired. All those years there, all the sleepless nights, late night shows, the stress, the pressure of constantly coming up with new ideas and new shows. Yes, it was interesting at first, but I need a change, a fresh start."

"Don't put in your notice! That's a huge step; you have to think about it."

"We can think seriously and plan everything step by step," Alexandria said and casually put her hand on the table. "I'm going to check what the rental prices are in Amsterdam, see what we could manage there…you know, if it's a good place to live or just our first stop."

She touched Marilyn's hand lightly.

"All of that sounds nice and exciting, but the reality is different." Marilyn felt herself somewhat swayed by Alexandria's fairytale plan.

"I understand, no rush. Let's just think about it, what you say?"

Marilyn stayed silent. Alexandria didn't want the conversation to go off in the wrong direction, so she began digging into her coat pocket.

"I got you something. It's a symbol of what I first told you tonight—a symbol of my forgiveness and an apology for what I did wrong." Alexandria pulled out the small box and set it on the table.

"You didn't have to buy me anything because I

came here tonight. I don't need anything," Marilyn said.

"I know, but please—take it."

Marilyn took the box and opened it. "It's very beautiful."

Alexandria took the necklace from her hand, got up from her chair, and went to place it on Marilyn's neck for her.

"Please eat what we ordered," Marilyn said while her whole palm over the small gold heart around her neck.

"Can I ask you something? Did you pick this restaurant on purpose?" asked Alexandria asked as she took a bite from her plate.

"Don't think this is easy for me." Marilyn needed to pause before she continued, feeling the tears welling up again. "Leaving our home was one of the hardest decisions I've ever had to make, and the days without you were awful. Do you know how hard it was for me not to call you or text you? And the whole time I was waiting for *your* call."

Alexandria felt that the tension in her throat might actually be releasing just a little. Marilyn's words no longer seemed so cold and final.

"So to answer your question, this place takes me back to a year ago, when everything between us was just butterflies in my stomach. The pain, mixed with nostalgia, and some weird masochistic desire made me want to turn back time and meet you here."

Alexandria took Marilyn's hand in hers.

"Listen, I'm not asking you to promise me anything, and I'm not deluding myself into thinking that things are fixed. I know everything is actually more complicated than ever. But can you at least think about it?"

she asked softly, her voice trembling slightly.

"It's very hard for me to make any decisions right now." Marilyn fell silent. Alexandria didn't want to press her, so she didn't say anything. She asked the waitress to bring the bill.

"We can split the check," said Marilyn.

"No, I invited you. Dinner is on me."

They exited the restaurant into the warm evening air of August. There was a light breeze, and the streetlights cast a soft glow on the sidewalk, illuminating the path. They walked side by side in silence, thinking about everything they had said to each other in the last hour. Alexandria broke the stillness.

"If you don't have anything else going on tonight, would you like to come home with me?" Alexandria's eyes were filled with a mix of hope and uncertainty. "Without any strings attached, just for a drink. Your stuff is still there; everything is just how you left it. What do you say?"

"I don't know if that's a good idea." Marilyn felt torn between her lingering feelings and the knowledge that it might not be wise. But the warmth in Alexandria's words and the sincerity in her voice made it hard to say no.

"I…I don't know…"

Alexandria gently squeezed her hand, giving her a small, encouraging smile. Marilyn stayed silent a few seconds longer, then took a deep breath and got in Alexandria's car.

Chapter 20

August 2012

"HERE, LET ME take your jacket." Alexandria hung up the light summer blazer that Marilyn had been holding in her hand.

"Thank you." Walking into the familiar apartment, Marilyn was engulfed by its scent and the sight of her belongings, which had remained untouched since the day she left. A wave of memories washed over her. She let herself look around. Her own portrait, the certificate from their symbolic wedding, her clothes on the hanger, the scent of the vanilla candles…it all seemed like a time capsule, preserving the memory of their love. Marilyn's mind raced with memories of lazy mornings, intimate dinners, and passionate nights in each other's arms. Her feelings for Alexandria hadn't changed since the first day they were together, and the time they were apart made her want her even more.

"Wine?" Alexandria asked as she opened the fridge.

No answer came.

"Are you going to drink wine, or something else?" she asked as she turned around. Marilyn stood behind her and met her eyes. Alexandria felt the refrigerator door close behind her on its own, but she didn't dare take her eyes off of Marilyn. There was just one step between them. Marilyn felt as though she wanted to move, but something was stopping her. At last, she took the necessary step, and pressed her starving lips into Alexandria's. Insatiably. Longingly.

Alexandria responded eagerly, her arms wrapping around Marilyn, pulling her closer. The kiss was at once familiar and new, unburdened by their absence from each other. Marilyn's hands moved through Alexandria's hair, her fingers raking through the soft waves, then lifting them out of her way and slightly shifting her head so that she could kiss more of her. They broke apart for a second, panting and flushed, eyes fixed on each other, then dove back in for more.

"I missed you," Alexandria managed to whisper as she pulled her mouth away from Marilyn's.

"I missed you too." Marilyn took a step back, pulling Alexandria with her. The two moved as one. Alexandria opened her eyes for a moment and located the couch directly behind them. She moved Marilyn gently toward it, until she could feel the edge of the sofa pressing against the back of her legs. Alexandria gently supported her back and lowered her onto it. Alexandria's fingertips gently traced Marilyn's belly then slid upwards, as she peppered Marilyn's neck with kisses.

"May I?" Alexandria asked while indicating her blouse. Marilyn didn't answer but rose slightly and, with a flourish, rid herself of the unnecessary garment. She then grabbed hold of Alexandria's shirt and with an unexpected motion, ripped the buttons off, tearing it wide open. The tiny buttons scattered across the floor with a metallic sound. Alexandria pulled off the rest and grabbed Marilyn by the waist. Her knee moved between Marilyn's thighs, which made Marilyn writhe in ecstasy. Alexandria couldn't get enough of the scent, the sounds, the heat, the small beads of sweat on Marilyn's body. Both felt on the edge already, wanting to release the charge that had built up. Marilyn took Alexandria's hand and placed it on her abdomen, then slid it slowly inside her pants, whispering, "Fuck me…"

~

"I'm happy you came," Alexandria said, holding Marilyn in her arms as they lay on the couch. Marilyn smiled mischievously at her. "Haha, no I mean that you came *home*."

"I didn't plan for any of this to happen."

"Me neither, but I really believe we can start over. Everything that I told you in the restaurant…I mean it, we can start over. Me and you…" Alexandria felt only a pleasant breeze now, after the terrible storm she had been through.

"I already told you—it's not that easy." Marilyn stood up and looked at the clothes scattered all over the room.

"Why not?"

"There's something we need to discuss that I didn't mention earlier." Marilyn passed Alexandria's torn shirt to her and started collecting her clothes from the floor.

Alexandria was worried. Something was happening and it didn't sound like it was going to be pleasant. She dressed quickly and sat next to Marilyn.

"I went on a few job interviews a couple of weeks

ago. I got a call today, and got offered a position."

"That's good news, isn't it? What kind of job is it?" asked Alexandria. She relaxed slightly. This sounded manageable.

"Yes, it is good news. They made me an offer I can't refuse."

"Yeah? So tell me." Alexandria was getting a little impatient.

"AirLux Airline—that's one of the largest and most prestigious airlines in the world—wants to hire me on a two-year contract. As a flight attendant."

Alexandria fell silent. She felt like she couldn't take any more.

"What does that mean?"

"Well, I start in less than two months. The first eight weeks will be intense training. After that, I'll have to pass a few exams and if I do, I get certified and can start flying. They provide everything—accommodation, food and utility, medical insurance, free tickets for friends and family. Everything! And you get paid for the training too."

"Accommodation? Why wouldn't you live at home during this training? Where is it?" asked Alexandria anxiously.

"Qatar."

"Are you kidding? You never said you wanted to be a flight attendant! I don't understand?"

"Well, I never wanted to be an erotic model either. I guess that's how things happen in my life. Unplanned."

"Yeah, but...we talked about options to try again, you and me… starting somewhere fresh, both of us. And now out of the blue, you're going to Qatar for two years. What am I supposed to do for those two years?"

"First of all, you'll remember that I didn't promise you anything. Second, the initial contract is for two years, then it can be renewed. We are not talking only for two years…" Marilyn squeezed Alexandria's hand. "It's not an option that's given to everyone. You know how many girls dream about this job and they never get chosen? The recruiting team goes all over the world and interviews thousands of women; they choose only the best. Interview dates are once a year. When I signed up, I didn't even expect to get an interview. You know that things between us were not going well at the time. I didn't think that we'd ever be together again, much less that they would pick me. It was a shock, and a difficult decision for me too. I love you and I know you want to change. I can see that things between us could get better and possibly go in the right direction, but this came out of the blue for me as well. It's a great opportunity, Alexandria."

"What are the options?" asked Alexandria. "Can we go there together?"

"It's not that simple. In the first two years, flight attendant trainees live together on campus. Even if you rented a place nearby, we wouldn't be able to see each other very often. I know you…you wouldn't like that. Even though you want to work on your jealousy, how are you going to feel? Going to a foreign country where you won't know anyone, you won't have your job, you'll have to start from scratch. You'll be alone most of the time, and no one even knows when we'll be able to spend time together. All of this just to follow me? It's going to kill you. To leave everything here for something like that? On top of that, we're talking about Qatar! Homosexuality is illegal there. They can put you in jail for kissing me. Maybe even worse…"

"No one needs to know we're a couple! We can say we're cousins, best friends. We'll stay underground for two years," Alexandria insisted.

"Two years is a very long time—and I'm not sure it will be just two years. I told you, this is an opportunity many people dream of. It's a chance to travel the world while earning money and having no living expenses."

"I can give you all that here! You know money is no problem. We can travel the world while we're on vacation. You're graduating now, you have a prestigious degree, and we could even set you up in your own dental office with my savings. Or if you don't want to do that, we can find you another job." Alexandria paused and searched for more convincing words. "I know this job seems like the best thing that could happen to you right now, but there are so many other options. Two years is a long time. If we had to be separated for that long, I don't know how I could live here without you."

"I couldn't make you wait two years for me. That's an awfully long time to put your life on hold. Just like I can't promise you that I'd put mine on hold."

"You sound like you've already made a decision."

"I told you, it's complex. Your jealousy is killing me. I don't think I'm ready to close myself up in a cage again. I fought my mom and her need to control me all my life, and instead of enjoying my freedom once I had it, I jumped into the next relationship, then the next."

"But you were the one who took the first step in our relationship!"

"I know. I was in love with you." Marilyn paused. "I still love you, but I need to be alone now. This job is an opportunity, for the first time in my life, to be completely on my own. I need to figure out who I am outside of our relationship, far from my mom, family, friends. And this is something that I chose, not the profession or the life that my mom picked for me."

Alexandria was on the floor again. Marilyn was supposed to be her reward for all those failed relationships. She couldn't believe she was losing Marilyn again.

"You can't just dump me, after everything we've been through! You want to forget about everything and be free? We're married! You are my wife, and I'm yours!" Alexandria shouted this in Marilyn's face.

"You know what—I'm *not* your wife, and you're not mine! You know very well that this marriage wasn't real; it was a theatrical production, a fabrication by a drama teacher! Forget about it, and stop saying that, will you— once and for all!"

Marilyn snatched the marriage certificate from the wall, lifted it high in the air, and threw it with all her might at the ground. The glass and frame shattered into thousands of tiny pieces all over the room. She grabbed the piece of paper out of the mess on the floor and tore it to pieces. Alexandria roared like a wounded animal, fell to her knees, and sobbed.

"Enough! That's it! You can stop saying we're married. Here's our marriage—in pieces!" Marilyn shouted at Alexandria. A shard of glass had lodged in her wrist, and drops of blood fell to the ground. "I promise you, this is the last moment you'll ever see me. Don't contact me again. I'll have someone come get my things tomorrow."

Marilyn slammed the door behind her, leaving droplets of blood in her wake.

Chapter 21

October 2012
Bucharest, Romania

"DO YOU KNOW what time Marilyn's flight is?"

"Um, noon. Why?" asked Mel. "Don't tell me you're going to do something stupid."

"No, don't worry."

"Are you ready to start looking for a job yet?" asked Mel.

"No. For now, I don't think I'll do anything. I'm going to take a break.”

"They're still talking about you at the studio, you know. And they probably won't stop any time soon. I never thought that after so many years, and giving them your heart your soul, it’d end up like this. I know what happened with Marilyn ruined you, but couldn’t you find the strength to at least keep going to work?"

"You know I didn't even want to live anymore without her. Work was the last thing on my mind," Alexandria said.

"I know, but you could’ve taken a vacation, you could’ve waited a little while for things to get back to normal, and then made some decisions."

"No, I couldn't. I couldn't even set foot in the studio

again. Everything there reminds me of her. Every corner of the studio, every piece of set, every detail, every part of my work brought a flood of memories. That studio is a cursed place. It's brought me nothing but suffering—all my relationships have begun and ended there. After all that, how could I keep showing up there every day? And you know I played my last card by starting my relationship with Marilyn."

"But you're also the best and most talented director on television, the most creative camerawoman *and* director!"

"Yes and also the director who's cost them all their best models! I talked to Mr. Lupan. We're parting ways on good terms. They paid me in full; everything is settled."

"Zara left too, did I tell you that? At least they can't put *her* on your list…there are rumors that she quit because of Nando—her boyfriend caught them in bed! You know my rule: stay away from models! But no one listens to me when some gorgeous woman comes around." Mel paused. She saw Alexandria's empty eyes and knew she wasn't really there. "I'll be sad not to see you all the time in the studio. You were always there. That place won't be the same without you," sighed Mel.

"Nothing is the same anymore, Mel."

~

On the day of Marilyn's flight to Qatar, Alexandria went to the airport. She leaned against a column some distance from the baggage counter for the flight to Qatar. She had a good vantage point, to hopefully spot Marilyn somewhere in the crowd, but she'd made sure to hide her face behind large sunglasses. Soon she spotted Zara and her boyfriend pushing a large suitcase. Behind them were Marilyn and her mother, and a few other family and friends. They had all come to see her off. Alexandria watched every detail: the hugs and kisses, the way their lips moved when they spoke…she could make out the wishes for success and luck in the new job.

She hadn't seen Marilyn in two months, and this might be the last time she would ever see her. She wanted to memorize every part of her: every expression, every movement, her smile and gestures. She wanted more than anything to run out and grab her in a hug, to scream in front of everyone how much she loved her, to beg her to stay…but she knew she couldn't even get close to them.

Marilyn left her suitcase and took her ticket. She walked back to her group and started hugging each of them.

"I'll miss you so much! We'll come visit you the first chance we get," Zara said while squeezing her tightly. Tears glistened on almost every face.

Marilyn's mother was the last one. She was crying. "Call me when you get on the plane and then as soon as you land," she said through tears, not wanting to let her go.

It was finally time for Marilyn to head to the security check. She handed her passport over, then turned to wave goodbye one last time. At that moment, among the crowd of people, she thought she caught sight of Alexandria in the distance. She tried to get a better look. She wasn't sure if it was her, but she didn't really believe she'd come, and she certainly hadn't told her about her flight. Alexandria was staring straight at her, as if an invisible string had been stretched through the crowd of people in the middle of the airport, holding the two of them together.

"Did she forget something?" asked Marilyn's mother.

"Ma'am, please move forward," said the officer "This way, please."

Marilyn touched the golden heart that hung from her neck and continued forward until she was lost among the crowd.

Two hot tears dropped behind Alexandria's large sunglasses. Marilyn's family and friends slowly made their way to the exit. Alexandria was left staring off in the direction where Marilyn had gone.

Chapter 22

June 2017
Frankfurt, Germany

"ALEXANDRIA! OH MY gosh, it's been forever! How are you?" Mel's voice trembled slightly over the phone.

"I'm good! Just got back from a trip to Tokyo, and I have a day-long layover in Frankfurt. How about you?" Alexandria leaned back in the hotel bed while holding her phone to her ear.

"Wow, Tokyo! That sounds great. When are you going to upload the video; I'd love to watch it!"

"Yeah, maybe next week."

"Nice, cool...well...I'm good, great. Work and home, you know."

"How's Miss DJ?

"Are you going to keep calling her that forever?" Mel's laughter echoed through the phone. *"Everything has been great, honestly. We've had our ups and downs you know, but I guess that's how it is in every serious relationship. I didn't know it was possible to love someone that much... but how about you? Still not tired of traveling after the last five years?"* Mel's voice held a hint of concern; she wondered if her friend was truly happy.

"Oh, I'm not tired, but even if I was, you know I can't stop. That's my job now. My life, my happiness."

After Alexandria quit the studio, she'd bought several plane tickets to various destinations that offered rock-bottom prices. New places, new sights, small tucked-away streets or shiny skyscrapers… the thrill of seeing something that she hadn't seen before gave her the strength to move forward. She traveled everywhere, always taking photos and videos. It didn't matter where…there were interesting cultures, people, nature, and traditions everywhere. She filmed everything she saw during the day, edited it in the evening, and eventually posted it on YouTube.

"I know, you'll always be a workaholic." Mel was silent for a moment, trying to remember something. "Do you know what, recently someone asked about your first video, the one that got thousands of views overnight. Where was it?"

"Prague, Czech Republic," said Alexandria without hesitation.

That video had gone viral, and thanks to the algorithm, it boosted the popularity of her other videos and her whole channel. Alexandria realized that what she was doing was monetizing. She booked her next trips without even considering the destination; the choice was determined by the low price of the tickets. In a few years, her channel had gained immense popularity, passing one hundred thousand subscribers. She now made enough money to choose her own destinations where she wanted to visit and film.

"Oh yeah, right. Can I pick your next destination for you?" Mel laughed.

"In fact, you can. Sometimes people leave comments under the videos, about which destination they'd like to see on my channel. I take that into consideration sometimes when I plan my next trip."

"You know, I never thought there'd be a more perfect job in the world for you than filming naked women, but I see you found it!" Mel joked.

"Funny, Mel. You know, I just bought a drone. With this little photographic bird, I can capture the most breathtaking aerial shots. You'll see."

"So tell me about your love life! Do you ever hook up with some exotic woman on any of these trips?"

"There are some women here and there," Alexandria laughed. "It's funny how you and I seem to have traded lives, isn't it?"

"Yeah, you're right—you were always the one in a serious relationship, chasing love…and there I was, just chasing women!" She laughed at her own joke. "It feels like we've stepped into each other's shoes. Ironic, isn't it?"

"I know, but the important thing is we both found happiness. I'm glad you feel good as a wife. Who knows, if they ever legalize gay marriages in Romania, you could have the biggest wedding ever."

"Oh, I will—believe me!"

~

Alexandria stood in line for the security check at the airport, listening to the voice making announcements over the PA system about flight changes and delays. She shifted nervously from one foot to the other. The line was moving slowly, and it was cutting it close with her flight. When she finally reached the front of the line, she glanced around at the bustling crowd. Her eyes played over the unfamiliar faces, then she glanced at the next line, where a flight crew in sharp uniforms was passing through. Alexandria's heart skipped a beat as she caught sight of Marilyn. Marilyn happened to glance in Alexandria's direction. Alexandria's hands trembled as they clutched her boarding pass, but Marilyn moved along and didn't notice her.

"Next!" the employee said, waving to Alexandria to step forward and enter the full-body scanner.

"*Next!*" the employee shouted again.

What are the odds? Alexandria wondered as she raised her hands in the X-ray booth. She watched as Marilyn disappeared into the crowd, knowing that she may never get another chance to reconnect with her lost love. She grabbed her carry-on and jacket from the bin and walked quickly after the crew, barely making her way through the crowds. Approaching them, she saw Marilyn's crisp uniform and impeccable bun. Even among this well-dressed and well-trained group, Marilyn was set apart from the rest.

"Marilyn!" Alexandria called out with a shaky breath.

Marilyn turned around and her eyes met Alexandria's with a flicker of recognition.

"Alex?" The bustling airport around them faded away. Time stood still as they simply stared at each other there in that airport, caught in a moment that reminded them of the weight of the years that had passed, and the words that had been left unspoken.

"I wasn't sure if that was really you! What are the chances, huh?" Alexandria's fingers clenched the strap of her carry-on. She wasn't sure what to do or say next. "The uniform suits you. You look great," she said.

"Thanks. Yeah, I would never have thought I would run into you again here. What are you doing here? Sorry, I don't have much time to chat; they're waiting for me."

"Just connecting through Frankfurt. My flight takes off in a bit."

"Wow, small world. How are you?"

"Yeah, I'm fine. Traveling," replied Alexandria curtly, her heart still racing.

"For pleasure or for business?"

"Oh, both."

"Well, I'm glad you're okay. You look good too! I'm sorry, but I really have to go."

"Wait…do you mind if we keep in touch?" asked Alexandria.

"Yes, I'd like that. Here, I have a new number," Marilyn said and pulled a small notepad out of her purse. She leaned down to support the pad on her knee, then tore off the page and handed it to Alexandria. "Text me if you have time. We should catch up."

She waved her hand and hurried to rejoin the rest of the flight attendants. Alexandria watched Marilyn go, unbelievingly. It hardly felt real, to reconnect like this. She looked at the paper with the phone number written on it, then carefully folded it and tucked it into her wallet.

It was time to board. She thought about the chance meeting and the incredible coincidence that had sent them to the right place at the right time. She wanted to text Marilyn right away, to find out what how her life was going, and if she was happy with the choices she'd made—even how many new places she'd visited. She didn't want to seem too eager or pushy, and the boarding announcement for her flight snapped her out of her reverie anyway. With a deep breath, she gathered her suitcase and followed the stream of passengers toward the gate.

~

Alexandria texted in a couple of days. *Hey, just wanted to say hi and see how you are. I still can't believe we met yesterday.*

Within seconds a reply came.

Hey, I'm fine, how about you? That was crazy. It really is a small world. I don't have much time right now, but I'll text you later.

Alexandria reread each word over and over, closing the message but then reopening it a moment later to read it again. She willed herself to be patient. After a few hours, her phone buzzed again.

I have a few free hours - tell me how you are, what's new with you? Where were you flying to the other day?

I had a connection via Frankfurt, I was going to London.

A tour of the British capital?

Something like that. Taking pictures, videos of landmarks, beautiful places. And how are you? Have you traveled around the world yet? Alexandria typed and retyped this several times, looking for the right way to word it.

I've been lucky enough to see many beautiful

places! In the beginning, I was sent mostly to Asia. Now most of my flights are to and from Europe, but sometimes we fly to the Americas.

Marilyn didn't send another message that day. But the next day, she texted first.

Hey, how is your day going

Alexandria responded with a picture of Big Ben and The Houses of Parliament. The reply came right away.

Wow, I only managed to see it once and it was at night. If you have time to see it then, I recommend you do, it's very beautiful.

Thanks for the advice, I will! Where are you now? Anywhere interesting?

Alexandria deliberately ended with a question to leave the ball in Marilyn's court. Not long after, Marilyn responded with a photo of with several cocktail glasses in what was clearly a bar.

Cheers. I see you're enjoying yourself. What are you drinking? Alexandria used the same technique of asking a question, since it had worked so well the first time.

We always try different cocktails. I don't know how the night's going to end, I'm starting to get drunk, haha.

Marilyn seemed to be in a good mood, which was possibly fueled by alcohol, but she seemed inclined to continue the conversation.

Haha, are there a lot of you?

A couple of girls, flight attendants. I think we're the funniest group in the whole bar.

I'm sure of it. Heading out to some club after this?

No, after this round, we're going back to the hotel to sleep. And you - who are you exploring London with? Some new beauty around?

This question was perfectly placed, and Alexandria lobbed it back to her.

I'm traveling alone. There are no beauties around me. And you? Is there a lucky woman or man around you?

Big line, haha. Just kidding. I'm single right now. I had a brief relationship with a steward, then something more serious with a woman who was a pilot in the airline, but it didn't work out. We don't have much time for that sort of thing, you know how it is.

A crazy idea occurred to Alexandria and she quickly reviewed popular European destinations where AirLux Airline flew. She began a new message.

It's getting late and I'm going to bed soon. Great to catch up with you. By the way, do you fly to Lisbon often?

Not very often, but I think I have a layover there in 2 weeks. Why?

My next destination is Portugal, we can meet up and have a drink if you have some free time. I'd love to.

Really? That's great. I'll text you exactly when I'll be there. We'll keep in touch.

Over the next couple of weeks, Alexandria and Marilyn texted each other regularly. Alexandria felt a warm sense of nostalgia and excitement with each message. She was really looking forward to seeing Marilyn again.

~

Two weeks later, Alexandria was in Lisbon, staying near the airport. When Marilyn told her when she was arriving, Alexandria planned to come the day before her, armed with all the patience in the world. Finally, the long-awaited message came; Marilyn confirmed that she would have time and would come to Alexandria's hotel to see her. Alexandria didn't want to plan anything, didn't want to strategize. She decided to go with the flow and see where it might take her. She felt fate was on her side.

Marilyn arrived in the elegant hotel lobby with its chandeliers and marble floors. She observed the guests and finally saw Alexandria seated at the hotel bar. As she approached her, the people's conversations and clinking glasses faded into the background.

"Hey…" Alexandria said as she noticed Marilyn behind her. "I'm glad you came." She gave her a hug and asked, "What are you going to drink?"

"What are you drinking?" asked Marilyn.

"Whiskey."

"A glass of white wine for me." Marilyn sat down next to Alexandria but with some distance between their chairs.

"How's it going? Where are you coming from? Tell me about the job," Alexandria prompted.

"From home—I mean, from Qatar." Marilyn laughed and her face lit up. Alexandria felt the butterflies in her stomach that she'd felt on their early dates. "It's very interesting. It's fast-paced work, it's tiring, and the time difference has an effect, but I'm not complaining. The people I work with are very interesting, from all over the world. I'm really enjoying it. After my two-year contract expired, I extended it, so I just keep flying."

"I see. Do you have enough time to explore?"

"Sometimes, but other times, we have to leave again so quickly that there's only time to get to the hotel and sleep for a few hours. Sometimes the crew goes out together to explore the city. Unfortunately, we're in Lisbon for just a short time. I have an early flight tomorrow morning and won't be able to enjoy the city."

"That all sounds great," Alexandria said "I'm happy for you. How is life in Qatar? Do you like it there?"

"I like it; I don't spend much time there though." Marilyn paused for a second while the bartender set down her glass of wine. "It's pretty hot this time of year. But as I told you, I don't spend that much time there. It's just the base; most of the time I'm off somewhere else." Marilyn sipped her glass of wine. "And you? Two weeks ago, you were in Frankfurt, then London, now here? Are you on vacation?"

Alexandria started to answer, but Marilyn continued, "I heard you left the station a long time ago. What are you doing now? What's your new passion?"

"Well, after I quit the studio, I decided to travel. I wanted a change of scenery." Alexandria cradled her glass and swirled the ice cubes and whiskey inside it. "While I was traveling, I filmed everything and then edited it. It turned out that people really liked my videos on YouTube. Long story short, I can make a pretty good living this way, and kind of mix business and pleasure…sort of like you. In a way, we're in the same industry again, huh?" laughed Alexandria.

"Yes, you're right. You should give me the link to your channel; I'd love to watch your videos. Knowing you, I'm sure they're as polished as a work of art. I still can't believe you left the studio. I honestly thought you were going to retire there. Do you miss it? Don't you miss the models?" Marilyn smiled while tracing the rim of her wine glass with her finger.

"Sure, there are things I miss… I miss Mel…but it was the best decision I could have made. And I don't regret it. Speaking of Mel," Alexandria laughed, "can you believe she's still with Miss DJ? They're living together, a happy family. I should probably call her *Mrs.* DJ." Alexandria burst into laughter. "I thought Mel was never going to settle down."

"I'm happy for her. She deserves a woman who loves her."

"I'm happy too," Alexandria said.

Marilyn asked, "Are you?" She paused "I mean…you know…well, I'm not talking about Mel."

"Yeah, I am happy…Are you?"

"I'm happy…a flight attendant's life is super interesting and exciting, but a little lonely." Marilyn felt the wine loosening her inhibitions. "I guess it's hard to make any lasting connections when you're in a different part of the world every week. I thought it might be smart to be with someone who is part of the crew too. My ex was a pilot. We tried to work the same schedule, but that was so hard. She also wanted to grow and fly bigger planes; in the end, she moved to another company…so it didn't work out. That's the only thing that's missing in my life. But I'm sure the right person will come along, sooner or later." Marilyn smiled through the tinge of melancholy in her voice. "What about you? I thought you'd be happily married well before now! Especially with this interesting job; I can't believe there hasn't been a woman special enough to steal your heart!"

"Oh sure, there were a few, but no one special enough to make me stay and commit to something serious, no. And I don't have time to stay still. It's pointless to start anything when next week I could be far away. You know how it is, right?" Alexandria smiled, brought her glass to her mouth, and took a sip. After a short pause, she continued. "How is your mom? Did you ever have the chance to come out to her?"

"I did. It didn't go very well…as I expected. She was shocked at first, then angry. She accused me of betraying our family and our values. We argued, and now there's this awkward silence between us. She's hoping it's just a phase, but I don't know if things will ever be the same again between us."

"Oh, I'm sorry to hear that."

"And you?"

"I talked to my parents too. At first, they also were shocked, and it was hard to digest, but with time, they've been coming around. I felt heard and understood, and I think they're proud of me. I guess they needed time…but I'm really sorry you didn't experience the same."

"It's okay. I'm happy for you."

"So, where are you off to next week?" Alexandria asked, deliberately changing the subject.

"I have a flight to Paris on Tuesday that I'm excited about. I'll have a slightly longer layover and I hope to be able to explore as much of the city as possible. Why do you ask—are you gonna come with me?" Marilyn added with a flirtatious smile.

"Well, Paris is on my list for my next videos. I've already filmed there, but I can do Part Two. Maybe we'll meet there…what do you think?"

"Is it that easy to just pick a destination and go? With no preparation, no plan?" asked Marilyn.

"Oh, I have a plan! I didn't say I was *just going*. I always research my locations in detail. I read guidebooks, opinions, reviews, recommendations, you name it. I watch videos by other people who have been there; I research the area. And then I just book my plane ticket and hotel. One day when I've visited enough places, I might pick one to settle down in."

"You're definitely lucky to always do what you enjoy and enjoy what you do."

"That's been my plan since I was little. Well, first it was to become an astronaut, but that didn't happen," she laughed.

Marilyn glanced at her watch, its silver band catching the soft light of the chandeliers. She sighed as she realized the evening was slipping away. "I really have to go. I have to get my required beauty sleep hours and be there early tomorrow for pre-flight preparations. But I'm glad we met here. Something tells me we'll be seeing each other again soon," Marilyn winked.

Chapter 23

September 2017
Paris, France

IF YOU'RE ALREADY in Paris - would you like some company as you explore this amazing city? Alexandria texted Marilyn.

The smiley face response arrived with no delay.

Here's the address of my hotel. Come when you're ready and we'll go together. I already have an itinerary for the most memorable sights. We'll end by drinking champagne at the foot of the Eiffel Tower.

I'll be there in about an hour, Marilyn texted back.

An hour later they started on their adventure. They took a boat ride on the Seine, a quick tour of the Louvre, strolled the bohemian streets of Montmartre, and ended up in front of the magnificent Eiffel Tower, as promised. Alexandra bought a small bottle of champagne and two plastic champagne flutes. They sat on the steps on the Trocadero as Alexandria pulled out the bottle.

"Let me help you," Marilyn said, removing the plastic packaging from the glasses. Her hand involuntarily touched Alexandria's arm. Alexandria didn't show it, but it felt like electricity coursing through her body.

Alexandria began to pour the champagne,

concentrating on keeping the rising bubbles from overflowing the glass. She handed the first to Marilyn and repeated the ritual with the second glass. She felt Marilyn watching her. She had always been able to feel her gaze even when her eyes were closed. Alexandria raised her glass into the evening air under the shadow of the Eiffel Tower.

"Here we are! Cheers, to the best view in the world!" Marilyn raised her glass as well and looked Alexandria in the eye. Her gaze was deep and warm. Her lips were juicy and red as if begging for a kiss.

"Cheers."

Alexandria slowly sipped her champagne.

Marilyn commented, "Never in my wildest dreams would I have thought that you and I would be drinking champagne and enjoying the Eiffel Tower. I wish things had started here…I wish we were just meeting now."

"At least we can enjoy the moment now," Alexandria said and looked at the Eiffel Tower. "Let's take a selfie—we need to capture this moment. Then I'll take some pictures of you for your Instagram, if you want?"

"Yeah, let's get a picture with the Eiffel Tower behind us," Marilyn said and squeezed next to Alexandria to fit in the frame. For the first time in years, Alexandria felt Marilyn's body against hers. She smelled the familiar perfume coming on her skin. Marilyn snuggled even closer for the camera. Alexandria reached forward, took a few pictures, and changed the angle slightly.

"Wait, I'll try opening the lens a little more so we can see the background better."

Marilyn brought her face closer to Alexandria's and she felt her warm breath; she inhaled it and held it in for a few seconds. Marilyn's lips were very close to hers. Alexandria kept adjusting her phone, trying to find the best angle, and also to hold onto this magical moment a little longer. The distance between their lips had almost melted away and Marilyn's breath became almost noticeably ragged. She could smell Alexandria's familiar scent as well. A cozy, comfortable feeling, with definite overtones of passion and desire, washed over her.

Another second, another millimeter closer, and their lips would have merged.

"Let's see the pictures," said Marilyn. Alexandria went through the photos.

" Got it! The whole Eiffel Tower is visible in the background," said Alexandria. "Okay, go over there and strike a pose, I'll take pictures of you."

"Okay, is that sexy enough for you, Miss Director?" Marilyn was hamming it up in various theatrical poses and laughing.

"That's it…play to the camera a little more. Make everybody at home want to give you a call."

Marilyn laughed, "I'm sure the phone lines are full. How many viewers do we have? Ah, it's been more than five years, but you brought me right back there! It feels like a lifetime ago. I think that was the happiest time of my life." Marilyn sat down next to Alexandria again.

"I feel the same way." For Alexandria, the past was a bittersweet place but being with Marilyn under the Parisian sky felt like a chance to rewrite their story, to rediscover what had once made them so happy.

"Do you remember that show we did together, the one where you wore the sexy wedding dress?"

"Of course I remember. I remember every show

that you ever put on! What was the name of it…oh, right! "My Dream Girl." Each model was dressed to represent various characters…remember, Aurora was the housewife from the 50s, and someone else was the businesswoman, the mechanic…" Marilyn sighed softly, lost in the memories.

"And you were the bride. Yeah, I remember how we arranged those small sets, each one reflecting the theme, making it seem like we were filming in eight different places." Alexandria proudly recalled one of her biggest successes as a director.

"That was one of my very first times on your show."

"I don't think I ever mentioned it to you, but that whole time, I couldn't stop looking at you. Do you remember when one of the cameramen went on break?"

"Yeah, and you took the camera…"

"I just came closer to you with the camera, I can still remember how my heart was pounding. Through my lens, I was imagining what it would be like to be with you, picturing us together. At that moment, with the camera hiding my gaze, I realized how much I wanted to be with you. After that show, I couldn't stop thinking about you. You were always the most beautiful woman there. Your eyes were so blue and memorable that people sometimes just stared at you. And you were always so nice to everyone, so diligent in your work. It was enjoyable just to be in the studio together."

Marilyn's eyes softened as she heard this. Without saying a word, she wrapped her arms around Alexandria, pulling her into a tight hug. Alexandria closed her eyes, rested her chin on Marilyn's shoulder, and wrapped her arms around her in return.

"I think we should finish the bottle and get going. Do you want to take the Metro?"

"Yeah, do you know which line we need?"

"I've never taken the subway here, but I don't think it could be that complicated. I managed the New York City subway just fine," said Marilyn proudly.

"And so began an adventure," laughed Alexandria.

"You don't think we'll make it? Let me prove it to you. The subway entrance is just around the corner."

The two women quickly got their bearings and found the subway. Just like in old times, they could hardly stop laughing. The train arrived while they were still descending the stairs. They ran and shimmied through the doors just before they closed. The train was packed.

"Hold on to me," Alexandria said, grabbing a handle with one hand. There were so many people around them, pressing them into each other.

"We made it," said Marilyn with satisfaction.

"We managed to get on a train, but are we even sure it's the right one?"

"Yes, I'm sure it's the right one! But we could ask someone if it would make you feel better. Someone has to speak English."

Marilyn looked around to see who she might ask, but the train had pulled into a station. Most of the crowd got off.

"I don't think we'll ask anyone," Alexandria said and smiled.

The two women were left alone in the middle of the Metro car, but they stayed pressed against each other. Alexandria still held the handle with one hand and kept the other wrapped around Marilyn's waist. They stared at each other without uttering a word. Marilyn moved her head, slowly closing the distance between them. Marilyn closed her eyes, and Alexandria gently pulled her in, erasing the last millimeters between them. Their lips fused together perfectly, like two puzzle pieces. It was a kiss that brought out all their desire, their passion, their love. The kiss tasted of second chances, of forgiveness, of new beginnings.

~

In the morning, Alexandria and Marilyn lay cuddled in the bed of the little Paris hotel room. The windows were wide open, and a gentle breeze refreshed the room.

"I want to stay here with you all day. I want to make love again, then have breakfast, then have sex again, and so on for the rest of the day. I really don't want to leave," Marilyn said and hugged Alexandria tightly.

"Do you think the universe fights for souls to be together? Some things seem too strange to be coincidences."

"Oh, I think we're proof of that," Marilyn said. "Sometimes the timing just isn't right though. Even if two people are perfect for each other, it might not be the right time."

Alexandria confessed, "I missed you a lot. Your kisses, your touch, your scent, your skin."

"I missed you too. Even though I meant what I said when we broke up, I couldn't stop thinking about you. I wanted so much to call you, to see you again, to hold you. Sometimes I dreamed that you would show up in Doha, do something crazy to find me. The day I left for Qatar, I even thought I saw you at the airport. I thought I was daydreaming, or that you'd made me start hallucinating."

Alexandria hugged her tighter and fell silent. Then she said, "Tell me where you'll be next week. I'll wait for you there."

"I have a flight to Rio de Janeiro, but isn't that too far for you?"

"There's no place on earth I wouldn't go for you," Alexandria said. "And not just on Earth—I'd go to Mars too. Send me the dates and I'll wait for you in Rio."

"Are you sure?"

"More than sure."

"Why don't I send you my schedule for the month, so we can plan everything out? That'll be better for you too, won't it?" Marilyn looked at her watch and jumped. "Oh! I have to go. I'll text you as soon as I get to the airport, then when we land, I'll text you all the time. I wish I could stay here with you."

"We're going to spend a whole day in a hotel room in Rio, and we're going to do whatever we want. I want to make love with you in every city in the world."

Chapter 24

April 2018
New York, United States of America

"ARE YOU SURE you know where we're going, and if it's the right train?"

"I told you, I've never gotten lost on the New York City subway," Marilyn said while holding Alexandria's hand. "You're in safe hands with me. The next stop is ours. When we get above ground again, you'll see the Empire State Building in front of us."

They walked down the street, entered the Empire State Building, and showed their tickets. They made their way through the exhibit and up to the 86th Floor Observatory Deck.

"Wow, the view is amazing! I've seen a lot of pictures and movies filmed here, but in person…it's indescribable," Alexandria said. The wind was blowing her hair and she held it back with one hand.

"This was the place that impressed me the most when I was here on the student exchange program. I hoped I would come back here one day," Marilyn said.

"Thank you for sharing this with me."

"That's not the only thing I want to share with you,"

Marilyn said. "You're the person I've loved the most in my life, the person who has made me the happiest, and made me feel the most wanted, respected and loved."

"You too, sweetheart."

"We both made mistakes…and we both paid for them." Marilyn paused for a second. "My job as a flight attendant was a dream come true and I'm grateful that it happened, but it was also one of the reasons our paths separated." The wind played with her hair as she continued, "My contract expired with that last flight, and I decided not to renew it."

"Are you serious?"

"Yes. I think I achieved everything I wanted to there, and I was proud to be a flight attendant for one of the most prestigious airlines."

"I don't know what to say." Alexandria's voice mingled with the wind at the top of the Empire State Building.

"I was so happy to be your wife once, even though our wedding wasn't real or legal. I'd like to do it right and be your wife again—but for real this time."

Marilyn fumbled in her coat pocket and pulled out a small box. She opened it and took out a beautiful diamond ring. Alexandria trembled with excitement as Marilyn got down on one knee and asked, "Will you marry me?"

"Yes, yes, yes! I love you!" Alexandria couldn't hold back her tears of happiness. She hugged Marilyn tightly, then kissed her. Marilyn placed the ring on her finger. "I can't wait to be your wife again."

After the euphoria had subsided just a bit, and they had spent enough time at the top of the skyscraper, they headed toward the exit.

"Where do you want our next flight to be?" Alexandria asked, holding Marilyn's hand. "And this time we won't just meet there—we'll go together."

"Wherever you want. I'll follow you," Marilyn said.

ABOUT THE AUTHOR

Hailing from the enchanting landscapes of Europe and now making waves in the USA, Avery A. Voss is a dynamic voice in sapphic fiction. With a gift for weaving intricate tales of love, resilience, and self-discovery, she captures the hearts of readers around the globe. Her stories resonate with a deep understanding of the complexities of relationships and the pursuit of true happiness.

In "Love in Prime Time," Avery invites you into the glamorous yet tumultuous world of erotic entertainment, where passion and heartache intertwine. Her ability to create vivid, relatable characters and emotionally charged narratives has earned her a dedicated following and critical acclaim.

When she's not writing, Avery A. Voss enjoys immersing herself in new cultures, seeking inspiration from the world around her, and celebrating the diverse experiences that fuel her creativity.

CONNECT WITH AVERY ON:

Website: https://aavoss.wixsite.com/averyavoss
Email: aavoss@yahoo.com
Instagram: avery.a.voss_author

We hope you enjoyed reading *Love in Prime Time*. Your feedback is incredibly valuable to us. If you could take a moment to share your thoughts and leave a review, it would be greatly appreciated. Your reviews help us improve and reach more readers like you. Thank you for your support!